Ocean City Lowdown

A Jamie August Novel

Kim Kash

Cape House
GREENBELT, MARYLAND

Cover design and illustration by Jake Clark, jcalebdesign.com

Book Layout & Design ©2013 - BookDesignTemplates.com

Ocean City Lowdown / Kim Kash. -- 1st ed.
ISBN 978-0-9895022-1-4

For Michael: my partner and co-conspirator,
my love

1.

Trina and Big Mary always get me into trouble. If they hadn't taken me to that dive bar down at the inlet last night, I never would have met that guy. If I hadn't met the guy, I would not have put away six Fuzzy Navels and ended up in the backseat of his SUV at closing time. But I did. Now my head was about to split open and spill my brains out on the orange Formica counter.

The old phone rang, and when that thing rings, there's an actual metal bell jangling in there, no joke. My skull cracked open a little. I lifted my head from the counter, shifted on the stool, cleared my throat, and picked up the heavy plastic receiver.

"Beach Getaway Rentals, this is Jamie," I croaked.

"Jamie, it's Tony."

"Hey Tony, what's goin' on?" I said, resting my chin in my hand and letting my elbow slide forward so that I was practically draped across the counter. I closed my eyes again. This call might take a while.

Tony the plumber launched into his usual plumbing tirade. He said that only a miracle from heaven could restore the pipes at Sunrise Paradise—a name so hideously off the mark it was just right, like Smalls, my 300-pound cousin on the Pittsburgh side of the family.

"Listen, hon," Tony said, his Maryland accent carrying through the phone like he was shouting—which he usually is. I held the receiver away from my ear. "All them pipes has gotta be replaced. I can't keep 'em goin' forever. I'm tellin' you, ya gotta tear out all the pipes in the whole building and replace 'em with PVC, and ya gotta do it now, in the winter, so it's ready when people start comin' back down the ocean in the springtime." He said it like *downy eoshun.*

He was right. But hey, I don't make the decisions around here. And this morning, I cared even less than usual. "Yep, thanks Tony, I'll let Abe know. So, is apartment Number 3 okay?"

"Yeah—wait, no. The kitchen ceiling's drippin' because the toilet's leakin' in Number 6." He pronounced it *terlet*. "Number 4's okay—for now," he warned.

"Number 4 it is. Take it easy, Tony," I said and hung up.

As the fog of my hangover began to lift ever so slightly, details of last night came into focus. I stared into space, blushed (although nobody was here but yours truly), and giggled.

Just then the front door, the glass steamed from the heating system, opened with a squawk of aluminum on aluminum. A family of four squeezed inside. They all looked grumpy, like they had been squashed into a car that was too small. Then again, just about any car would have been too small for them.

"Welcome to Beach Getaway!" I said, willing myself into customer service mode. "You're here to check in for Sunrise Paradise?" The pasty father halfheartedly straightened his comb-over and grunted in the affirmative. I had him fill out some paperwork and handed over the keys to Number 4. The wife looked around appraisingly at the vintage office decor. The son, maybe 12, scowled and scratched his butt. The daughter, a little younger, picked her nose.

I dropped my eyes to the rental contract and picked out their name. "Thanks, Mr. and Mrs. Slomkowski. So, you just take the main road up a few blocks and turn right on 43rd Street. It's the, um, reddish building on the left. Enjoy your stay," I said with as much enthusiasm as I could dredge. The bell on the door clanked as they left, possibly rupturing my eardrums.

I dropped my smiley face and checked the time on the plastic pre-digital-era clock, the kind with flaps that drop each minute. It was hanging slightly askew on the fake wood-paneled wall. I felt guilty about sending those people off to Sunrise Paradise, which has to be the ugliest, worst apartment building in all of Ocean City. But really, what did they want for ten bucks?

The owner of Beach Getaway Rentals and my uncle, Abe Vello, was running a promotion. "Stunning" Vacation Rental with "Old Ocean City Charm" (well, the "old" part is true.) Ten dollars a night for a minimum of three nights any time in January. "Enjoy the beach without all the traffic and crowds!" the ad proclaimed. For those of you not from around here: Ocean City, Maryland reaches a high of about 28 degrees on a typical January day. No crowds here.

Anyway, according to the forms, the Slomkowski family lived in Baltimore, so at least they knew Ocean City is no tropical paradise. But they could not possibly have anticipated the building on 43rd Street. My mother's crazy brother was under the impression that painting things in, shall we say, vibrant colors, was just as good as actual maintenance. The three-story cement-block beauty was a neon orange shade we at Beach Getaway Rentals poetically describe as "Sunrise Red." The paint was starting to peel and show the "Tropical Lemon" (read: "Safety Yellow") color beneath it, so I guess it actually had a sort of cloudy sunrise effect.

I feel like an idiot sometimes being associated with a rinky-dink operation like Beach Getaway Rentals, but I know that deep down, Uncle Abe is not a bad person. It's just that somehow he's gotten a name for himself as the go-to guy if you're looking for dry-rot, vintage wiring, and majestic views of the backs of strip malls. Well, I was lucky to have work through the winter in this mid-Atlantic beach town.

I waited for the phone to ring, certain Mr. Slomkowski would be calling to give me an earful. I stared at the dingy yellow telephone, and my eyes drifted out of focus, then slowly closed. My mind slid back to last night—a much nicer place. I was in the back of this bar with no name in the old part of downtown, making out with a guy I had just met. John? Jim? Jim, I think.

Trina and Big Mary may have already taken off by then. Maybe I sort of told them to leave without me. But then they did! They left! What kind of friends do that? My best friend Tammy never would have left me drunk in a bar making out with a stranger. Nuh-uh. She would have stuck around, even if I told her to take a hike.

This guy, though? He was a great kisser, not too pushy, and his hands went places they should not have gone, but it felt like they belonged. I sighed, reliving the moment. My head throbbed, but I smiled a little.

We went out to his car, some kind of upscale SUV, to keep the party going when the bar closed. Oh, man, it had been so long: four months. This guy was a little older than me, maybe in his 30s, and he was smooth and easy. The back seat was really big. Once Jim started the engine and got the heat going, it was nice and comfortable, like a living room. As The Rolling Stones' "Start Me Up" blared through the sound system and a little snow spit from the sky, those hands removed layer after layer of my clothing, and soon my leopard-print panties were dangling from the passenger seat headrest.

My eyes snapped open and my throbbing, day-after brain took over. I'd had sex with that guy. I sure had. I shuddered with nervous energy, with thrill and dread. I mean, it's not the first time I'd jumped right into the deep end with a guy I'd just met, but I sure don't make a habit of it. Especially not in the backseat of a car. That's just tacky.

I rooted around in my big, faux Gucci bag and found my wallet. I checked the inside zipper compartment, and sighed with relief. The little pocket was empty. The condom I carry for just this kind of unexpected fun was gone. I blew out a big breath, then my face bent into a sleepy grin.

When the phone jangled a few moments later, I yelped, then braced myself as I picked up the receiver. "Beach Getaway Rentals, this is Jamie," I winced and held the receiver away from my ear, waiting for an earful.

"Hello Jamie, it's Donald Brightland." I breathed an enormous sigh of relief that it was the editor of the *Ocean City Weekly Breeze*.

"Hi Donald," I said. "I'm so glad it's you."

"Oh," he said, sounding puzzled. "How sweet of you. Listen, I have a *Lifestyles* feature assignment for you. Can you come by the office to get the details after you're done there at Addams Family Beach Rentals?"

I snorted at Donald's remark. "Maybe if you paid me what I'm worth as an investigative reporter, I wouldn't have to hold down this junky job to keep the heat on," I said.

"Jamie, sweetie, I could not possibly pay you what you're worth. So get down here."

"Sure Donald. You know I'm always up for a *Beach 'n' Bay Lifestyles* feature," I said, eyes rolling. "It's what I live for. I'll be in this afternoon."

Donald doesn't fully appreciate my investigative reporting skills. He's always sending me out to cover American Legion awards dinners and grand openings of Dumsers Dairyland locations. *Beach 'n' Bay Lifestyles* pieces. But I don't stop there. No, someone needs to take a good, hard look at the tough issues, and that's me. Even though it's a free weekly, the *Weekly Breeze* is Ocean City's only paper. Donald just nods vaguely when I remind him of our journalistic duty to cover, well, news. But so far he hasn't fired me. He just reminds me that the *Weekly Breeze* is supposed to be just that: breezy. "Leave all the muckraking to the *Washington Post*," he says. "Our readers want to know about happy things, local people doing good, the latest in rattan furnishings." Then he would breeze out for a latte.

But this is my calling. Washington, all the way across the Chesapeake Bay and completely self-absorbed, might as well be on the moon. So I square my shoulders and soldier on. Jamie August: investigative reporter, *Ocean City Weekly Breeze*.

"Oh, and Jamie?"

"Yes?"

"Don't forget, I need that piece on trends in dog grooming. Poochy Curlz is running an ad in next week's paper, and I want that story to run with it."

Looking around the Beach Getaway Rentals office I pondered, not for the first time, what it would be like if I had money like Donald had money. Well, actually it's Donald's partner Wesley who has the money. Tons of it. Wesley retired a few years ago from the family import/export business. They live in a huge condo on the 25th floor of a building in north Ocean City overlooking the ocean.

I absently twirled a strand of long, dark hair, listening to the radiators ping. I brought the strand in for a closer look, and snipped a few split ends with scissors from the office drawer. Someday, I thought, I will be a famous reporter and make real money. I wondered, if I had plenty of money, like Wesley or maybe like the guy from last night, would I still ride the bus in winter and a rusty beach cruiser in the summer? Would I still wear clothes from Daffodil's Department Store? Daffodil's is the local chain that stocks factory-second acid wash jeans with rhinestones on the butt, cheap plastic patio furniture, wooden plaques painted with Jimmy Buffet lyrics, and cheese curls with expired sell-by dates. And where would I live? I guess if I had money I could rent an apartment instead of living on a rusting houseboat docked at the cement plant. But why?

My parents are seriously puzzled about their 26-year-old daughter's sketchy life choices. Most of my girlfriends back home in the Baltimore suburb of Dundalk are already divorced and fighting for alimony and child support. All things considered, I think I'm doing pretty well.

By the end of my shift at Beach Getaway, I had finished the dog grooming article and felt human again. The hangover was mostly gone and my memory of last night was mostly back. I applied a quick swipe of blue eyeliner, which most think is for blue eyes, but mine are very dark brown and I think blue looks great.

I put on my heavy ski parka and was out the door in a flash. On the sidewalk locking up, I heard the phone ringing inside. I felt a twinge of guilt for the renters at Sunrise Paradise, but not enough to make me open up and answer the phone. Sucks to be them. I walked down the block to the bus stop.

At the corner I took a seat in the bus shelter to get out of the chilly January wind. I opened my bag, which I noticed was starting to crack at the seams, and fished for my pink gloves. I disentangled them from my computer's power cord and put them on. My trusty MacBook, the most expensive thing I own by a mile, gave off warmth in the depths of the bag. The wind whipped under the shelter walls. I pulled my wool cap over my ears.

When you rely on public transportation, it's important to put yourself into a state of suspended animation. Otherwise you'll go crazy waiting. I stared off into the middle distance directing warm thoughts at my nose until, finally, the bus pulled up. I showed the driver my all-day pass and slid into the first seat. I was the only passenger, which is not unusual in the middle of winter. As the bus started down the block, the driver, who was a dead ringer for Santa Claus, said, "Keeping warm this afternoon?"

"I can't complain," I responded. "I hear there might be snow later this week."

"Yep," Santa said. "That's what they say. You never can trust the weatherman, though."

"True."

We sat in amiable silence as the bus chugged down the nearly deserted Coastal Highway in the twilight, the sound of its diesel engine sharp and loud in the absence of other traffic noise. I watched the neon signs go by, advertising motels, all-you-can-eat buffets, and liquor stores. I mentally filled in some of the other signs that weren't lit: signs for the crab shacks and night clubs and mini-golf courses shuttered for the cold months.

"This is my stop," I called out as we neared 178th Street, and the driver pulled to the curb. "Take it easy," I said. He waved as I stepped down. The empty bus drove toward Delaware, bright in the gathering night.

I walked across the street and through a small parking lot, empty except for Donald's white Acura, to the little strip shopping center office of the *Weekly Breeze*. The wind cut sharply across the un-sheltered expanse of asphalt. As I walked into the harshly lit storefront, my senses were assaulted by a blast of pineapple air freshener and Whitney

Houston. "Didn't we almost have it aaaaaallll?" she demanded. Donald looked up from his desk at the back of the room and waved cheerfully.

"That is obscene," I shouted, looking at the Bose Wave Radio on the maple file cabinet behind Donald's desk. He grinned and turned the volume down using a credit card-sized remote control. He had to reach farther for the remote than for the radio. I put my bag on the reporters' desk. "Any messages for me? Did any of my sources call in?"

"Your sources?" Donald arched one perfectly shaped eyebrow. "Well, Jerry Mulvaney from the Chevrolet Dealership out in Salisbury called for you, and I put him through to your voice mail. I think he wants to invite you out for an evening of romance." Jerry Mulvaney was as old as my grandfather, and had hair growing out his ears.

"You know you'll never love that way agaaaain," Donald crooned along with Whitney. A jaunty, highlighted lock of hair fell across his forehead, and his laugh lines accentuated the twinkle in his blue eyes. He had a combination of good genes and a great hairdresser.

"Gross!" I laughed and pulled off my coat and hat, and smoothed a wild case of static electricity out of my long, straight hair. I plopped in front of his desk, throwing one leg over the arm of the chintz barrel chair. Donald cringed at the sight of my knockoff Ugg boots.

The office is furnished with the stuff that came from Donald and Wesley's apartment after its latest renovation. They junked the English country cottage look for the über-masculine black and beige chunky look that is probably already out of style in Los Angeles. Not that I would know.

Donald reached a strong, manicured hand for a sheaf of promo materials on the corner of his desk. "Bayview Preserve is a big new traditional home community near the wetlands on the bayside. Have you heard of it?"

"Oh, that place! It's not near the wetlands, it's right on them—well, what used to be them," I grimaced.

"Don't get your panties all in a bunch," Donald said, perusing the press kit. I blushed for all kinds of reasons, including that I was wearing a red satin thong, the first thing I grabbed from the drawer in my morning fog.

"Right, okay! So, Bayview Preserve, what about it?" I changed the subject.

Donald did a little twinkly smile and continued. "Bayview Preserve is the new flagship community for Ivory Enterprises, and they're putting the finishing touches on it right now. They're planning a

14

grand opening celebration just after Easter. Have you heard of Ivory Enterprises, Jamie?"

"They're the largest developer in Ocean City, right?"

"Definitely. Do you know anything else about them?" he asked. I shook my head.

"They started about 20 years ago, buying beach bungalows as teardowns and building small apartment buildings on the oceanside streets. Their projects got bigger and bigger, and over the years they have built high-rises and condo developments all over Delmarva," Donald said, using the term for coastal Delaware, Maryland, and Virginia. "Their focus, though, has always been on Ocean City. More recently, they've been doing bayside development, because more land is available there and the building trend has been away from apartment towers and toward new traditional communities with front porches and a small-town feel."

Donald leaned forward earnestly. "Bayview Preserve is the biggest and most high-end of all the Ivory projects. It will have its own main street, with a Reynauld's Steakhouse, a sushi bar, a Starbucks and some retail gallery space with artists' lofts above them. This establishes Ocean City as an upscale place for people from Washington, Baltimore, Philadelphia, and even New York, to own a beach

15

home," he said. "It's going to change the way the world looks at Ocean City! *Coastal Life* magazine is going to be featuring Bayview Preserve in an upcoming issue, and of course, the opening is going to be front-page news in the *Weekly Breeze*."

I envisioned a pod of plywood houses sprouting out of the reeds of Assawoman Bay, within earshot of a dinosaur-themed mini-golf course and a teen nightclub in a metal agricultural warehouse. I examined Donald's face, and didn't see any hint of sarcasm. Hmm.

"Okay, so what kind of coverage do you want? Should I look at the history of the company? Market trends for bayside development? I could talk to the engineers who figured out how to fill in the marshland..."

"We're going to devote most of *Lifestyles* to Bayview Preserve, and you'll actually need to do a couple of stories," Donald said. "So, sure, talk about the real estate trends and maybe a little about the engineering if there's a story there, but we are not doing an expose on the big, bad developers, okay? Forget it. This is a *Beach'n'Bay Lifestyles* feature."

"Got it."

"I'm serious, Jamie. There is nothing to investigate here."

"Okay. No investigating. I promise." I held up my hand, Girl Scout style.

He still wasn't satisfied. "Remember what happened when you tried to link the Russian mafia to that string of bicycle thefts?"

"Hey, I traced those stolen bikes to a chop shop in the garage of a guy named Alex, didn't I?"

"Yeah, Alex O'Shaughnessey, a high school kid from Ocean Pines."

"I still say that kid was mobbed up."

"Knock it off."

I shrugged and gave him a weak grin.

"And I want a whole story about the design choices. Talk to the decorators, the landscape designers. I want to hear about the artist who created the sculpture for the fountain..."

"The fountain?"

"Yes, it's part of the entryway, just past the guardhouse. It's a 30-foot-tall bronze osprey in the middle of a Bellagio-inspired interactive water display. I've seen the artist renderings of it," Donald said. "Exquisite."

I swallowed my snarky remark about the osprey statue probably replacing real osprey mating grounds. "The guardhouse? Who are they keeping out, my cousins from Pittsburgh?" I asked instead. I picked at a loose thread on the arm of the barrel chair.

Donald gave me a warning look. "This is high end, Jamie. It's the future of Ocean City. Get used to it."

He was probably right, but I didn't like it. The days of ramshackle beach cottages with surfboards leaned against the porch rails were fading. Beach-front—and now bayfront—real estate was too valuable, and little enclaves of weather-beaten bungalows with crab pots on the porches and sun-faded lawn furniture in the yards were being replaced with high-density, large square-footage vacation villas.

Anyway, why was I complaining? My nostalgia about the old days of Ocean City was mostly secondhand, gleaned from barroom conversations with weathered old-timer fishermen and surfers-turned-carpenters. Plus, I thought with a shudder, Bayview Preserve had to be easier on the eyes than Sunrise Paradise. I shook my head to get rid of the image of that moldering bunker of a building.

"It sounds like a great project, Donald," I said. "A lot of research to do, and plenty of people to talk to. Thanks for this." I took the promotional materials from Donald, then we talked several minutes about other stories I had in the pipeline. I confirmed he had received the dog grooming story, and he complimented my thoroughness. "I never would have thought to throw in that sidebar on the best dog hairstyles by breed."

I beamed as I moved over to my desk. I was the *Weekly Breeze's* only staff writer, but I shared the desk with several freelancers. I checked my in box, which was one slot in a vertical metal set of office trays. Tossed a couple of advertisements disguised as press releases in the trash. Then I checked my voice mail. Jerry Mulvaney from Chevy Country had left a message.

"Hey Donald."

"Hmmmm," he said, engrossed in editing, or the next song on the Whitney Houston CD, I'm not sure which.

"Jerry Mulvaney's putting a '72 Impala on the roof of his Chevy dealership on Wednesday night."

Donald chuckled. "You'd better be there to see it happen."

"Are you kidding? I wouldn't miss it."

About 7 o'clock, I closed down my computer and packed to go. As I wound my scarf around my neck and put my hat on, Donald said, "Oh, Jamie. Wesley and I are having a little dinner party next week. Will you come?"

"That sounds great, Donald!" I said, buttoning my parka tight around my scarf. "What's the occasion?"

"Occasion?" he grinned. "I don't know. No, Wesley's brother just sent a couple of cases of good Spanish Rioja." Since Wesley's retirement, his brother Vincent has been running the day-to-day operations of the family business, which flies in a lot of European wine. Wesley was thrilled to no longer be schlepping between Ocean City and Newark, and was spending his time cooking and being generally domestic. This seemed to suit Donald just fine.

"And, sweetie, bring someone," he said. It was clear that Donald relished witnessing my adventures and (mostly) misadventures in dating.

I quickly looked away and felt my face grow hot. It had been a long, dry season since my breakup in September with Brian, a bartender at Liquid Assets.

"Jamie! Are you blushing?" I couldn't sneak anything past Donald; he could tell when I was getting some. He knew even better than my best friend Tammy. This sometimes made for awkward employer-employee relations.

"I am not blushing."

"You are." His wide smile lit his face. I blushed even more.

"Who's the lucky boy? Did you and Brian patch things up?"

Brian was nice enough, but I couldn't really see us together for the long run. I hadn't spoken to him in months. The real drag was that I couldn't go back to my favorite restaurant in Ocean City. I really couldn't, not after I walked into Brian's apartment—with the key he gave me—and found him doing the deed on the coffee table with Tatiana, a Liquid Assets waitress. Asshole. I heard they never became an item. I hoped they hated seeing each other all the time at work.

"Not Brian," I said. "Just some guy I met in a bar last night. It was nothing."

On the trip south on Coastal Highway to nearly the end of the Ocean City peninsula, I had a classic Zen bus ride. I settled into my seat, stared out the window, and my mind went blank. The lights slipped by, in contrast with the darkness of the bay beyond. My breathing became slow and deep. Some people pay big bucks for meditative retreats, but I'll bet they've never tried taking the Ocean City bus down Coastal Highway in the middle of winter. By the time I got to my stop at First Street, I was totally mellow. And hungry.

I walked down First toward the bay and approached the gate in the tall chain-link fencing. A sign hung above: "Lombardo Concrete, We Dry Harder." With gloved hands I fumbled to open the padlock on the gate. I went through, then relocked behind myself.

An orange sodium light on a tall wooden pole lit most of the concrete plant's small parking lot and glinted off the metal roof of the office, a trailer in the middle of the lot. The office windows were dark. I continued past toward the lighted pier. As I walked down the pier, the wind whipped hair across my face and bit through my clothes. My home, an ancient tugboat converted to a houseboat about 30 years ago, bobbed in the water at the end of the pier. I clomped up the narrow, rickety wooden ramp to the deck, steadying myself in the wind with both hands on the railings. I'm sure this ramp is in violation of about 20 safety regulations. And the houseboat itself? I'm surprised the Coast Guard hasn't towed it.

On deck, I quickly crossed to the cabin and let myself in, switched on the lights and closed the door behind me. Larry Lombardo, the cement plant's owner, rigged the electricity when I moved in last spring. I pay him $100 a month, and I can't imagine that even covers the cost of heat. I think

Larry is simply happy someone thinks his old tugboat is habitable.

It took some elbow grease, but now the boat
feels like home. The kitchenette has a fresh coat of
high-gloss paint in vivid islandy colors, and some
Indian cotton bedspreads brighten up a
secondhand futon. I have an old bentwood rocker
and a bookshelf next to it that also serves as a table,
piled high with political science textbooks from an
online course I dropped, a Timothy Leary biog-
raphy, and a bunch of paperback mysteries. On the
floor is a scrap of green shag carpeting left over
from a Beach Getaway renovation project.

I cranked up the heaters and pulled the makings
for dinner out of a cabinet and the apartment-sized
fridge. Soon pasta was boiling on the tiny stove,
and steam was fogging the cabin windows.

After dinner, I wrapped myself in a blanket,
curled up on the futon, and called Tammy to give
her the exposé on last night's adventures with the
handsome stranger. The stars shone, the water re-
flecting their icy light.

2.

AMIE, SWEETIE, you gotta talk to Abe," Tony's voice hollered over the phone the next morning at the Beach Getaway counter. "I don't think he understands the situation here. See, what I gotta do is, I gotta shut the water down in the whole building and get in there and replace them pipes before they all freeze and burst. You hear what I'm sayin'?"

"I hear you, Tony," I said, my eardrums throbbing. "I'll be sure to let him know. And Tony, you can't turn off the water at Sunrise Paradise. There's a family staying in Unit 4."

"Oh yeah," Tony said, his voice filled with wonder. "I can't believe it! I went over there this morning to see if any of the pipes was froze, and they're actually in there. There was a lady out on the balcony. She was lookin' at the ocean or somethin'. They haven't said nothing?"

"No, I haven't heard anything from them," I said, then remembered the phone ringing as I was locking up last night. "Well, I guess we'll have to wait and see what happens. The weather isn't supposed to get any colder this week, is it?"

"No, but it's droppin' in the teens at night, so them pipes oughta be freezing by now. It's some kinda miracle they haven't already."

Abe was on a fishing trip in South Carolina all week, but I was under strict instructions not to call him unless there was an actual catastrophe. Tony has been pestering Abe about the plumbing in Sunrise Paradise for years. I agreed with Tony, the building was a disaster waiting to happen. But I guess Abe figured if the plumbing had held out for sixty years, it could hang on for another week.

"Well, let's hope the miracles continue at Sunrise Paradise. Hey, coffee in ten minutes," I said, and hung up. When I quit smoking six months ago, I had to do something besides take smoke breaks. So I started putting out coffee and doughnuts. I make a stop on the way into work at The Fractured Prune to get them hot out of the ovens. The calories are a bitch, but I did switch from Dr. Pepper to Diet Coke.

I got the coffee brewing, then I arranged a half dozen doughnuts on a platter with a fuchsia and chartreuse floral pattern that I found in the office storeroom one day while looking for a wrench to fix the restroom sink. I also put out several coffee cups in a competing bright green pattern. There surely wouldn't be any actual customers on this January Tuesday, but word was out that Beach Getaway had coffee and doughnuts. One or two people usually drifted in for a mid-morning snack.

The morning coffee setup complete, I hauled my bag onto the counter, perched on a stool and opened my laptop. I pulled out the Bayview Preserve information Donald had given me last night. I knew from press releases that Jonathan Ivory, son of company founder Bernard Ivory, was the company's spokesperson for the project. I picked up the phone to call the offices of Ivory Enterprises.

"Good morning, Ivory Enterprises, this is Corinne," said a silky voice.

"Good morning, this is Jamie August from the *Ocean City Weekly Breeze* calling for Jonathan Ivory."

"One moment please," she said, and put me on hold, where I was treated to an audio infomercial about Bayview Preserve. "Do you remember how small-town life used to be? Visiting with friends and neighbors on the front porch... Spending family time at the park... Walking downtown for an ice cream cone... Ivory Enterprises is bringing that back to Ocean City in a beautiful new traditional Main Street community, Bayview Preserve." The music rose a bit for effect. "Experience seaside living and old-fashioned small-town comfort with state-of-the-art security"— the line picked up.

"Thank you for holding, Ms. August. Mr. Ivory is on another call right now. Were you calling about the Bayview Preserve grand opening?"

"Yes, exactly. *The Breeze* is going to devote an upcoming *Lifestyles* section to the opening. I'll be handling the coverage, and I'd like to schedule some time to talk with Mr. Ivory and tour the community," I said.

"Of course," she replied. "Mr. Ivory has some time this afternoon around 4 o'clock. Would that be convenient for you?"

"Yes. That would be ideal," I murmured, already easing into the dulcet phone tones of Ivory Enterprises corporate-speak. I got the office address— uptown—and promised to be there at 4.

I hung up and considered today's outfit: flat, slouchy grey suede boots, grey tights, and a maroon cowl-neck cable-knit dress. This is about as dressy as it gets on a 20-degree day that is threatening snow.

Then I dialed the library. "Tammy, it's Jamie."

"Hey Jamie, what's going on?"

"Listen, I need to come down there in a little while and do some research on the Bayview Preserve, that big new bayside development that's about to open. I'm doing a big feature on it. Do you know the one I'm talking about?"

"Sure thing," she said. Tammy knows everything, the way librarians do. She's also smokin' hot, with long, blond rocker hair and a closet of skinny jeans and plunging necklines. "What do you wanna know?"

"Oh, geez, where do I start?" I said, thinking aloud. "Let's see: Is this the largest housing project in the history of Ocean City? I want to take a look at the permits. Was there anything on the land before—or *was* it land before now? Did they do any filling in of marshland? Were there any significant complaints from environmental watch groups? Is it legal to have a main street with businesses but have the community completely gated off? I'm wondering who they had to pay off to get this thing built. I want to see all the press coverage that there has been so far about the project, and I want to read about some of Ivory Enterprise's other projects."

"Yeah, and how much're you paying me?" Tammy snorted.

"Oh, no, no! I'm really just talking it through. I mean, I wasn't asking you to do all that research!" I lied. "I'm just telling you what I'm up to." Yeah, right. I knew she'd have half my work done before lunch. I was going to owe her some daiquiris at Fager's Island. Cost of business.

Tammy chuckled. "Well, you are looking for trouble, now, aren't you?" I could hear the eagerness in her voice. "I've got some new titles to check in, but not much else is happening. I'll see what I can scare up." Tammy worked in the new library in the northern part of town.

"You're the best. I'll be there around lunchtime, and I'll bring you a meatball sub from Belly Busters."

"Yeah, you will."

I hung up, poured myself a cup of coffee and grabbed a chocolate cake with chocolate frosting doughnut. Why mess around? I returned to my perch behind the counter and spent the next hour doing internet research on Ivory Enterprises and its many building projects. I read a *Baltimore Sun* story from two years ago about Ivory Enterprise's plans for the bayside development. The article included the views of several environmentalists who had opposed the construction. Dr. Vernette John-son of Eastern Maryland College was quoted ex-tensively. She was on a crusade against the development. "Bayview Preserve is going to be a travesty for several wetland species, including os-preys and blue crabs," she was quoted as saying. "It's ironic that the very things we come to the beach to experience—sea birds, Maryland Blue Crabs—are being destroyed by large-scale con-struction projects like Bayview Preserve, which is filling in and paving over our largest remaining expanse of wetlands."

I wanted to hear what Dr. Johnson would have to say about the project now that it was done. I checked the faculty listing on the college's web site, but she was not listed. I called the college, and learned she was no longer with the Environmental Sciences department. I'd have to track her down.

As I continued surfing, I absentmindedly kicked my boot against the back side of the wood-paneled counter. Thud, thud, thud. The 1970's "digital" clock dropped a flap— 10:48. The restroom sink dripped intermittently. Not a car passed by Beach Geta-way's plate-glass windows. Outside the sky was leaden and the temperature hovered around freez-ing.

At 11:03, Tony's work truck pulled up. He hauled himself out of the cab and slammed the door. Tony was in his late 60s, and recently, in addition to being hard of hearing, was moving a little bit stiffly. His salt-and-pepper hair and mustache were, as always, neatly pomaded into place, and he wore a heavy blue work jacket with a patch that said "Tony."

The bell tinkled as he strode into the office. "Good morning, Jamie, how you doin'?" he boomed.

"I'm doing great, Tony. Have a doughnut and some coffee," I said, gesturing to the plate at the end of the counter.

"Thanks, sweetheart, I don't mind if I do. You put out such a nice spread here," he said. "Real nice. I always tell Tony Junior, 'you ought to come down the office, get yourself a doughnut.' I guess he's pretty busy, though. Maybe he'll make it in tomorrow."

"Sure, maybe he will," I said. Every day Tony said the same thing. It was soothing, like hearing the same stories over and over from my grandpa as a kid. Tony Junior, a plumbing supply store delivery guy, was painfully shy. I couldn't imagine him stopping to shoot the breeze, but I thought it was sweet that Tony held out hope his son would discover this enjoyable little daily ritual. I could also hear what Tony wasn't saying. He was trying to play matchmaker, but neither party was taking the bait. And no wonder. Socially awkward men in plumbing supply don't hook up with reporters on the lookout for the next big story and the next all-wrong guy.

Tony made himself comfortable in one of the vinyl lobby chairs and we chatted about nothing much until lunchtime. When Abe was here, the two of them would argue about football and horse racing. I didn't know anything about horse racing, and I only know enough about football to cheer when the Ravens score and wear my purple jersey like a Maryland girl should.

So Tony had to talk to me about other things, but that was no problem. He told me about his plans to repave his driveway; the linguine and clams his wife had made for dinner last night; what he thought of the Monday night TV lineup. At about noon, I cleaned up the coffee and doughnuts (I had eaten two; Tony polished off three, so I tossed one). I packed my bag and put on my coat and hat, with Tony keeping up a steady stream of chatter about the trip he and his wife had taken to the Delaware shopping outlets, the economy, and his new favorite brand of socks. As I shuffled him out the door, he was still bellowing about how he was thinking of changing to a different cell phone plan and isn't it terrible that the price of electricity keeps going up?

He got into his white work truck, with a "Tony's Plumbing" logo in blue lettering on the side, and drove off. I stepped to the curb as the bus rolled up, and hopped on for the ride to the sub shop, then to the library.

The new branch of Ocean City's library had opened less than a month before, and a new carpet smell mingled with the unmistakable, intoxicating smell of books and *information*. I spotted Tammy pushing a cart of children's books down the aisle. She was wearing all black: a slouchy sweater with a tank underneath, mini-skirt, heavy tights, and boots with big, clunky heels. I headed in her direction, waving the Belly Busters bag.

"What's with the Goth look?" I said, giving her a quick hug.

"All my virginal whites are in the wash," she said as she parked the cart at the end of a book-shelf. "I'm starving! Come on back and let's eat."

We walked through a door marked "Employees Only" and into a bright, comfortable lounge with a few round tables and chairs, and a small sofa tucked in the corner. A kitchenette hugged the far wall, and a reasonably fresh pot of coffee sat on the warming burner. The fact that I had just eaten two doughnuts did nothing to curb my appetite. As we settled into lunch—steak and cheese sub with mushrooms and onions for me; meatball sub for Tammy—she filled me in on what she had unearthed that morning.

"So here's the deal. Are you ready for this? Bayview Preserve was built on a couple of parcels of land. The largest one was previously owned by someone named Frank Donnelley. Donnelley had a house on the property, and he died when the house burned down in 1995. Shortly after the fire, Ivory Enterprises bought the property from the estate. For $75,000."

"What? A big parcel with bay frontage would be worth over a million today, wouldn't it? Even back then, wasn't that too low?"

"Yeah, I would think so," Tammy said.

"How long had he owned the property?"

"Thirty-five years," Tammy said. "Maybe they didn't know what they had, you know, the estate."

"Wow." I took another bite, strings of mozzarella stretching from the sandwich to my mouth. I found some napkins in the bottom of the bag and wiped the grease off my chin. Heaven!

We finished lunch, cleaned up the aftermath of our feast, then Tammy led the way up to the second floor. She set me up with research materials in the OC Room, where the library has collected all things relating to Ocean City. I studied maps, read about the history of bayside development, and the recent attempts at environmental preservation. All background, but all necessary for my understanding of Bayview Preserve. The sleet pelting the window did not break my concentration. At 3:30, my cell phone alarm startled me to action.

I closed up my laptop and tucked the materials back on the shelves. With a grim look out the ice-glazed window, I put on my scarf, coat, and hat. Tammy, now at the circulation desk, waved good-bye. I sprinted across the street to the bus shelter for the northbound bus, and thankfully it pulled up just a few moments later. Minutes after I stepped on the bus, the toes of my wool tights grew cold and damp as the ice on my suede boots melted.

As the lone passenger, I sat in the front of the bus. I found a stick of gum in the depths of my bag, and popped it in my mouth. Didn't want onion breath for the interview.

The driver was a woman in her 50s, with white-blond hair shellacked into orderly waves marching back from her forehead. Her lipstick, which looked

fresh, was frosty pink, as were her perfectly manicured nails. She drove with just the toes of her tiny
white tennis shoes touching the pedals. She had
bright blue galoshes tucked neatly into a side compartment next to her seat. She drove slowly and
carefully. Being on the road when it's icy makes me
more than a little nervous, but this driver inspired
confidence.

When the bus deposited me in North Ocean
City, I was surprised. Ivory Enterprises was an
enormous, hulking 1970s-era high-rise building,
with black-glass windows supported by industrial-
looking gray concrete. But it wasn't an office building: it was residential. A sign by the entrance called
it "Ocean Mirage."

The foyer inside the smoked glass entry door
was cramped and dim, with low ceilings and recessed lighting circa 1977. Pushing through a second set of doors, I emerged into a giant square
lobby, devoid of furniture, with floors and walls of
black marble. Hanging at least three stories up
were four enormous '70s-modern chandeliers that
looked like monstrous, illuminated surgical instru-
ments. I felt a little nervous walking under them as
I crossed to the elevators. My boots echoed against
the marble, and I noticed with surprise that this
cold, empty space smelled musty. Where could the

smell have even attached itself? The place seemed deserted, and for the most part, it probably was—just like the rest of town.

As I reached the elevators, a security guard approached, his hard leather shoes clicking smartly. He wore a well-made blue blazer and a tie. His eyes were the color of his jacket, and looked as hard and cold as marbles. His skin was pale, nearly translucent, and looked like it would be cold. Where had he come from? "May I help you?" he said politely, but he didn't smile.

"Oh, hey! Hi! Wow, where did you come from?" I said with a nervous laugh that echoed in the room. He stared at me with a neutral, vacant expression.

"Um, I'm here to visit Ivory Enterprises. Have I come to the right place?"

"Your name?"

"Jamie August," I said with a grin.

He studied me until I stopped smiling and popped my gum. Then he turned to the elevators and carefully pressed the up button. We stood in silence and I looked sideways at him while he watched the display track the elevator's descent from 24 all the way to L. A rich, deep bell sounded and the doors slid open. The guard stepped in and placed his hand across the opening to hold the door for me. I stepped in, and the door closed. He pressed 22 and stood in silence on the shiny black floor. I didn't understand why he would ride the elevator up with me, but he didn't seem like one for chitchat. So I stood quietly, studying him as discreetly as I could in the black mirrored surface of the doors. His clean-shaven jaw was sharp; he was fit in a lean, economical way; and he smelled slightly musty, like the lobby.

The silence in the elevator was shattered by the sudden shrill ringtones of my cell phone, which plays Bon Jovi's "Dead or Alive." The guard looked at me as though I had vomited on my shoes as I rooted around in my huge purse trying to find the damn phone. Fuck that creepy security guard. Bon Jovi is the best American band since—well—since ever.

Finally I had my phone in my grasp, then it lost its signal and stopped ringing. I smiled wanly, and threw the phone back into the bag's depths.

When the doors slid open at 22, we stepped into a hushed corridor that stretched about 50 feet in either direction. The floors were carpeted in thick, black shag, and the walls were papered in smoky, silvery paper. Lights were recessed into a low, nubby, acoustical-tiled ceiling that must have been the height of modernity about 10 years before I was born. Everything in this building looked like it was the pinnacle of cutting-edge style around 1974, and it was all perfectly preserved.

The security guard turned left, and I followed. When he reached the door at the end, he rang a small bell at the side and stepped back, nearly bumping into me. As I moved aside, he turned to look at me again. I smiled, chewed my Trident. He stared back, considering me as if I were a dung beetle crawling across the silverfoil wallpaper.

Then the door opened.

"Jamie August to see Jonathan Ivory," he said to the striking, auburn-haired woman.

"Thanks for the lift!" I said as I entered the office, laughing at my pun as the two of them considered me dispassionately. Holy crap! These two were making me so nervous I was babbling. The woman wore a winter-weight wool suit in turquoise, nipped in at the waist and accessorized with a razor-sharp gold and silver brooch on the lapel. Her high-heeled pumps matched her suit, and her magenta lipstick was flawless.

The security guard shut the door behind him, and the woman said, "May I take your coat?" I recognized the voice as Corinne from the phone this morning.

"Yes, thanks," I said, handing her my parka. I felt a chill as Corinne's critical eye swept over my sweater dress, which looked hopelessly worn and sloppy next to her suit. These people were not making an ironic, fun statement with their '70s decor and fashion. They might not have taken a single step outside since the Ford Administration.

"Please have a seat," Corinne said, indicating a pair of mustard-yellow nubby wool chairs with a floor lamp/table combination thing between them. The chairs actually looked great with the thick charcoal carpet, which extended from the hallway. I sat, and rummaged in my purse to look for a gum wrapper to get rid of my chewed gum. No luck. Corinne disappeared silently through a heavy door to the right, and I sat, considering the sleety view out the floor-to-ceiling window behind her desk.

There was a carefully ordered rack of files on the desk, and a bank of file cabinets to its left. A heavy black phone sat on the desk's surface; there was no computer in sight. The silence was complete. Even the precipitation outside seemed to make no noise against the windows. The room was warm, but I shivered.

Just then the door to the right opened, and Corinne emerged with a smiling, sandy-haired man. He looked to be about 35, fit, and sporty. I

41

swallowed my gum and coughed sharply as Corinne looked at me with a mixture of concern and distaste. I forced myself to take a deep breath, felt the gum slide down my throat, and stood.

I pasted a smile on my face and looked at the man, whose smile did not quite conceal his shock. This was definitely the guy I fucked two nights ago.

"Hello there! I'm Jonathan Ivory, please call me Jon. Great to see you! So glad you could swing by!" He thrust a manicured hand past Corinne, and I reached to shake it as she stepped sideways to extricate herself from between us. His glance lingered on the sweater dress—or was it my boobs he was looking at? The dress may have shrunk a little in the wash last time.

"Hi Jon. Thanks for meeting with me."

I picked up my bag and followed him into his office. We lurched forward a decade as we crossed the threshold. I focused intently on the furniture, the carpeting, willing my heart rate to slow. The carpet switched abruptly to a thick but tightly plush green, with two black leather sofas and a coffee table punctuating the expanse of space in front of a massive black and chrome desk. The coffee table's glass top enclosed a display of Ivory Enterprises brochures and booklets. On the right side of the desk sat a Newton's cradle, one of those desk ornaments with the row of suspended steel balls that knock against each other as they swing. In the corner was a golf putter; shelves behind held what looked like a display of more items from The Sharper Image catalog. By the window there was a small wet bar.

I crossed the room and sat on the leather sofa, in the process knocking my knee against the coffee table's sharp edge. I caught a gasp of pain in my throat and saw that my sweater dress now had a hole that would soon start to unravel. Great. Jonathan, not noticing this, sat opposite me and chuckled.

"Hi," he said.

"Hi. Um. I had no idea...."

"Clearly. Well, I think we can make the best of an awkward situation," he said with a mischievous grin.

I smiled, my skin hot. "Definitely." I pulled out my notebook and pen, and a small voice recorder, which I placed on the table between us with a shaky hand. He motioned to a set of glossy promotional materials that were arrayed across the glass tabletop.

"Let's get the preliminaries out of the way," he said, clearly enjoying my embarrassment. "Bayview Preserve is the premier Ocean City address, as I'm sure you know." He leaned back comfortably, extending an arm across the back of his sofa and launching into a canned speech about the architectural details, the amenities, the conveniences, the luxuries of the gated bayside enclave. I took notes and made what I thought were appropriate comments as he spoke. After a few moments, Corinne came in with a full coffee service and a carefully arranged plate of cookies.

"Wow, thanks Corinne! This is great!" I said, earning a cool glance from the icy Corinne. I noted that the cookie platter was similar to the one I used at Beach Getaway. Mine was pink and green, and this was a muted black and grey—but the same pattern. Corinne left and I settled back with a weak cup of coffee and a hard cookie, and listened to Jonathan's smooth voice going on and on about the luxurious wonders of the crappy new housing development on the marsh.

I was not thinking about the housing development, not even a bit. I couldn't help but notice Jon's flat stomach. A different view of it forced its way to my mind's eye. I remembered looking up from between his thighs, as his fingers raked my hair, his breath caught in his throat and his head dropped back against the seat...

"And the environmentally sensitive nature trail rings the perimeter of the community," he droned, his voice growing quiet and silky. By the time he got to talking about the "green-themed" model homes, I had stopped writing. My breath was light and shallow, and our eyes were locked.

Focus, Jamie! Focus! "Green-themed?" I asked. "Who cares? No! I mean, how so?"

Jonathan's slow, sexy smile made me shiver. "Oh, you know, bamboo flooring, recycled paper towels in the model kitchen, the usual," he said. "Let's go take a look, shall we?"

"Yes, let's go," I said. With some effort, I shook off my hormone-induced lethargy and gathered my notebook and recorder. Good thing I recorded the interview; I couldn't remember a damn thing he said.

As we donned scarves, coats, and hats in the reception area, the outer door opened suddenly and in swept a much older, more padded version of Jonathan. As he let the door swing closed behind him, he turned to face me. The sour expression that looked to be the normal arrangement of his face, transformed itself into an ingratiating smile.

"Hello, Father," Jonathan said. "I'd like you to meet Jamie August from the *Ocean City Weekly*

Breeze," he said. "Jamie, this is Bernard Ivory, president and CEO of Ivory Enterprises."

"It's nice to meet you," I said. "I am putting together a series of articles about Bayview Preserve, and I am so grateful for Jonathan's help." Ack! Laying it on thick never hurts, though.

As we shook hands, Bernard Ivory responded with a brusque, "Yes, a pleasure. I'm sure Jonathan can give you all the information you need."

"Jamie and I are going to take a drive around Bayview Preserve and have some further discussion," he said, throwing a grin in my direction.

"Hell of a day for it, but knock yourself out," Bernard said, glancing out the window at the sleet and the steely expanse of ocean below.

We finished bundling up and headed out the door, down the strangely claustrophobic hall, into the elevator and out into the sleety afternoon.

3.

ADMITTEDLY I WAS NOT thinking clearly, not with all those visions of back-seat sex dancing through my head, but even so I had to wonder what we were doing heading out in this storm. It soon became clear.

"Yeah, she's good in any kind of weather," Jonathan said proudly, patting the dashboard of the Cadillac Escalade. "Platinum edition, 6.2 liter V8, all wheel drive with over 400 horsepower in this baby." One smooth hand rested on the burled wood and leather steering wheel as he drove south down the empty but slick Coastal Highway. He smiled at me confidently and sailed right through a series of red lights. "Um, Jon," I stammered.

"Nobody's out here today, why worry?" he said, as I double-checked that my seat belt was fastened.

He made a right turn onto a service road and we soon coasted up to a guard shack, its gingerbread trim clogged with icicles. A narrow bar blocked the street, which raised when Jonathan pressed a button on a remote clipped to his sun visor. "The guardhouse is staffed 24/7. If you don't belong at Bayview Preserve, you're not coming in," he said with finality. He waved at a guy sitting inside the little building and the guy waved back.

I made a note in my book. "I know that gated communities are becoming more and more common," I said. "What's the point of living in a gated community here?"

Jonathan looked at me like I was a dimwit. "If you've just spent a million-two on a Bayview Preserve condo, you're not going to want just anybody walking past your front door, am I right?"

"I guess so," I said. "But this is Ocean City, not some ritzy neighborhood. I mean, blue-collar and white-collar people come here for their vacations, and everyone feels comfortable. Do you think a gated community really fits in?"

"We're over 80 percent sold out and it's not even spring yet, so yeah, I think the concept works," he replied.

"Fair enough," I nodded.

We drove slowly into the compound, and passed through a fake cobblestone roundabout. The lane curved into a tiny, one-block "downtown" area, with a town square and a series of shopfronts, most completed but not yet occupied. "This is downtown Bayview Preserve," Jonathan said, easing into well-practiced patter and sliding a hand onto my knee. I did not protest. "There will be a coffee shop, a general store, an ice cream parlor, a salon and day spa, an art gallery, and a casual bistro. To our left is the home sales showroom, and over here ..." he paused for effect, "is the interactive fountain, modeled after the Bellagio fountain in Las Vegas."

"Yeah, this I have to see. You really modeled the fountain after the one at the Bellagio? That thing is enormous, and it's timed to music!" I looked out into the sleet, trying to get a sense of the space, but could only see a foggy void beyond the corner of the sales office. I was also trying to remember the one glimpse I had of the Bellagio fountain, but that memory was dimmed by too many rum punches in the back of a stretch limo with six girlfriends on a bachelorette weekend. That was the furthest I'd ever been from home.

"Well, it's not as big as the Bellagio's, of course," he admitted. "But it'll play to music every evening in season!" When I think of music in Ocean City, I think of Billy Squire, AC/DC, and whatever is the most sexist and offensive gangsta music of the day. I had a moment's mental flash of the arcs of water cascading gracefully to "She was a fast machine, She kept her motor clean." I smiled, then snorted a little when I thought about what the fountain might do with "She told me to come but I was already there."

"Wow, this is really something," I said aloud, composing myself. "Maybe later this week the weather will clear up and we can take another trip through so that I can actually see this thing and get some pictures."

"I'd love to, Jamie," he said, flashing a brilliant smile.

As the storm grew more fierce and the ice marched across the SUV's roof in waves, we continued with the tour. We drove past a series of three-story condominium buildings, all trimmed in faux wooden siding and painted in sunny pastel shades. Mid-Atlantic beaches have a forlorn look about them in the off-season, with their jaunty summer colors and thatched-hut decor shaking in the winter winds. Here, the sky blue, butter yellow, and peach buildings with their fancy old-town trim looked fragile and out of place, like tropical birds caught in a snowstorm.

As we drove past the condos, Jonathan rattled off pricing and features. "The classic package has your vinyl and wall-to-wall, in-unit washer dryer, basic appliances, and then your upgrade package includes solid surface counters, hardwood and tile options, upgraded trim and stainless steel appliances." I went through the motions of taking notes, but my brain kept tuning out. "The Green Living package has been a big seller for us in the condos but even more so with the townhomes and villas. That includes your bamboo flooring, Energy Star appliances, low-VOC paints in your eco-style colors..."

"What are eco-style colors?"

"Oh, you know. Brown. Come on, I'll show you the model."

He parked and we dashed for the model condominium, its front walk lined with frozen tufts of sea grass.

Jonathan's master key opened the door to a unit decorated in muted beiges and greens, with arty sand dune photographs on the walls.

"Pretty," I said, strolling through the living room.

"Like you," he said, putting an arm around my waist and guiding me down a hallway.

I grinned, and my stomach did a little flip as he led me through a bedroom door, then pinned me against the wall.

He kissed me and those easy, practiced hands rested on my shoulders. My arms went around him and I kissed back. I wasn't sure my brain really liked this guy, but my body was seriously into him.

When I noticed that he had inched my sweater dress all the way up into one hand and he was starting to roll my tights down, I came up for air.

"Hey, wait, no."

"It's okay, there's nobody here but us." He caught me in another mind-melting kiss, and I lost track of all reason. His fingers inched inside my black and pink lace panties, and I knew he could tell how ready I was to have him again. Part of me said what the hell. We already did it once. The other part...

"No. Jon, stop." I nudged him away and pulled my dress more or less back into place. "I want to stop."

"What's wrong?"

"I don't ... we don't even know each other."

"Well, actually, biblically speaking, we do," he said, rocking back on his heels, hands in his pockets to minimize his erection.

"That's true. But this time we're sober."

"We can fix that."

I laughed, then I gazed at him, feeling a little foolish. "It's just too fast."

He gently smoothed a strand of hair from my forehead and kissed me. "I can go real slow."

My knees nearly buckled with lust, and I let myself get lost in one more kiss. Then I took a step away from him. "Okay, seriously, no. Let's continue the tour." Jon blew out a frustrated sigh, then nodded.

Am I nuts? This guy is hot, and I already know he's got mad skills. But I can't help it, I'm a modern girl. It's okay to have sex with a stranger, definitely exciting and sort of excusable after several drinks. But having sex on purpose with someone you already know? That actually means something. That makes me a little nervous.

With a hand on the small of my back, Jonathan led me back through the door of the model and into the cold afternoon.

"Were environmentally friendly practices used in the construction of the buildings?" I asked later, when we were back on the road that circled Bayview Preserve.

"Of course, of course," he said. "Everything here complies with the latest building codes, which emphasize environmental concerns. We used double-paned windows, high-efficiency HVAC systems, all the latest in environmental, uh, technology."

"Wait, but this is just in order to meet the local building codes, though?"

"Definitely. All of our buildings are constructed 100 percent up to code," he said.

"But any new construction has to follow current building codes," I pointed out. "Isn't Bayview Preserve supposed to be designed specifically to be ecologically friendly?"

"Absolutely, and I'm glad you asked that question," he said with a disarming smile. "As we round the bend here, ah, look at that view!" he said, and we squinted through the windshield at the bay: slate-colored, choppy and nearly invisible in the fog and freezing rain. "As you can see, over there by the water's edge, there is the eco-walking trail." I couldn't see what he was talking about, but I took his word for it. He stopped the car again and turned to face me.

"The trail is made of reclaimed, recycled rubber and encompasses the whole property," he said, drawing a circle with his hands to illustrate this tricky concept. "At several key points," here, here, and here, went his gestures, "we have put up educational signage about the area wildlife. There's one on the Maryland blue crab, one on the osprey, one on the native grasses that grow at the water's edge. All of this is designed to bring greater awareness to our residents about the importance of the fragile local ecosystem," he said in a concerned, earnest voice.

I nodded and scribbled. I was thinking, they may as well change the slogan from "Maryland is for crabs" to "Maryland *was* for crabs." Soon the blue crabs that Maryland is famous for will be gone, along with the other land and sea creatures that used to thrive on the marshy shores. But all that was just my inside voice. My outside voice remained silent.

"Ivory Enterprises is very proud of our environmental stewardship at Bayview Preserve, and our residents are committed to it as well," he continued.

"Mmm-hmm," I said as I wrote. "That's great, Jon! Let's see the rest of it." I looked across at him with a cheerful smile.

55

"Sure, I'll show you the villas and the executive estate homes," Jonathan said as he wheeled the car down the lane, which curved left into a tightly packed section of tall, narrow houses with steeply pitched roofs and front porches. Alleys ran behind the houses, and a line of garage doors and trash enclosures lined either side of the alleyways. In front, there were sidewalks with park benches here and there. The houses stood about 10 feet apart.

"These are the Villas at Bayview Preserve," he said, rattling off more prices, features, and other real estate patter. As he spoke, I noted the same gingerbread details on the porches, the same beachy pastel colors on the "wood" siding on the fronts of the houses. The sides and backs looked to be vinyl. A powerful gust of wind blew in off the bay, and a section of siding flapped loose. Jonathan drove on.

Beyond this neighborhood, the streets widened slightly and the yards got more spacious. Centered on each plot was a gigantic, three-story faux-farmhouse with shake-style shingles, screened front porches, skylights, two-story windows, three-car garages—the works. The houses on the right side of the street backed directly onto the bay. The shoreline was neatly lined with rocks, and a dock extended from each back yard into the steely, half-frozen water.

The community beach, clubhouse and dock were next on the tour. The dock was black with wet ice. The clubhouse, a rambling one-story wooden structure with a jaunty island-style tin roof was buttoned up tight. Jonathan said that inside was a bar and restaurant, a snack bar, a gym, and a party room.

All these perks looked nice. The thought crossed my mind that someday I ought to think about owning a place of my own, though God knows I couldn't afford anything like Bayview Preserve. My development would be more like Cornfield Vista or Mini-Mart Acres.

"So what do you think, Jamie?" said Jonathan as he wheeled the Escalade to the main loop that led back to the guard shack and out of Bayview Preserve.

"Very impressive," I punted. "There's definitely nothing else like it in Ocean City."

"Absolutely. Now, let's continue this conversation over a drink, shall we?"

"A drink. Not six drinks and a roll in the back seat!"

"As you wish."

57

We drove past several bars and restaurants before we found a place that was open on a Tuesday during an ice storm. Jonathan parked in the surprisingly full lot, and we dashed through the slush into AJ's, one of those restaurant/pubs that has random stuff hung from the walls and ceiling as decor. I had hoisted many a green beer here on St. Patrick's Day.

On the TV behind the bar, the pre-game show was just starting for the Steelers vs. Browns game, and the place was already filling with Pittsburgh fans. Ocean City is almost 400 miles away from Pittsburgh, but make no mistake: it's a Steelers town. Things can get a little tense when the Steelers and the Ravens play.

Smells of fried everything wafted from the kitchen. We sat at a booth by the window. The waitress, wearing jeans and a black Steelers jersey, approached. She narrowed her eyes and stared daggers at me. She looked at Jonathan, smiled slyly and tossed her blonde ponytail. "What can I get you all?" she said.

Jonathan gave the waitress a knowing smile. "Hey there," he said. "Are you hungry at all, Jamie?"

Before I could answer he said, "We'll have the fried sampler platter, a Heineken and ..." he paused and looked at me.

"A Coors Light," I said, smiling sweetly at the waitress and flipping my hair over one shoulder. The waitress looked at me and did one of those "Oh no you di'int" neck rolls. Then her eyes cut to Jonathan, and she grinned and winked at him. His eyes lingered on her ass as she walked away. Then he returned his gaze to me, absentmindedly twisting a signet ring.

"If you don't mind, I'd like to talk some more about Bayview Preserve," I said, ignoring the waitress drama completely and setting my tape recorder on the table.

He sighed patiently. "Absolutely, love to," he said. The sounds of the Star-Spangled Banner drifted over the crowd as the Steelers game neared kickoff. The waitress brought our beers over, a little smile on her face as she arranged coasters and glasses and did not make eye contact with either of us. Then she swished away. Jonathan's eyes strayed to the waitress, then up to the TV. How irritating.

My voice brought his attention back to the table. "Let's get back to the environmental focus that Ivory Enterprises has had with the Bayview Preserve project," I said, fanning out the promotional materials, all unbleached, heavy textured paper with elegant yet homey woodblock images of bayside scenes. "With so much focus on the bay's ecosystem, and the decline of the Maryland Blue Crab population, I'm sure you had to jump through some serious hoops to get this thing built."

Jonathan raised his beer bottle and took a swig. "Hell, you got that right," he said, looking skyward. Then he got his game face back on. "It was a lot of work, and we were glad to do it," he said, salesman-speak rolling into place. "We formed a working partnership to study the area with the Environmental Sciences department at Eastern Maryland College. We took a look at what was happening on- and offshore right there, at what is now Bayview Preserve, and found that the topography and the currents in that particular spot actually made it difficult for crabs to mate. It might have to do with the dredging that was done for the Route 90 bridge construction in the early '70s. We don't know for sure why, but that's what the Eastern Maryland report said. And so, we went on with the construction."

"What would you have done if the report showed that the construction would have been a problem?" I asked.

"Actually, in my book it was a win-win situation," he chuckled. "Plan B was to build an environmentally friendly golf course. It wouldn't have been as profitable, of course. But it sure would be nice to play a round of golf right here in Ocean City, wouldn't it?"

Just then Miss Thing arrived with our plate of fried goodies, plunking it down right on top of the press kit. A turkey platter-sized dish of fried cheese, fried mushrooms, fried chicken tenders, fried green beans, and fried onion rings. Oh, and French fries, of course. Marinara and tartar sauce nestled in the middle on a leaf of lettuce—greens! Jonathan and I dove in, silent for a few glorious, salty moments of joy. I grinned at him between bites and he smiled back.

When the food was gone, I pushed myself back from the table, greasy and sated, and finished my beer. The pub erupted into a thunderous cheer at the Steelers' first score. Jonathan gave a hoot for the team as well.

"So Jonathan, do you live in Ocean City?" I asked, languid and happy.

"Yes, right in the Ocean Mirage building. When Father consolidated the Ivory Enterprises offices here in Ocean City a few years ago, we moved down from Philadelphia."

"And when you say 'we', you mean?"

"I, uh. That's a little something we haven't covered yet. I can't lie to you, Jamie. I moved down here with my wife. I'm married." He said it earnestly, like he was telling me he had cancer.

Son of a bitch. How had I not seen this coming? I dropped my eyes to the table.

"Hey, but don't worry about it, it's not a problem. She's in Boca Raton for the winter."

I could taste the fried food coming back up my throat. I didn't trust myself to speak. My hands shook as I pulled the press kit out from under the wreckage of the appetizer platter. I shoved everything randomly in my bag, including a few stray French fries. I grabbed my coat and slid out of the booth.

"What are you doing?" He looked more annoyed than concerned. "Okay, come on. There's a snowstorm outside. I can take you home."

I kept walking and bumped into our waitress, who gave me a withering look as she attempted to rebalance the huge tray of food on her shoulder. "Girl, you better watch it," she hissed. Without breaking stride, I flipped her the bird, then used the finger to give a little push to the underside of the tray. The whole thing came crashing down, a waterfall of chili, mashed potatoes, gravy, and fries all over her shiny blond hair. As the waitress hollered obscenities at me and Jonathan yelped in horrified embarrassment, I pushed open the front door and walked out into the night.

The air was frigid with wet, and I knew it would be hard to get warm on the boat. Nevertheless, I caught the bus heading south on Coastal Highway. I sat in the back, letting the tears stream down my face. After a few minutes, I sniffled, straightened up, and gave myself a good talking to. I might be a lousy judge of boyfriend material, but I'm a good reporter and I'm on deadline. Tonight, I will put all my notes together. I will do my job.

By the time I got off at the First Street stop, I was feeling steadier. I made myself sing Gloria Gaynor's "I Will Survive" as I trudged down the deserted street, crunching on the icy sidewalk. I opened the padlock, locked up behind myself, and crossed the parking lot. I noticed that the lights were still on in the office trailer and Larry Lombardo's car was next to the door. I walked over and opened the trailer door.

"Doesn't anybody know there's a bunch of ice all over the roads?" I said by way of hello.

"Oh hey, Jamie, what's goin' on?" said Larry in his usual, weary voice. Larry wore a frayed fisherman's sweater, jeans, and work boots. His gray hair, in need of a trim, curled out from the edges of a heavy wool cap. He was drinking coffee, smoking a cigarette, and, as far as I could tell, not doing anything else. The surface of his desk was clean.

"Hey, Larry. Seriously, it's treacherous out there! What are you doing here?" Larry lived near Salisbury, about 40 minutes away.

"I got it covered, don't worry about me," he said gruffly. "I got some coffee on." He nodded across the room at the grimy Mister Coffee machine. I grabbed a chipped "I'm Crabby" mug decorated with a big orange crab, and poured myself a cup. The secondhand smoke felt great. I breathed it in greedily.

"Yeah, I'll have some coffee, thanks. It'll be a late night for me. I'm working on a big story. Couple of stories, actually," I said, trying to match his gruff attitude.

"Oh yeah? What about?"

"That monstrous new housing development up near the Route 90 Bridge, Bayview Preserve. Heard of it?"

"Yeah, I know about it," Larry said sharply, and took a big swig of hot coffee.

"Really? What do you know? Have you done work for Ivory Enterprises?"

"No, I have never worked with those assholes," he said. "They are a bunch of thieves, and I wouldn't sell them a pile of dog shit." He slammed his cup down.

"Well, yes. I agree they're a bunch of slimy, no-good, two-timing, sleazy-ass dickheads—or at least Jonathan Ivory is—but what happened between you and them?"

Larry barked out a laugh. "Sounds personal. What, did you sleep with him?"

"Oh my god, how'd you know?" I planted my forehead in my palm.

He shook his head. "Ah, hell, you really did sleep with him. I'm sorry."

Tears welled up in my eyes again, and Larry, looking extremely uncomfortable, patted me on the shoulder. "He's a piece of shit."

"Thanks, Larry."

He retreated, squinting out of the smudgy trailer window, and stared for so long that I wondered if he had gone off into a reverie, as he often does these days. His wife, Martha, died of cancer just a year ago, leaving Larry and their grown son, Dan, who runs a charter fishing operation.

"Anyway, whatever," I said. "It happens. As for Ivory Enterprises: I know these guys are slimeballs who must have cut every corner in the construction process. Hell, the cornerstone of their advertising campaign is that Bayview Preserve is 'environmentally friendly,' but do you know what they mean by that?"

Larry shrugged.

"It means they followed the current building code, which is becoming more environmentally stringent. They followed the building code! Like they had a choice!" I fumed. "So, if you know something about how the place was built, or if they screwed any of their building contractors, or maybe they are hiding something about the construction, or anything, please ..."

"No, I don't know anything about Bayview Preserve, okay?" Larry said. "Just leave it. Just leave those people the hell alone." He gave me an angry, almost threatening look.

"Okay, Larry. Listen, if you change your mind, or there's anything ..."

"No, Jamie! Now, get out of here. I'm going home." He softened just a fraction. "I'm sorry for what happened to you, but forget it."

I took a final swig of the potent coffee, put the mug down on the desk, and walked out, closing the trailer door softly behind me.

What the hell was that all about?

The parking lot was slippery. I made my way carefully down the dock and onto the houseboat. Once inside, I turned the heat all the way up, switched on some lamps, and put another pot of coffee on. When I'm this wired, having more or less coffee in my system doesn't matter. I settled down at my desk, my coat and hat still on. The cabin would warm up soon enough. Sort of.

What had gotten Larry so bunched up? Had he tried to be a part of the Bayview Preserve construction project, but they gave the job to one of his competitors? Did they screw over their contractors? Was there something sub-par about the concrete work? I pondered. What else could get Larry so upset about them?

I set up my laptop and did some internet research to try and find out who the various construction contractors were. It took some digging, but I pieced together a list, including an outfit called Eastern Concrete, based in Dover, Delaware. I made note of a phone number for Eastern, and wrote down the names of the owners.

Next, I began entering all of the day's notes into the computer, a job that has to be done while the information is fresh. It was almost midnight when I finished. I saved the file and backed it up online. Then I connected my digital recorder to the computer, backed up the recording of today's interviews, and saved that online. Even though my MacBook is going strong, I have had two computers shit the bed in the last three years, so I no longer take any chances with my work.

I walked over to the window with my coffee cup, sipping the cold dregs. The night sky had cleared in the last hour, and starlight gilded the edges of the last wispy clouds.

Larry's troubled face haunted me as I gazed at the inky bay. Larry was a hothead, but business is business with him. He has run his company long enough to roll with it when he gets passed up for a job. It didn't add up.

I put my cup in the sink, folded out the futon, and switched off the lamps. As I lay gently rocking in the dark, the sting of hurt and anger fell over me again in waves, but each one rocked me a little less. I should have known. A guy like that doesn't go for a girl like me. Then I thought, what does that even mean? As my little houseboat gently creaked and bobbed in the bay, I wondered, what kind of a girl am I?

4.

DO YOU THINK those people at Sunrise Paradise are still alive?" I asked Tony over coffee and doughnuts the next morning. I brushed stray chocolate crumbs from the front of my purple scoop-necked sweater and jeans.

"I don't know. Do you think them pipes made it through last night?" he wondered. We considered the situation, leaning against the orange countertop. I picked at a loose spot of Formica.

"Let's go see," I said, and like a flash we were out the door, me locking up while Tony started his truck.

We cruised down the icy street, squinting at the sunny, freezing morning. We turned left onto 43rd

Street and the orange building loomed ahead. Tony slowed to a crawl, and pulled over at the curb. Silence, except for the calm, rhythmic crash of the surf.

"Should we go knock on their door?" I didn't really want to face the cranky family; they looked sullen when they picked up the keys. They were probably murderous after two days of "vacation" in this moldering place. What if they came at us with a frying pan, or a toilet plunger? On the other hand, what if they were frozen to death?

"Oh boy, I don't know," Tony said, blowing out a big exhale. We sat staring at the building for a minute, and then—"Wouldja look at that? There she is!"

The woman walked out onto the balcony and leaned on the railing—"Uh-oh. Is that wood rotten?" I asked Tony with a shudder.

"I think it's okay," he said. "Kinda rotten, but frozen good." She leaned out further for a glimpse of the sea, breathing in the clean, cold morning air. The wind blew gently through her permed red hair.

"I don't believe it," I said. "It looks like she's kind of enjoying herself."

"Maybe she's going through the change a' life," Tony said. "You know, hot flashes and that." I gave him a scornful look. "What? Gotta be something like that; the heat don't really work in there."

"Maybe she killed the rest of the family," I said. "Maybe they're all in there, stacked up and frozen solid in the bathtub." Tony grimaced.

"Hope not. Could cause real problems with the drain pan, all that weight," he said thoughtfully.

The woman stretched her arms overhead luxuriously, turned, and went back inside.

"Amazing."

"Never woulda believed it," I said. Tony turned the truck around and we headed back up the street.

Back at Beach Getaway, I found a phone number in the Salisbury directory for Vernette Johnson, the former Eastern Maryland College professor, and got her voice mail. "Dr. Johnson, this is Jamie August, reporter from the *Ocean City Weekly Breeze*. I am putting together a series on Bayside Preserve, which will be opening in the spring, and I understand you had some concerns about its environmental impact. I am interested in talking to you about it." I left my contact information.

Then I called Tammy. "Girl, have I got a wild night planned for us," I said. "They're putting an Impala on the roof at Mulvaney Chevrolet out on

Route 50, and I'm covering it for the paper." Tammy guffawed. "You in?"

"I wouldn't miss it. Come over for dinner and we'll go after. Dustin's coming, and we're puttin' steaks on the grill," she said.

"You sure you want me over there, getting in the way?"

"Naw, you won't be in the way. Anyway, there's a game on tonight. We were going to watch it at my place, but he'd probably rather be down at Buffy's watching it with Chris, Dave, and Sanchez. So this is perfect. We'll grill at my place. Then he can go hang with his friends, and we can go see this Impala. And your boyfriend."

"Shut UP," I said. "That is even less funny today than normal." I told Tammy about my meeting with Jonathan Ivory yesterday: the good, the bad, and the ugly. She let out a horrified cry.

"Get the fuck out! What a fuckin' dirtbag!"

"Yeah. Thanks, Tammy."

"Only good thing is, at least he told you about his wife. He could have strung you along," Tammy said.

"I'm a reporter, doing a story on his company. Of course, I'm gonna find out. He probably figured this was the best way to do some damage control, and maybe keep getting some on the side."

"Maybe he's got, you know, an arrangement with his wife."

"Yeah, well that arrangement doesn't extend to me. He should have laid his cards on the table before he laid me out on the back seat." I giggled. That was a good one. Maybe I was going to come through this okay, I thought with fresh hope.

"Maybe he did. You were trashed, you said it yourself."

"Tammy, seriously, would you shut up? I'm trying to be the blameless victim here, all right? You're not helping."

"Oh, okay. Right. Sorry."

"Okay, no worries, I'll be there at six o'clock."

I was dreading the next phone call. I took a deep breath, and dialed the number for Ivory Enterprises. After exchanging icy pleasantries with Corinne, I was put through to Jonathan. "Jamie, how are you? Did you make it home okay last night?"

"Safe and sound, thanks."

"That was quite a show you put on there at AJ's."

"Mmm. So, the reason I'm calling is I need pictures of Bayview Preserve to go with my story. I'm hoping you can send someone over there to let me in this afternoon."

"I know you're upset, and I am sorry for not talking to you about my, uh, personal situation sooner."

"No need to talk any more about that."

"I couldn't seem to find the right moment."

I snapped. "Honey, the right moment was in that bar the other night, before you ever laid a hand on me." I was waving a finger at the telephone.

"I know, and I'm sorry. I was lonely. You were beautiful—you are beautiful."

I squeezed my eyes shut and felt myself softening. God dammit. "I didn't call you to talk about this. Can you please send someone to meet me at Bayview Preserve so I can take some photos?"

"I'll pick you up, Jamie. I have some time this afternoon and I'd be happy to do it."

"Thank you, but I'd rather you just send someone to let me in the gate."

"Do you want in or not?"

I was silent.

"I'll come by at 2 o'clock. Where do you live?"

"Fine. Pick me up at the *Weekly Breeze* offices." I gave him that address. No way was I letting him pick me up here at the Beach Getaway offices—though the decor was actually of a vintage he could relate to. This little three-card monty would mean

74

I'd have to take the bus all the way uptown, past Bayview Preserve, to the newspaper offices.

Next I called Eastern Concrete and spoke to the foreman on the Bayview Preserve job, a guy named John O'Hagen. I didn't really know where to go with my questions. "So, did you all cut any corners on that Bayview Preserve project? Use any sub-standard materials? Bury any bodies in the building foundations? You know, stuff like that?" I mean, what can you say? O'Hagen seemed perfectly open and honest in his answers to my questions about how the work had gone, how big a project it was for the company—the biggest in Eastern's history. It didn't feel like this was leading anywhere.

Next I called Sergio, of Sergio's Water Fantasies, to discuss the fountain masterpiece. His assistant told me he was in Milan, but would be calling in, and took a message.

Just then my friend Traci called me, and asked if I wanted to go with her, Angela and Jenn to see the ultimate East Coast beach town cover band, Fuzzy Bunny Slippers. They were coming to town next month. "Um, hello? Yes!" I said. I wondered how old those Fuzzy Bunny Slipper guys must be, since Donald once talked about seeing them on the Jersey shore in the early '90s.

I ate one more chocolate doughnut. I figured I could get away with that if I ate only half the sandwich I had stuffed into my purse this morning. Then I ate half of the sandwich. Then the other half.

After lunch, I locked up and took the bus to the newspaper offices. Twenty minutes later, Donald was working at his desk while I was confirming with my pal Jerry Mulvaney that I would be at the car dealership that night. Jonathan Ivory walked into the office and gave me an easy smile. I said goodbye to Jerry, then stood and coolly shook Jonathan's hand. He was sporting the hearty woodsman look today, with jeans and a heavy flannel shirt. Hot. Hot. Hot. Damn.

I introduced Jonathan to Donald, and they exchanged handshakes and confident smiles. They looked like they had both stepped off the pages of a J.Crew catalog. I wondered if I should give them time alone to swap grooming and shopping tips. I checked my own manicure and noted that the French tips were starting to look like chipped Wite-Out. Next time, I was going for something more tropical. Magenta, or orange. I tapped the toe of one Caterpillar boot on the carpet discreetly, ready for them to finish their preening and get on with it. I wore the construction boots because they've got style, and also because I had hoped to be tromping around in the snow taking pictures this afternoon.

The two suave gents finished up their small talk, and I zipped up the parka and hoisted the fake Gucci on my shoulder. "Ready?" I said, popping a bubble with my gum.

Jonathan Ivory flashed me a winning smile. "Absolutely, absolutely," he said. I was happy to note that he was getting on my nerves. Then he turned and I got a look at his butt in those Levi's. Dang.

Jonathan and Donald exchanged cards and another manly handshake, then Jonathan opened the door for me and we stepped out into the cold, sunny afternoon.

"How did you all manage to put together this incredible parcel of land, anyway?" I asked Jonathan, keeping things stridently businesslike as we cruised in the Escalade down the Bayview Preserve road that followed the curve of the glittering bay. I was happy for the heated seats after the several stops we made to take photos of the downtown area, the condos, the fountain, and the "environmentally friendly" walking path. Muddy ice from my boots was melting into the carpeted Escalade floor mats. Good.

"We needed a big, really spectacular location for this community. We knew this kind of development was the future of Ocean City, so we put this together with a series of purchases from private owners," he said.

"Like Frank Donnelley?" I asked, and he looked at me attentively.

"I believe so, yes. Or, perhaps his estate. I don't recall the details of the land purchases. They happened many years ago, of course."

"Of course," I said. "You got a pretty amazing deal from the Donnelley estate." Jonathan made no comment.

I looked out at the windswept bay and remembered many afternoons fishing and crabbing on those waters when I was a kid. Dad and Uncle Abe would take my sister, Lindsey, and me out in Abe's sun-faded Bayliner motorboat with two coolers: one for beer and one for bait. We'd put chicken necks into crab pots and throw them in the water, letting the line trail way out on them. Then Lindsey and I would be set up with fishing rods. We'd be really into it for about 20 minutes, then it got boring.

My sister, who was three years older, would arrange herself, movie-star style, on the cracked vinyl bench seat and sunbathe. I would curl up on the dingy, wet floor of the boat and stick my nose in a Nancy Drew mystery. Eventually we would jump in the water for a swim to cool off. I can remember sitting in our wet bathing suits eating bologna and cheese sandwiches and Utz potato chips for lunch, the salty bay water drying on our skin. Dad and Abe would listen to Orioles games on a little radio, kicking back with their feet up, National Bohemian beers in hand.

Jonathan continued around the curve of the road, and as we approached the clubhouse, I asked him to stop for some photographs. When we pulled up in front of the low building, I got out and asked him to drive a little beyond the building so the photos would not include his SUV. I took a few shots of the big houses across the bayfront road, and some of the clubhouse with the sun glinting off the tin roof. I walked out onto the dock, slippery with melting ice, to get more photos. A dinghy with an outboard motor was tied up at the end.

Just then I heard Jonathan's voice ring out: "Hey! What are you doing?" I ran down the dock and around the clubhouse to find Jonathan facing a middle-aged woman who was a foot shorter than him. She had deep black skin, wire-rimmed glasses, and a heavy wool cap jammed down tight on her head. She was clutching a small Styrofoam cooler to her chest.

The two were yelling at each other. Quickly, I snapped a few photos. "Whoa! Whoa!" I shouted while pocketing my camera. "Calm down, both of you! What is going on here?"

"Doctor Johnson is just leaving. That is what's going on here," said Jonathan, whipping out his cell phone and dialing.

"Tom?" he said, glaring at the woman as he spoke into the phone. "We've got a trespasser on the property out here by the clubhouse.... I don't know how she got in, and that's a problem.... Yes. Regardless, please come out here and escort her off the premises." He disconnected the call and took a step toward the woman.

"Hand over the cooler," he said, reaching for the small Styrofoam box as she deftly stepped back and turned.

"Don't you lay one finger on me, or you're going to find yourself in bigger trouble than you're already in," she warned, wagging a finger at him. Her tone was steely, her accent a bit southern. Maybe Virginia. Jonathan stepped back.

"I'm leaving. I have what I need." She gave him one last vicious glance, turned to look me up and down, and walked away.

"Where do you think you're going?" Jonathan called after her, as she rounded the corner of the clubhouse. We followed, and watched her walk to the end of the dock and step into the little boat. She untied the lines, started the engine, and motored away.

I turned to Jonathan in astonishment. Just then, an SUV with the woodcut Bayview Preserve logo on the side sped down the road and screeched to a halt next to the clubhouse.

"Where is she?" the excited security guard asked, craning his neck.

"Excuse me," Jonathan said quietly to me, then turned to the security guard. "Tom, are the dock security cameras not working?" His tone was acid. Tom shook his head. "A problem with the monitors in the guardhouse? Is there some reason why just anyone is apparently able to pull up to our dock and wander around our private property doing God knows what?"

I stood to the side, and watched Tom wilt.

"I'm sorry, sir. I guess I missed it."

"How could you miss all that? Somebody tied up to our dock and walked around like they owned the place!"

"I—well, sir, Steelers' pre-game was on, and I guess I got distracted."

"Pre-game? Pre-game?!" Jonathan was disgusted. "If it was fourth quarter, Steelers against Ravens, and the game was tied up, then maybe. Maybe I'd have some sympathy. But pre-game? That's pathetic."

Tom hung his head in shame. "Sorry, sir. It won't happen again."

"You got that right," Jonathan said. "You're fired. Get off the premises immediately."

Tom looked stricken. "But..."

"Now."

Tom's face crumpled. As he opened the door to the SUV, Jonathan said, "No, Tom. That's company property. Give me the keys. You can walk."

The orangey late afternoon sun caught the glint in Tom's eyes as his expression hardened. He dropped the keys on the pavement at Jonathan's feet, turned on his heel, and walked down the road, the wind whipping off the bay and through his thin security uniform.

Jonathan bent, picked up the keys, and said tersely, "Do you have all the pictures you need? Let's go."

We got into Jonathan's SUV in silence. He started the car and pulled onto the street.

"What the heck was that all about?"

"Just some crackpot who doesn't know private property when she sees it," Jonathan said. His knuckles were white on the steering wheel.

"But what was she talking about?" I asked. "What did she mean, she has what she needs?"

"That woman is a nut case who wants us all to move back into mud huts with no cable TV," he said. "She has gone too far, though. I've had it." He wouldn't say more. He turned his game face back on, upped the wattage on his smile, and asked, "Drink?"

I was too curious about what I had just seen to turn him down.

At Nick's House of Ribs bar, Jonathan downed two mugs of beer like a man just rescued from the desert and his nerves seemed to settle out a bit. I tried to approach him from a different angle. "I guess Vernette Johnson has been a real pain in the ass since the beginning of this project, hasn't she?"

Didn't work. Jonathan's eyes came into focus and bored into me. "What do you mean? How'd you even know who she was?" he asked.

"Well, you called her Dr. Johnson, so I assume she must be the same Dr. Johnson who tried to stop Bayview Preserve from being built."

"Vernette Johnson was fired from Eastern Maryland College," he said. "She is not a credible scientist. She is completely crazy."

"What do you think she was doing today?"

Jonathan turned to me, leaned in and said, "This is off the record." Grrr. Why do people love saying that so much? I made a show of putting down my notebook and pen, which I hadn't actually realized I was holding, and turned to him.

"Vernette Johnson is trying to prove that Ivory Enterprises knowingly destroyed the last breeding ground for crabs in the bay," he said.

"And did you?"

"No! The dredging sediment from the Route 90 Bridge got dumped on the Bayview Preserve shoreline before we even owned it. That's what ruined the breeding ground. Vernette Johnson won't let up, though. Eastern Maryland fired her because she wouldn't stop pushing when her department's environmental assessment of the land demonstrated just what I'm saying. She kept at it. She accused her colleagues of falsifying data, and she released information to the press and to scientific journals that contradicted their findings. She was the one falsifying information! Must be so, because they fired her.

"And what's she trying to prove now? The development is built! The work is done! Even if she was right—which she's not—what does she want us to do about it now? It's ridiculous." Jonathan finished his mug of beer and thumped it on the bar.

"Why did Ivory Enterprises have Eastern Maryland do that environmental assessment in the first place?" I asked. "Kind of unusual, isn't it, for a developer to take that step?"

"Yes, it is an unusual step," Jonathan said emphatically. "We did it because we care about the environment. We wanted to do the right thing, and that meant weighing the importance of this kind of community for the image and the economy of Ocean City with its possible environmental consequences."

"Sure, and the Maryland Department of the Environment made you do it, didn't they?"

"Well, there was that," he grinned. I winked.

"Nothing gets past you, Jamie. I like that. Have dinner with me," he said suddenly.

"No. I have other plans," I said, happy that this was actually true. I was thinking with relish about the steak dinner awaiting me at Tammy's place. Oh, and Jerry Mulvaney. These men, they never stop.

"I would love to talk to you more, to get to know you and try to make things right between us," he said, placing a hand on my forearm, which was resting on the bar. "I find you fascinating."

"Thank you, Jonathan," I said, briefly taking his hand in mine with a delicious little electrical shock, and removing my arm from underneath it. "But I'm not into married men. I am not going to be one of your other women."

"You say it like there are so many."

"I'm getting that impression, yes."

"If only that were true!" he said with a laugh.

I let go of his hand, slipped off the barstool, and considered leaving a five for the beer but decided not to. I gave his arm a light squeeze and headed to the door.

He looked surprised, but quickly rearranged his scowl into a tight grin and turned back to the bar.

Outside, I crossed Coastal Highway and caught a southbound bus downtown. I had to run home to change into something more appropriate for a major news event at the car dealership. A reporter's life is full of glamour.

5.

I PICKED THROUGH the clothes in my closet and found what I was looking for: black low-rise jeans, a fuzzy maroon sweater that reliably falls off one shoulder, and high-heeled black ankle boots. A pair of dangly gold earrings and a swipe of frosty lipstick, and I was good to go. I was out the door and back uptown to Tammy's apartment.

"Hey Jamie," Dustin said as he answered the door and gave me a quick hug, the beer can in his hand giving my shoulder a chilly jolt. "Hey, Dustin," I said. Tammy came out of the kitchen, wiping her hands on a Phillips Crab House apron. "Hey! Want a hard lemonade?" she asked, handing me a bottle before I could answer.

Tammy had done her hair curly and teased, grazing the shoulders of her purple Ravens sweatshirt. The ass of her grey sweatpants said "Pink" in black lettering. In the kitchen, Tammy opened a bag of mixed salad greens and dumped them in a bowl. She squeezed the enclosed package of ranch dressing on the salad, and opened a bag of croutons. "How did we eat healthy before these salad kit things?" she asked. I shrugged, took a swig.

Dustin was standing on the deck, huddled over the grill, a cigarette glowing in one hand. Dustin works as a boat mechanic for Larry Lombardo's son, Dan. Dan has built a successful fleet of charter fishing boats that sail out of Ocean City's harbor. Charlie's Charters, it's called. Who's Charlie? I don't know.

It's no coincidence Tammy's dating Dustin: I get invited to Dan's summertime dock parties because I rent his dad's crazy houseboat. I brought Tammy to one last summer, and she met Dustin there. They've been together ever since, and I would say it's serious except that I hesitate to apply that word to either of these two.

"So, I got a dinner invitation from Jonathan Ivory," I said as I ripped open a bag of frozen garlic bread and arranged the pieces on a cookie sheet.

"You saw him again?"

"I had to, for the story. I went out to Bayview Preserve with him today to take pictures."

"What a gentleman! He already fucked you and now he wants to buy you dinner."

"Yeah, well, now he loves me for my mind."

Tammy took a swig of hard lemonade and belched expressively.

"If you're gonna get it on with married men, you should hold out for Jerry Mulvaney. Hold on to your dreams, Jamie!"

"Yuck!" I gave Tammy a little shove, and put the tray of garlic bread into the oven.

Tammy went out to check on Dustin's progress. I listened to the murmur of their voices on the other side of the sliding glass doors. I pulled out three plates and set the table in the small living/dining room. I thought of my ex-boyfriend Brian and had a momentary pang of self-pity. Then I remembered that Brian used to leave dirty socks between the cushions of his couch, and I felt better.

The doors opened and a blast of freezing air blew into the room as Tammy and Dustin entered. Dustin carried the steaming steaks piled on a plate. A headlamp, still lit, was strapped to his head. He looked like Jon Bon Jovi the coal miner. They were chatting and laughing, and as I pulled the bread out of the oven and joined them at the table, I was really happy to be here instead of in a fancy restaurant fending off Jonathan Ivory.

As we gorged ourselves on the T-bones, Tammy said, "So Dustin, Jamie's got a new boyfriend, and he's not even a senior citizen."

I glared at Tammy. Winking at me, Dustin said, "Oh yeah? Who's the lucky guy?"

"Jonathan Ivory. She's chasing the money this time," Tammy said approvingly.

"Ivory? I know that guy," Dustin said. "Kind of an asshole. But he's an old dude."

"No!" Tammy and I both said.

I said, "Not Bernard Ivory the dad, but Jonathan Ivory, the son. He's in his 30s, and he's married." I shot a warning look at Tammy. "He's definitely not my type."

"Oh. Well, Bernard Ivory has been coming around Dan's office down at the marina recently. Last week he was there and Dan had him in the office with the door closed. I had one of the boat engines apart down next to the dock." He stopped to swig a Coors.

"Dude comes stomping out of the office and leaves the door wide open. Gets into a Cadillac, and he's driving off as Dan comes out the door telling him to fuck off."

"Wow!" I said. "I wonder what that was all about?"

"Yeah, me too, but Dan just told me to chill when I asked him."

"And you said he's been around other times, too?"

"Yeah. Well, I think so. I've seen his car in the parking lot a few times."

"What is it, an Escalade? That's what Jonathan drives," I said.

"No, it's a big, gold Sedan de Ville."

"Hey, tell me the next time you see him or the car down there, okay?"

"Jamie, don't get this Jonathan guy too worked up, all right?" Tammy chimed in. "If he's anything like his father, you probably don't want to tangle with him."

"You got that right!" I said, and told them about Jonathan's performance that afternoon at Bayview Preserve, and the security guard who got fired.

"Whoa," Dustin said. "But you know, the man's got a point. The security guard seriously got distracted by the pre-game?" He shook his head and took another bite of steak. We all grunted in reluctant agreement.

After dinner, Dustin went down the street to join his friends at Buffy's. I cleaned up the dishes while Tammy changed her clothes. She came out in acid wash low-rise jeans, a plunging purple V-neck sweater, and her super excellent black cowboy boots that were worn in, like she spent her days on the range, not behind the circulation desk.

"You look great. If I don't watch out, you're gonna take Jerry Mulvaney away from me," I said.

"You think I've got a chance with the big guy?"

We grabbed our coats and purses and left. Down in the lot, Tammy cursed as she struggled to get the key in the lock of her '96 Chevy Cavalier. The sea air was wet and frigid, and when she got the doors opened, we jumped in and slammed them tight. She turned the key and the voice of Ocean 98's deejay blasted through the speakers. As Tammy headed south on Coastal Highway, we listened to the end of the sports news, then an ad for Mulvaney Chevrolet.

"TONIGHT! Come on down to Mulvaney Chevrolet to check out DelMarVa's biggest selection of new and pre-owned Chevrolets, and be a part of history as Mulvaney Chevrolet puts a classic 1973 Chevy Impala on the roof! That's right, on the roof! No DelMarVa Chevy dealership has ever gone this far! Come on down to Mulvaney Chevrolet, check out the classic Impala, and enjoy the smooth sounds of Frankie and the Whalers in the show-room from 7 to 9 TONIGHT!"

We sped down the dark, nearly empty street, sailing through green lights to the inlet, where we turned right and crossed a metal drawbridge to head west on 50. When I looked right, I could see the orange light on my dock, upstream. To my left was the bigger, more sturdy dock of Charlie's Char-ters downstream, where the inlet widens to form the snug little Ocean City harbor. We left the lights of Ocean City, cruised through West Ocean City and into the darkness of eastern shore farm coun-try.

Mulvaney's dealership is on Route 50 a few miles west of Salisbury, a small city that's home to Eastern Maryland College, and also the world headquarters of Purdue Chicken. "It takes a tough man to make a tender chicken" was their long-ago motto; now everybody's jumping on the tough man for polluting the watershed. Or something like that. I put Purdue on my mental list of research projects.

As we drove past Eastern Maryland's floodlit campus, I decided to come back out tomorrow morning and talk to somebody in the Environmen-tal Sciences department. Maybe I could track down Vernette Johnson, or talk to somebody else who had been a part of the Bayview Preserve study.

Salisbury Mall and the lights of town were quickly behind us. Soon after, huge movie-premiere spotlights appeared on the skyline, then the high-wattage glow of Jerry Mulvaney's Chevrolet Country. The showroom was the height of 1960s space-age architecture, its glass walls leaning outward, and one corner of the roof jutting out practically over the roadway, forming a portico. Spotlights were trained on this corner of the roof. The front door was sheltered by the portico, and back in the day I'll bet salesmen would roll up with the latest Chevy, ready to take Ward and June Cleaver for a test drive.

The lot was filling up, and a crane sat next to the building. A pea-green Impala—apparently THE Impala—was parked next to it. The area was marked off with safety cones and lit by lights you see at nighttime road construction sites. A couple of guys were doing last-minute checks of the car and crane.

In the showroom a group of middle-aged gents in Hawaiian shirts, some with thermals layered underneath, warmed up on guitars, keyboards and drums. A bar had been set up next to a shiny blue Malibu parked at a jaunty angle on the showroom floor, and a trio of girls in shorts and Mulvaney Chevrolet T-shirts were circulating with trays of snacks. Oh boy! Free hors d'oeuvres! Free drinks! I had already forgotten the gigantic steak dinner I had just eaten.

Before we went in I told Tammy I needed to take some photos and that I'd meet her inside. I circled the Impala, getting shots from every side. Then I rushed to the warm showroom and joined Tammy, my boots clicking on the floor. A woman with a blond ponytail, sneakers, jeans shorts and a Mulvaney tank top came up with a tray of tiny crabcakes, heavily dusted with Old Bay Seasoning. As I reached for one, Tammy said, "Oh, my god, Tanya!" and the woman said "Tammy! How're you doin'?" The two of them did a little one-armed hug, Tanya carefully balancing the tray. "Tanya, this is my friend Jamie," Tammy said. "Jamie, this is Tanya." We said our hellos as Tammy said, "Tanya worked at Buffy's last season," which explained how they knew each other, since Tammy and Dustin practically live at Buffy's. "How'd you end up with this gig?" she asked.

"I'm working for Prestige Catering now," said Tanya, carefully controlling her shivering as a big group paused at the front entrance with the door wide open. "The Buffy's job was just seasonal. I've been with these guys for a few months. Hey, it's a job." My first impression of Tanya was that she was in her 20s, but as I looked closer, I could see that the blond came from a bottle and the boobs looked a little too perky. And one looked bigger than the other. I forced my eyes to Tanya's face.

As Tammy and Tanya chatted, the band finished its warm-up, and I saw Jerry in his Mulvaney Chevrolet golf shirt making his way across the room. I excused myself and walked over, pulling out my reporter's notebook and pen. When Jerry saw me, a huge grin spread across his face. He sauntered toward me, arms out, and greeted me with a huge hug and a kiss on the cheek. "Hey, darlin'," he drawled. "How's the best goddamn news reporter in the tri-state area?" I offered a modest curtsy, and we chatted as he steered me through the crowd, his sun-spotted arm heavy around my shoulder.

"Now, darlin', I gotta tell you, I've got a reporter here from the Salisbury *Daily Times*, and one who came clear from Dover, but I'm giving you the exclusive on this story. That Impala out there on the lot, the one that's gonna make history tonight? That was my momma's car," he said. "She loved that car probably more than she loved my daddy," he said with a booming laugh. "Now that she's passed, I can't think of a better way to honor her memory than to put her favorite Chevy up on the roof, lit up like Christmas, for the whole world to see." I scribbled in my notebook as he gazed out the window at the shiny green coupe, spotlights glinting off the chrome.

"She even had a name for that car." He paused for effect. Just then a woman patted him on the shoulder and he turned around with a booming "Hey, darlin'!" and a bear hug. A moment later, he returned to me. "Now, where was I?" He flagged down a girl with a tray of mini-puff pastries and took three. He continued his story, saying his mom would take his grandma out for Sunday drives about every week, and they'd go exploring up and down old country roads. They especially liked to drive to Assawoman Bay. Winter and summer, they'd wander along the coastal roads, sit on the bumper, drink bottles of Coke, and watch the birds.

"Momma, bless her heart, was a bit of a shutter-bug, too," Jerry said. "I have a shoebox full of pictures she took out there by the bay. She'd take pictures of grandma sittin' there on the bumper, but mostly she took pictures of the birds. She loved those ospreys."

Then he glanced at his watch and said, "Welp, it's showtime! Enjoy yourself, now." He strode up to the stage, waving to the crowd.

Jerry worked the crowd into a frenzy of flag-waving brand loyalty with a speech about his momma, Chevrolet, and the good people of the DelMarVa peninsula, then said, "Let's go outside and put that Impala up on the roof!" The crowd cheered, rushed out the dealership's doors and onto the parking lot, where the Impala gleamed, ready for its close-up.

The wheels of the car had been clamped with something similar to a Denver boot. Each boot was connected to a giant strap, which hung vertically from an I-shaped brace, suspended over the car from a pulley on the crane's long arm. A gust of wind blew across the flat land, rattling the straps. People pulled their coats tighter.

With a cheery wave, Jerry stepped into the cab of the crane truck (next to the guy who, hopefully, knew what he was doing), and eased up on what looked like a big gear shift. The chains retracted and the pulley eased upward, pulling the straps taut. Gradually the Impala's wheels lifted off the ground, and the audience drew in a breath. I was snapping photos like crazy, along with several others. Every inch the car rose, it felt as though the wind picked up a knot. Six, 8, 10, 15 feet up, chains groaning against the wind. Stars glittered hard in the frozen sky and the Impala's chrome sparkled.

After a minute that felt like an hour, the Chevy's wheels crested above the level of the flat roof. Two men were standing up there, waiting to do their part. The car hung like a horse in a sling, and then slowly, carefully, Jerry (and the crane operator) nudged the crane arm horizontally, easing the car sideways in space. The crowd was silent as the Impala hung a few feet above the roof, swaying, creaking. The car was lowered to settle on the gravel roof. The two guys removed the boots and, a moment later, the Impala was freed of straps and chains.

The crowd cheered and applauded, and a visibly relieved Jerry Mulvaney emerged from the cab, laughing and waving. The band struck up "Little Deuce Coupe" as the crowd rushed inside for warmth and more drinks. I saw the other reporters head for their cars. Amateurs. I was here till the end, or until the drinks ran out (which, by definition, is the end).

The party continued for another 45 minutes or so, with Jerry spinning every lady across the dance floor at least once. Finally, Frankie and the Whalers wailed its last tune. Tammy—who seemed to know everyone as well as everything—was chatting with a group I didn't know, so I approached Jerry. "Congratulations, Jerry! This was a really fun, and what a turnout. There must have been 75 people here."

"Yeah, and we managed to sell a few cars in the middle of it all," he said. I hadn't even realized the salesmen were at work.

"Listen, Jerry, I wanted to ask you about something, if you have a minute," I said. "I was thinking about those pictures your mom took of birds."

"Yep," he said, waving farewell to someone at the door.

"I'm thinking it might be nice to do a little feature on your mom and her Sunday drives in the Impala. You know, since it's her car up there on the roof, maybe we could publish a few shots of her and the Impala out by the bay."

"Hell, that's a great idea, Jamie. She'd be so proud to have some of her pictures printed in the paper. I sure do wish she was still around to see it."

"I'm glad you like the idea. Can I take a look at that box of snapshots?"

"Sure, no problem." He promised to bring the pictures to the dealership tomorrow, and offered me a loaner car to return. It would be the day to go to Eastern Maryland to talk to someone about the Bayview Preserve study. I let Tammy know I had my own wheels, and she headed off with friends to a nearby pub.

I left the showroom about 10:30 with the last of the stragglers, found the tiny red Aveo hatchback loaner and drove home. Thirty minutes later, I was crossing the bridge onto the island, looking forward to a good night's sleep on my rusting, creaky little piece of paradise. When I got out to open the gate, I saw Larry Lombardo's car still in the lot, the office lights still blazing. I knocked on the door and poked my head in.

6.

LARRY'S HAIR WAS frazzled from a distracted habit of running his hand repeatedly through it. He looked up and offered a half-hearted smile.

"Come on in, girl," he said, gesturing with a stained coffee cup. "Have some coffee." This late-night coffee thing was getting to be a bad habit, but I figured Larry would be less likely to roar at me if he had just served me a cup of his rotgut.

I told him about Mulvaney landing an Impala on the roof and he laughed, his eyes crinkling. He's got a great, booming laugh, not often heard. Sheesh! Do I have an old-guy crush on Larry Lombardo? Yeah, probably.

"So Larry," I started in. "How's your son these days?"

"Huh? He's fine. Same as ever, you know. Why?"

"Oh, well, we were just talking about him at dinner tonight."

"Oh, yeah?"

"Yeah, I was over at Tammy's, and Dustin tells me that your son threw Bernard Ivory out of his office the other day. Crazy, right?"

Larry's smile disappeared. So much for my smooth delivery. I plowed on. "In fact, he's been around there more than once. Dustin says he's seen the guy's car."

Larry stood up sharply, causing the casters of his vinyl office chair to squeak and roll backward into the scarred, wood-paneled wall. He clenched his jaw, then abruptly turned his head to look out the window, across the parking lot to the dock and the icy water. I could see the muscles working in his jaw. He was thinking.

"Thank you for telling me that, Jamie," he finally said. "You have got to believe me when I tell you to stay away from those bastards." I started to cut in, but he held up his hand. "I can't get into how I know that, or what's going on with them and me, but please trust me. Just print their promotional horseshit and forget the whole thing."

He sat back at his battered desk and busied himself with his work, clearly not seeing the papers in front of him. "I hope you change your mind," I said. "If they've done something wrong, I can expose it. Seriously. I can totally expose it."

"Drop it, Jamie," he said. "Go home." I put my empty cup on the edge of his desk, and stepped out. At the dock, I turned back and saw through the window that Larry was pacing, talking on the phone and gesticulating angrily. I checked my watch. Almost midnight. Was he talking to Dan? What was the connection between Dan Lombardo, Larry Lombardo, and the Ivory family? I trudged onto the dock and stepped onto my houseboat, suddenly weary with all of the drama of the last few days.

The next morning, it was a nice change to drive out of Ocean City instead of staring at the telephone at Beach Getaway. Wind buffeted the Aveo as I crossed the drawbridge onto the mainland. The stereo had no bass, which is a real problem when you're trying to rock out with some Nirvana, but it was still an adventure.

When I actually get to do some investigative reporting, it puts me in a great mood. I have rooted around at the county landfill on a story about illegal dumping (unfortunately I was thrown out before I could find anything) and I have taste-tested crabcakes for a Best of Ocean City review. I can honestly say that, professionally speaking, I preferred the landfill. It's more exciting. I had a good feeling about my trip to Eastern Maryland.

First, though, I had to pick up photos from Jerry Mulvaney. When I got to the dealership, I had to admit the Impala looked pretty on the roof, gleaming in the wintery light. I walked through the showroom to the back and knocked on the frame of Jerry's open office door.

"Hey, darlin', come on in!" he boomed. He came around the desk and gave me a smothering hug and kiss on the cheek and insisted I sit down. He carefully placed an old Hush Puppies shoebox in my hands.

"Here they are," he said. "All of my momma's Sunday drive snapshots. I haven't looked through these in years," he chuckled. I put the lid on the desk and dipped into the full box of faded photographs. Some were black and white, but most were in color. The first snapshot I pulled out was of the car parked along a dirt road, the bay gleaming in the background, between stands of cattails and grass.

Jerry grinned. "You'll see a whole lot of pictures of the Impala in there. She took more pictures of that car—and her mother—than she did of all the rest of us."

"I'll take good care of these."

I stopped for lunch as I headed for Salisbury, taking the box into the diner and thumbing through the photos as I worked my way through a bowl of chicken and dumplings. The pictures were repetitive: the Impala in the foreground with bay scenery in the background. There were, as promised, plenty of Grandma Mulvaney and plenty of birds; clearly Mrs. Mulvaney had a zoom lens on some of her Sunday outings, because there were close-ups of birds on branches, birds soaring over the water, birds in tall grass. I don't know much about birds, but I did recognize the leggy white egrets.

Two snaps were stuck together on one corner, and I pulled the back one gently away to find a shot of Grandma Mulvaney on the porch of a small bungalow. Leaning comfortably against the porch rail, back to the camera, was a black woman. She was gesturing, one hand bent at the elbow, finger pointed up for emphasis, and Grandma Mulvaney was smiling. The picture, like many of the others, had a date on it. September 17, 1989. The chicken and dumplings cooled in the heavy diner bowl as I gazed at the picture.

At the campus, I got out to check the map at the entrance gates and drove to the Biology and Environmental Science building. Finding parking was easy because the semester didn't start for another week. I locked the Aveo, with the Hush Puppy box on the passenger seat. A whoosh of warm air greeted me as I pushed through the glass doors of the two-story brick building. This one looked newer than the other 1960s buildings that squared off around a central quad of concrete benches and trees in boxy planters.

A wide staircase led to the Environmental Sciences department. The outer office had beige low-pile carpeting and was cluttered with plants, bookshelves, and cork boards papered with departmental memos, including one titled "Improving the Quality of Environmental Science Memos." Three other office doors opened into this reception space, one closed and two partially open. I could see into one of the inner offices, where a dark-haired man wearing tortoise-shell glasses and a green pullover was working at his desk.

The heat in the office was stifling, and the woman behind the desk was flushed. She looked to be in her 40s, and wore a short-sleeved, plaid cotton shirt, her light hair pinned casually up. She greeted me, and asked how she could help.

"I'm Jamie August, reporter for the *Ocean City Weekly Breeze*." She offered me a wide smile. "I called a few days ago looking for Dr. Vernette Johnson but was told she is no longer with the department." The man with the glasses looked up.

"Oh, uh, yes, that's right, she is no longer here," the woman said, her smile fading.

"I thought I'd just come by today to see if I could get some contact information for her, or maybe speak with one of her former colleagues." I locked my gaze on the man, as the receptionist turned in his direction.

"Oh, right, well, let's see, not a lot of people are here right now, but let me ask..." she rattled on and her voice faltered as a silver-haired man in a brown wool suit stepped through the other office door.

"Pauline, I can take care of this," he said. "I'm Dr. Paul Saunders, chairman of the department." He extended his hand and we shook. "And, I'm sorry, you are...?"

"Jamie August, *Ocean City Weekly Breeze*," I said, handing him a card. I made these cards up on my printer, and you can see the little perforations around the edges, but it's all I've got. Saunders looked at the card skeptically and offered a wan smile. "And why is it you're looking for Vernette Johnson?"

I could see no reason for deception, so I told him about the story I was doing on Bayview Preserve. "I understand Dr. Johnson was a lead investigator on that project until she, uh, left the college, and I wanted to talk with her about the work that was done."

Saunders put on a "stern professor" look and said, "Dr. Johnson is no longer with the department."

"Yes, I know. I am here to try and locate her or perhaps talk with one of her colleagues who may have some insight into her concerns about the project."

"There is no good reason to dredge up all the ancient history about the Bayview Preserve environmental study," he said with haughty finality. "It was covered in the local press years ago, when it was happening."

"I appreciate your insights on how to carry out my job as a reporter, Dr. Saunders," I said. He smoothed his tie and looked at me with disdain. "However, it is important that I gain a complete understanding of the project from start to finish in order to write my series of articles. The environmental survey won't be a big part of the story, but I will be mentioning it, so I need to learn about it from all angles. I've read the report itself, but I know that Dr. Johnson disagreed with the findings. That's why I'm hoping to speak to her, and to any colleagues who worked on the project with her. I'm sure I don't have to explain to a member of the academic community about the importance of thorough research."

He didn't like that last part. "We have no current information as to Vernette Johnson's whereabouts, and it would be irresponsible of you, as a journalist, to include her as a source for your story." He had the nerve to stick his fingers up and use air quotes around the word *journalist*. I shifted my weight, crossed my arms and narrowed my eyes. I remained silent.

"If you must know—and this is strictly not for publication—Vernette Johnson was fired for professional misconduct during the Bayview Preserve project that included falsifying data and repeatedly harassing government officials, project developers, and, frankly, her own colleagues. I don't enjoy dragging her name through the mud, but that is the unfortunate truth of the situation, and it's im-

portant for you to understand that as you put together your story."

"Dr. Saunders, please allow me," broke in the
tortoise-shell glasses guy, who had come out of his
office and stuck his hand out. "Please. I'm Fred
Western, and I also worked on the Bayview Preserve project. I'd be happy to answer any questions,
although all of the information you could possibly
want is in the final report, which I think you said
you already have." He paused, turned to the receptionist desk and pulled a couple of brochures off
stacks on the desk. "I'm tied up just now, but here
is some information about the department, which
you may find helpful for your article. Take these
and let us know if we can do anything else to help."
He thrust the brochures into my hands, and physically guided me out of the office. "Thank you so
much for coming in," and just like that, he pro-
pelled me out the door. I was left standing in the
hallway.

Stunned, I headed back to the car (which now
felt positively Arctic after the overheated department offices). I dropped heavily into the driver's
seat and tossed the brochures onto the passenger
seat. A business card slipped out of a flyer and onto
the floor. I picked it up. It was Dr. Western's card,

and on the back, in red ink, was written a phone number and the words "Call me."

So I did.

"Dr. Western, this is Jamie August."

"Uh, yes, hello, now's not a great time —"

"I know, of course it's not. But when can I talk to you?"

"Today at 4, Market Street Inn. You know the place?"

"Yep. I'll be there."

He hung up.

Well, this was certainly cloak-and-dagger. Perhaps my first real break in the case. I mean, story. Less Nancy Drew, more Bob Woodward, I scolded myself.

With a couple of hours to kill, I went to the mall and tried on shoes. I picked up a pair of clogs trimmed in pink fur, and on sale. Then I started trying on jeans. My size 6s were getting a little snug, but the department store prices were out of my range. The whole thing was starting to depress me, so I went to the food court. Over an order of cheese fries, I considered taking up smoking again to get rid of those extra winter pounds. Then I decided I couldn't afford the habit.

Market Street Inn is not an inn at all but a great restaurant on the Wicomico River. Fancy, but not uptight, especially on the back deck. Last time I was here was on a date with an Ocean City lifeguard a couple summers ago. We sat on the back deck, drank too many margaritas, sang Lynyrd Skynyrd songs, and watched the river flow by.

I arrived at the restaurant a few minutes early and ordered an iced tea at the bar. About 4:15, Fred Western rushed in looking agitated. He moved us to a corner table and ordered a bourbon, neat.

"I can't tell you anything on the record," he began without preamble. "I must be crazy for even meeting you here in the first place. This is absolutely crazy. I mean, I don't know what got into me when I heard you out in the office this afternoon, but I just had to say something. I just felt like—" he sighed.

"Hey, Dr. Western—"

"Fred."

"Okay. Fred, seriously, it's okay. I can just use what you tell me as background. I won't quote you. I won't —"

The waiter arrived with Fred's bourbon and he grabbed it, gave me a nod, and gulped it. I had been tempted to order a drink, but I was glad I went the sweet tea route. If Fred kept this up, I'd be driving him home.

He sat for a moment and pulled himself together. The waiter passed by and Fred ordered another. I pointed to my tea.

"Right," Fred said with a rueful laugh. I sat back and waited.

"So, 10 years ago Vernette Johnson and I were the co-leads on the Bayview Preserve study. We were asked to determine whether the land on which Bayview Preserve has been built was a significant breeding ground for blue crabs and ospreys, and to comment generally on the extent to which the subdivision would adversely impact water quality and wildlife diversity. The project was funded by Ivory Enterprises."

"Is that a weird arrangement, having the study funded by an interested party?" I asked.

"It's not as unusual as it ought to be," Fred said. "In this case, the project had been turned down by the Maryland Department of the Environment, but the state agreed to take another look at the proposal if an environmental impact study was done. So Eastern Maryland College got the job.

"Vernette and I were both new professors at Eastern, neither of us tenured. Paul Saunders dropped the project on us, saying it was a prestigious thing to be part of and would help to get our names out there. Politically speaking, I guess that's true, since the Maryland Department of the Environment was involved.

"He also hinted that our chances for tenured positions within the department hinged on how the report came out. And he told us in no uncertain terms that we were to find that there was minimal impact on the bay—and this was before we started our field research."

"Wait, you're saying that the chair of the department told you to falsify your data if necessary in order to write a report that would allow the development to be built?"

"Yes, that's exactly what I'm saying," he said glumly.

"What did you do?"

"Well, neither Vernette nor I was in a position to argue, really. We wanted to keep our jobs, and we wanted tenure. Hell, who doesn't? So we started making trips out to the property, taking samples, doing surveys of nesting areas and crab breeding grounds. It was clear that this land was tremendously rich in both. The rest of the Ocean City side of the bay was, even then, getting pretty built up, but this was a little oasis, the last oasis, for basically all of the wildlife that we associate with Del-MarVa's waterways."

The waiter delivered fresh drinks and a little dish of pretzels.

"And did your reports say this?"

"Vernette and I argued about this. She felt that we had to report what was actually out there, regardless of what Saunders was telling us. I was thinking about the three kids I had to feed. Still have to feed. They're teenagers now. My whole professional career is based on me lying for a greedy developer."

Fred gulped his second bourbon, sighed, and slumped in his chair.

"Why did Saunders put you two on this project in the first place? I mean, if either of you blew the whistle —which Dr. Johnson did, or tried to do— then he would be in trouble along with the Ivory Enterprises people."

"I guess he thought we both needed our jobs too badly to say anything. That was true enough for me, but not for Vernette." He stared into his drink, and it seemed as though he wanted to close his eyes and sleep the whole thing away.

"Anyway," he said with some effort, "she insisted that we report our actual findings. I got her to compromise. We wrote it up accurately, but we met with Saunders to discuss the situation before we shared our findings with the Maryland Department of the Environment—or with anyone.

"Vernette tried to convince Paul that we had to do the right thing. Saunders insisted on taking the report in order to 'try to put a more positive spin on things,'" Fred said, "given the 'delicate situation' with a huge endowment that Ivory Enterprises had just promised to the department. I handed everything over. Vernette blew up, called me a spineless hypocrite, and threatened to go to the *Washington Post*. Saunders fired her on the spot.

"Then he did just what Vernette predicted. He changed the numbers. All of it was modified, airbrushed, shined up to make the parcel look like the most strangely unpopulated marshland a developer could hope to stumble across." He chuckled. Then he laughed loudly. Too loudly. The bourbon was kicking in.

"So, what happened to all of your original research? The wildlife counts, all the raw data? And, you mean to tell me you only had one electronic copy of the report? No backups anywhere?"

"Not that I know of. Remember, this was back in 1996. The department was cash-strapped and we were using outdated computers—and much of our work was still paper-based. There must have been a disk we used to save the report, but that would be long gone by now.

"Isn't it funny? About a week after that white-washed report was published, there was a fire that burned the old Biology Building right down to the ground." He laughed bitterly.

"Was it arson?"

"Yes. They know the fire was started intentionally, but they never caught who did it. What a coincidence. All our samples and data—poof. Gone."

I was still having trouble believing that they gave up the fight that easily. "Sure, but the data could have been collected again. It's not like the marshland went away."

"Ah, but just a few days after the fire, Saunders published the cleaned-up version of the report and declared it final, finished. The Maryland Department of the Environment accepted the information and gave Ivory Enterprises the green light, then the whole parcel was fenced off and declared a construction zone. Vernette showed up there about a week later and got arrested for trespassing. Bayview Preserve is locked down, and has been since before construction began."

"How do you know about Vernette getting arrested?"

"She told me. She had just gotten fired; we were still in touch."

"But you're not now?"

"No," he said sadly, and swallowed the last bit of his drink. "At first she said she understood why I had to keep my head down. But she seemed to kind of change after awhile. She became obsessed with proving that the environmental report was wrong and that the development was doing terrible damage to the bay. And it was, absolutely, but it was too late. Now it's *really* too late.

"The last time I spoke with her was a couple of years ago. The development was well under construction and she was still trying to piece together something to present to the state, to the city council, to whoever would listen. She kind of ... cracked."

"Do you know how I could get in touch with her?"

Fred leaned back in his chair and stared at the ceiling. "She will lead you on a wild chase with this. She will not let you rest until she is convinced you're going to rip the story wide open and cause the whole place to get knocked down and returned to its pristine state."

I laughed. "Well, I'll see what I can do, but you know I write for an arts and entertainment weekly."

He sighed and belched softly, then pulled out his cell phone and read a number off to me. "That's Vernette's cell phone number, or it was two years ago. So, I can't have any of this attributed to me. I swear to God. I can't lose my job. It would be harder for me to be forced out of there since I've got tenure, but Saunders would figure out a way, I'm sure."

"I understand, Fred. Once I speak to Vernette, I'm sure she can tell me a lot of this information and be happy to go on the record with it."

"That's the truth," he said. "Just ... She has kind of come unhinged, and she may sound ... unreliable. Believe me, I saw the osprey nests. I was part of the surveying group. I know that marshland was a beautiful breeding ground for crabs. She might have some wild conspiracy theories about politicians and developers and all the rest of it, but the environmental damage that Bayview Preserve has done? That part is real." He picked up his glass for another swallow, but it was empty. He stood and walked away.

I stared after him, debating whether to call him a cab. He seemed pretty steady as he left the restaurant. I let it go, paid the bill and drove the loaner back to Mulvaney Chevrolet.

While there, I showed Jerry the picture that I'd been staring at over lunch. "Do you know this woman?" I asked, pointing to the young black woman on the porch.

He squinted at the snapshot. "Huh. Nope. Can't say I do. That was Grandma Mulvaney's porch, and folks would often stop in on her."

"She looks pretty young."

"Yeah, I guess that is kind of unusual for a young person these days to visit an old lady on her porch, isn't it? But Grandma Mulvaney would wave and say hello. And likely as not, she'd have some fresh cookies up there."

"Well, that'd do it, then, wouldn't it? There was probably a block party up on her porch every afternoon."

"Yeah, Grandma was a sociable sort."

"The apple didn't fall far from the tree. Well, I'll hang onto the pictures a little longer, if you don't mind."

"Take all the time you need, darlin'," he said. I thanked him, then one of the mechanics gave me a lift home. As the mechanic chatted away, I stared out the window, lost in thought.

We pulled up to the cement plant and found the gate open. The mechanic pulled into the lot and I stepped out of the truck. Just then a car engine started and a gold Cadillac sedan pulled out from behind Larry's truck. Its headlights caught me in the face as the sedan swung past. Bernard Ivory was at the wheel and our eyes met. I saw a glimmer of recognition as he slowed, then continued out and up the street, vanishing into the darkness.

7.

I FOUND LARRY inside the Lombardo Concrete office looking very old and tired.

"Larry! What was Bernard Ivory doing here?"

"You keep asking me about the guy, and I keep telling you, it's not your concern and you need to stay out of it. Those people will find your weak spot and hit you there."

"Weak spot? What weak spot? Seriously, what are you talking about? If you tell me, maybe I can help you."

Larry let out a defeated guffaw. "Jamie. You cannot help me. Let it go. I'm going home," he said, reaching for his jacket.

We walked out of the office, and I watched Larry as he drove out of the gate and locked up behind him. I gave him a little wave as he got back in his truck and drove away. The sodium light buzzed and flickered, and I felt alone and vulnerable. The houseboat bobbed at the dock, moonlight shining on the bow. I sighed and went aboard.

I am a sound sleeper, but that night I tossed and turned. The boat's creaks and sighs usually lull me to sleep, but that night my dreams were full of strange footsteps on deck, shadows on the dock, rattling at the security fence. About 4 a.m., I got out of bed. Wrapping in a blanket, I turned on a lamp at the galley table and sorted Mrs. Mulvaney's photos into piles. Egrets and ospreys, songbirds and seagulls in one pile, pictures of the beloved Impala, some with Grandma Mulvaney in another. A third stack was of landscape shots, taken mostly from the western side of Assawoman Bay, looking east at Ocean City. A water tower with spindly legs rose above the landscape in many of the shots. In others, I could see the Route 90 bridge.

I realized I was looking at the landscape that would become Bayview Preserve. I peered more closely at a few shots and could make out a rooftop in the reeds. Was that the Donnelley house? Had to be. It was the only one there. I wondered again what would have made the Donnelleys sell to Ivory Enterprises for so little money.

The next photograph was a closer shot of the house with two men standing next to a black Cadillac. One looked like a much younger Bernard Ivory. He was pointing a finger at the other man in a gesture of anger, or threat. The other man seemed to be yelling back. There might have been a blurry figure inside the car. Or was I just woozy? I decided I'd have another look in the morning. I wrapped the blanket tighter and padded back to bed. I awoke with a start to sunlight streaming in the windows.

After a bowl of Frosted Flakes and a cup of coffee, I called Vernette Johnson.

"Who is this?" she answered on the third ring.

"Uh, yes, hello. This is Jamie August from the *Ocean City Weekly Breeze* calling for Vernette Johnson."

"The weekly what?" she asked sharply.

"Breeze. The *Weekly Breeze*."

"Huh."

"Right, so, I'm doing a story on the grand opening of Bayview Preserve. I left a message for you. Maybe you heard it?"

A pause. "Well, they think they're gonna have a grand opening, but they've got another thing coming. Meet me at Piezano's at noon," she said, and hung up.

The clock said 11:20. Yikes! I threw on a pair of old grey corduroys, a fisherman's sweater, and my Uggs, nearly poked my eye out with a speedy mascara application, and was out the door by 11:35. If I hurried, I'd make it to the boardwalk by noon.

The breeze on the boardwalk was cold enough to make the insides of my ears ache. The waves were small and tight. I walked towards Piezano's Pizza, one of the few boardwalk businesses that stays open all year. You can fool tourists with bad pizza but not the locals. Piezano's makes a fresh, crunchy-crusted pie, and I can really get behind that. On the other hand, sometimes I gotta have their cheesesteak sub. I was thinking about what to order when, as I approached the door, I saw Vernette arrive. I recognized her from the showdown with Jonathan Ivory at the Bayview Preserve marina.

"Vernette Johnson? Hi, I'm Jamie August," I said, extending my hand.

I had surprised her and she scowled. She looked up and down the boardwalk, then ushered me through the door. "Let's hope for your sake that they didn't see us out there," she muttered.

"Who saw us? What do you mean?" I asked as she hustled us through the restaurant, pushing me past the lunch counter and into the dining room, where she chose a booth in the farthest corner.

"Bernard Ivory has had somebody on my tail for years," she said matter-of-factly, settling into the booth and unwrapping a big green scarf from her neck.

"Really? Why?" I asked, playing along. Fred was right. This woman was unhinged.

She pursed her lips and looked at me over the top of her glasses. "If you've been talking to Fred, then you know why," she said. "You were the one with Jonathan Ivory the other day, weren't you?"

I nodded.

"Then you were there. So you know I was there."

She was getting excited. "I got the last water and soil samples right there at the dock, and you saw me."

I stared at her. "I saw you there, sure, but I don't know what you were doing."

"I was getting the last samples. Oh, this is better than I could have asked for," she said and burst into a beautiful, deep laugh. "The press was there to see my last sample collection. What paper did you say you're from?"

129

"*Ocean City Weekly Breeze*. It's the arts and entertainment weekly."

Her smile dimmed for a fraction of a second,
then she beamed again and said, "Well, Jamie, you
are about to get your big break. *The New York Times*
is going to be knocking at your door because I have
got a story to tell you." She stopped and stared at
two teenage girls who came into the dining room,
chatting and giggling. They glanced our way, saw
Vernette's glare, and fell awkwardly silent.

Hoo boy.

Luigi, the restaurant's owner, came over, and we
exchanged air-kiss greetings, Italian-style. I love
Piezano's Pizza and had said so more than once in
the *Weekly Breeze*, so, of course, Luigi loves me.
Vernette stared dispassionately at us, and had no
preference when I asked her what she liked on her
pizza. Luigi and I conferred and decided veggie
pizza might work best. Really, I had no idea what
Vernette might take offense at, and you can't go
wrong with veggie. After another minute of gossip
and chitchat about the cold snap, Luigi headed to
the big open kitchen at the front to make our pizza
from scratch.

"Are you all finished with the Italian love fest?"
Vernette said, sulking like a child who wants more
attention. "We have a lot of ground to cover here."

"Of course we do, and I can hardly wait," I said with more sarcasm than I intended. She glared at me over her glasses, then leaned back and crossed her arms.

"Here's the deal, Miss Restaurant Critic," she said acidly. "Bayview Preserve killed off the last of the blue crabs in Assawoman Bay and I have the data to prove it." She held up a shiny green thumb drive in the shape of a fish.

Well. Now she had my attention.

"Are we on the record?" I asked, pulling out my notebook, pen, and recorder.

"You're damn right we're on the record," she said. Then she unwound her tale.

In the mid-1990s, Ivory Enterprises acquired a large parcel of land on the Assawoman Bay and proposed to build a housing development. Their initial proposal was rejected, but the Maryland Department of the Environment agreed to take another look if they could produce a detailed environmental analysis that proved filling in the marshland would not have a serious impact. Then Bernard Ivory said he'd build a new Environmental Sciences building at Eastern Maryland College and give them a handsome endowment, if they would be so kind as to put together an environmental impact study that radically downplayed the damage that Bayview Preserve would do to the wildlife.

"The department chair, Paul Saunders, was on that like a dog on a pork chop. He told Fred and me to create a bogus report once it became obvious this area was actually a critically sensitive region. I said no way, and Saunders fired me. Fred caved, and now he's a spineless, useless alcoholic. But that's not important here."

She interrupted her story to scrutinize an aging biker couple who sat down opposite our booth. She lowered her glasses to the tip of her nose and stared at them until they decided they preferred another table. Then Vernette continued.

"The genuine report and all of the data samples and notes were destroyed in a fire. Almost all the data." She paused with a gleam in her eye.

"I held onto a single disk that contained the raw numbers from the water samples and the wildlife counts," she said, and leaned back with satisfaction. "Bernard Ivory hired a bunch of clowns to start following me. They tried to steal it a couple of times, but I saw that coming and gave the disk to an old friend for safekeeping."

"What happened to the disk?"

"Oh, it's in a real safe place." She barely paused as our pizza was delivered to the table on a silver stand. We both ignored the food.

"Anyway, this new data"—she held up her drive—"shows levels of pollution in the water consistent with the runoff that would be caused by the new construction. That pollution, combined with the destruction of the marsh when they filled it in to build those damn McMansions, is what knocked out the last of the blue crabs, and decimated the osprey population. I've got the numbers, before and after."

"I could use both sets of data."

"Yeah," she said thoughtfully. "I'll check into that."

Vernette said she had been doing bird and crab counts and taking water and soil samples roughly once a month since the environmental survey, so she had nearly 12 years of data illustrating the decline. Shortly after the marshes were filled, the wildlife counts plummeted. Soon after, other contaminants started showing up in the samples, including stuff you'd expect to run off a sloppy construction site. In the last few months, since the occupation of some houses, the water samples have been contaminated with sewage.

"So now, on top of everything else they already did, you think they're dumping raw sewage in the bay?"

"Positively."

The pizza was cold.

My recorder's green light blinked brightly. My pen was flying in my notebook. I finished and we sat in silence for a moment.

"I keep trying to tell the city council what's going on, but they don't want to hear it," Vernette said. "My apartment has been broken into three times, my car has been stolen, and somebody hacked my email and sent child pornography to all of my contacts. The Department of the Environment won't take my calls any more, and I've been barred from city council meetings. I have the proof, but nobody will believe me."

"Why not hire a lawyer, and fight this in court?"

"Please. The only lawyers I can afford are idiots."

She sat back and squinted at me. "And you probably don't believe me either." She took a mouthful of cold pizza and chewed distractedly. Then she looked over my shoulder and her eyes grew wide. I heard the sounds of other people coming into the dining room, and turned to see two men sitting at a booth on the other side of the room. I didn't recognize either, and they glanced at us and then away with no apparent interest. I turned back to the table to see Vernette grab her things and slide out of the booth.

"They found us," she said in a hoarse whisper. She roughly grabbed my arm and pulled me out of the booth, fear etching her face. I snatched my bag and winced as her fingers dug into my forearm. She made a beeline for the ladies room, coat on, scarf trailing. The two guys at the other table were engrossed in their conversation and hardly looked up as we passed.

In the restroom, Vernette dashed into the last stall, trying to pull me in with her. The back wall had a window of frosted glass at about shoulder height. The bathroom must have been reconfigured after the building's construction, because the door to the last stall nearly bisected the window.

Vernette unlocked the window and forced it open with a powerful grunt. She stood on the toilet seat, grabbed the vertical support of the stall and hoisted herself through the window.

"Hurry up! I can't be standing out here waiting on you."

Shit! She's loony tunes. I jumped up onto the toilet seat and stuck my head out the window. Vernette was already halfway down the alley. She turned back and yelled, "Get the disk from Jeanine!"

"Jeanine? Who's Jeanine?"

Vernette kept going down. I saw no point in chasing her.

When I walked back to the dining room, the two men were gone and Luigi was at my table.

"Those two assholes were trying to steal from you," he said. "I walk in here to take their order and find you and your friend gone, and those two guys at your table going through your coat pockets. I ran them off, though, and I don't think they got anything."

I told Luigi there was no harm done and no need to call the police. I saw, though, that they hadn't left Piezano's empty-handed. My recorder was gone.

I slumped back into the booth and waited for my heartbeat to slow. Then I fished out my phone and, after several failed attempts due to poor signal, managed to reach the *Weekly Breeze* office. "It's a good morning at *Weekly Breeze*," Donald chirped.

"Donald, it's Jamie."

"Good, I was getting ready to call you. Are you going to come by later with the Bayview Preserve feature?"

"Yeah, about that? I need to talk to you."

"Oh, here it goes. You're going to miss your deadline and ruin my weekend, aren't you?" he asked, only partly in jest.

I didn't rise to his bait.

"Donald, this is a much bigger story than I thought it was going to be, and I need a little more time. I just interviewed someone who claims to have proof —" I stopped, looked around the room, and convinced myself nobody was listening. Then I lowered my voice to continue, "— that they killed off the bay's last blue crab breeding ground to build Bayview Preserve, and now they're dumping raw sewage."

I heard a deep sigh. "Jamie," Donald began gently. "I want to know about the Bellagio-inspired fountain. I want to read the details of the eco-inspired decorator palettes in the model homes." His voice was raising. "I want to know what restaurants are going to open on Main Street, and I do NOT WANT TO READ ABOUT RAW SEWAGE!"

"But Donald—"

"Just. Wait," he choked out. I heard him take a couple of deep breaths, then he said, "Okay, Jamie. If there are open cesspools of raw sewage (I could almost hear his eyes rolling) at Bayview Preserve, then, of course, we need to report on it. We also need to cover any and all confirmed alien landing sites and dinosaur hatcheries. I want the story in my hands by the end of the workday tomorrow."

I started to speak, but he continued.

"And I fully expect your next phone call to be to Jonathan Ivory, so he can respond to these fantastical allegations."

"Don't speak to me like a high school intern," I snapped. "I know how to write a balanced news story. And when people follow my sources and steal my recorder, it makes me just a little bit suspicious that maybe I'm onto something."

"Somebody stole your recorder?"

"Yeah. Swiped it right off the table when I was in the restroom."

"Ah, your recorder. Probably somebody thinks they can pawn it for 20 bucks," he said, but I could hear a little doubt in his voice. "Can you still write the story without it?"

"Of course. I was taking notes the whole time."

"Okay, then do it. I want that story tomorrow."

We hung up and I immediately dialed Jonathan Ivory. I didn't want to give myself any extra seconds to lose the edge of my anger, which was giving me the courage I needed to make the call.

"Jamie, how nice to hear from you," Jonathan oozed.

"Great. So I have a few additional —"

"I want to see you."

My heart skipped and my skin grew hot. I had to figure out how to get my sex drive under control. Maybe I'm a sex addict. I'd have to ask Tammy if she could recommend a self-help book.

"Well, you're in luck," I said, steering the conversation back to the straight and narrow. "I'm tying up some loose ends on the story and some things have come to light that I would like to talk to you about."

"Really? Sounds interesting," he said, like he hadn't even listened to my words. "How about over dinner?"

"Fine." I really didn't want to torture myself with another episode of fighting off this guy, especially when part of me didn't want to fight him off at all. However, I needed to have this conversation in person. It's hard to get a real sense of someone's reactions over the phone. Especially over my cheap phone, which randomly disconnected and regularly ran out of battery.

"I can pick you up around 7," he said. "Where do you live, Jamie?"

Ah, so his father hadn't yet mentioned seeing me at the cement plant. Or maybe he wondered why I was there but didn't put it together that I was living on the houseboat.

"Why don't I meet you at the restaurant?"

He seemed personally affronted, and said that he wanted to surprise me with his restaurant choice. I was beginning to think he just liked driving me around in his fancy SUV. Whatever. "Okay, then pick me up at the *Weekly Breeze* office," I relented. Crap. Another bus ride from one end of town to the other.

"I'll see you this evening, Ja—" and then my phone died. I decided if I win a Pulitzer for this story, first thing I'm going to do is buy a better phone.

Luigi returned with a soft serve ice cream sundae. "On the house," he said.

"Luigi! How sweet!"

"Someone tries to rob you right in my dining room!" he fumed. "That's not right. You are suppose to be comfortable in my restaurant. You are a suppose to be safe." Luigi has been in this country for more than 20 years, but his Italian accent creeps in when he gets passionate.

"I'm sure it was just a fluke," I said. "It's not your fault, and I do feel safe here! I'm sure those guys will never come back."

"Yeah, they better not," he said, puffing his chest out. "I chased them out of here with a pizza paddle! Gave one of 'em a good whack on the back-a the head."

A few minutes later I bundled up and left. I looked up and down the boardwalk but saw no sign of the two guys. An elderly couple walked arm in arm towards the pier, and a group of eight teenagers went past. "Situational awareness" was my motto on the walk home. I wasn't suspicious of any people or cars, but how would I know what to be suspicious of?

Home again, I called Fred Western, who did not sound at all happy to hear from me.

"I told you everything I know, and more than I should have, and I do not appreciate —"

"Right, Fred, I know, I'm sorry, but do you know anyone named Jeanine?"

He spluttered at the interruption, then said, "Jeanine? Jeanine who?"

I told him about my meeting with Vernette Johnson and her strange parting words.

"Jeanine ..." He thought a minute. "No. I don't know who that is."

"A colleague? A family member? Did you know any of her friends?"

"No, no, I really don't have any idea. If you find out, though, call me. I can take a look at the data."

"Would you be willing to do that?"

"As long as my name's not in the story. I'm in it this far. Might as well at least make sure you don't screw up the story because you don't know what you're looking at."

I thanked Fred and worked the rest of the afternoon on the story, including a couple of hours in Larry's construction trailer using his landline to interview decorators and landscape designers, and to leave another message for the elusive Sergio of Sergio's Water Fantasies. His assistant assured me Sergio had received my message, was in Zagreb, and would return my call at the first opportunity.

As the sun set, I returned to the houseboat to change into something less comfortable for an expensive and pretentious dinner with Jonathan. Hmmm. High-heeled black over-the-knee boots and a black-and-grey striped knit dress. The dress was a little tight, like everything else in my closet after this recent junk food bender.

Back on the main drag, I caught the bus north. Behind the wheel was a lady who looked like my fifth-grade teacher, Mrs. Cod. She had iron-colored hair, hands like a bricklayer, eyes that could bore right into your soul, and a voice like a long-haul trucker. But no foul language. About half a dozen people were on the bus this time, and I took a seat a third of the way back.

While digging in my purse for a lipstick, I came across the two photographs I'd been carrying. Vernette had bailed out before I got a chance to ask her about the shot that looked like Bernard Ivory in front of the Donnelley house. I stared at the other photo, the one of the young woman on Grandma Mulvaney's porch. It occurred to me that she was about the same age as Vernette would have been in 1989. And something about that gesture looked familiar, that finger raised in earnest discussion. It was a weird coincidence, but there are lots of those in a small town.

By the time the bus reached the *Weekly Breeze*, I was the only passenger. I swung to the pavement with a thanks to the driver.

The office was dark and I used my keys to open. Inside, I turned on the lights, checked my mailbox, and looked over press releases. The Lions Club was having a dinner meeting. St. Andrew's Church was doing a fundraiser to renovate its social hall. Organizational meetings were scheduled for the White Marlin Open in August. That's the world's largest billfish tournament. Just ask Ocean City's hardest working reporter: I can rattle off the tournament stats going back to after World War II.

I had just finished adding all the meeting dates to my calendar when Jonathan walked in, looking comfortable but moneyed in a pair of silky grey trousers and a dark red cashmere sweater. I stood and we exchanged greetings, his eyes lingering on my various assets.

"Where's Donald this evening?" he asked.

"He ran out to get some dinner a while ago, so he'll be back any minute," I lied. I had no idea where Donald was, but if I had to guess, he was at home at his penthouse drinking a vintage burgundy. "Shall we go?"

Jonathan helped me into my coat. He held the door and then opened the passenger-side Escalade door as well. This guy was smooth. I had to stay strong. Where I grew up, if a guy had a car you could hear it coming down the block. And he'd only open the door for you if it was stuck.

We glided south on Coastal Highway to the refurbished Hobbit Restaurant. Actually, it wasn't refurbished; it was in a new building, on the bottom floor of a high-end condominium called Rivendell. (Would I make this up?) The Hobbit used to be in a house that was Hobbit-tiny and Old World charming. Now it's spacious and glassy and very West Coast flash meets East Coast money. Which is great, if you're into that kind of thing, but The Hobbit?

Inside, the sleek, long-haired hostess greeted Jonathan by name and they exchanged air-kisses. I really hoped I wouldn't have to dump a tray of food over this woman's head.

She escorted us to a table next to a glass wall with a view of marsh grasses dramatically up-lit. The restaurant was quiet, with maybe six occupied tables. For once in my life, I remembered to switch off my cell phone.

Jonathan ordered a bottle of wine. I hate that! He didn't ask me, and I am not really a wine kind of girl. Coors Light will do fine, or if we're going fancy I'll take a Sam Adams. I found a scrap of paper, and stuck my gum in it. Jonathan looked away.

The waitress opened the bottle. Jonathan swirled the deep red liquid in his glass and took a slow, ostentatious sip.

"Very nice, yes," he murmured. I shifted impatiently in my chair. Our glasses were filled and Jonathan raised his.

"To new friendships," he said, his eyes boring into mine. I raised my glass, lowered my eyes, took a sip. I'd rather be drinking a Jack and Coke, but I could choke this down.

Oh, who was I kidding? The wine was delicious.

"I had a long conversation this afternoon with Vernette Johnson," I began, and Jonathan shifted in his chair, his expression neutral after a flash of impatience. "She made some serious accusations about Ivory Enterprises and Bayview Preserve, and claims to have evidence. I need to hear your side of the story."

"You have now spoken to the woman, so you know it's true: She's insane."

"She says she has proof that Bayview Preserve knocked out the last blue crab breeding ground and that it's now spewing raw sewage into the bay," I said.

Jonathan made a show of choking on his wine, but I noticed he didn't spill a drop. "Is that what she's claiming now? First it was that we paid off basically everyone to get the development built. Then it was that we somehow got her fired from Eastern Maryland. Then she accused us of breaking into her house, following her around, what else? Hacking her computer, beaming signals into her dental fillings, have I about covered it?"

"Except for that last one, yes, exactly."

"Oh, for God's sake! And you believe this crackpot?"

"It doesn't matter what I believe. I'm just trying to do a complete reporting job. She is a marine biologist who says she has proof of an environmental disaster and a cover-up. I can't just ignore that, can I?"

I took a calm sip of wine.

"I don't see why not," he said with a clever smile. "What proof does she have?"

"She says she's got water samples and wildlife counts dating back to before construction."

"How do you know where she got these samples?"

"Well, I saw her collecting one set when I was with you the other day."

Jonathan grimaced.

"And I suppose she is testing these samples in her kitchen sink using a child's home chemistry set?" His voice was heavy with sarcasm.

"I'll tell you something odd, too, Jonathan," I said, ignoring his last dig and looking him in the eye. "A couple of guys came into the restaurant where we were meeting, and Vernette thought they were people who have followed her before —"

"You see what I mean about her? She is paranoid and delusional."

"Yeah, but she took off; went out the restroom window. I started to follow but wasn't quick

147

enough. When I came back into the dining room, the two guys were gone and the owner said he caught them going through my stuff. They stole my recorder."

"Well, that is unfortunate," he said, feigning concern. "Does that mean you'll have to start all over with our interviews?" he said, eyes twinkling.

"Not at all," I said with finality.

"That's a relief," he said, again hitting an unconvincing note. Then he leaned forward earnestly. "Jamie, the woman was fired for incompetency. She has no affiliation with any scientific institution and she has decided that her own failed career is somehow the fault of my company. She has made it her mission to drag Bayview Preserve through the mud, but she's got no credibility. Nobody believes her nonsense."

The waitress arrived with our meals, and we paused to devote our attention to the food: roast prime for Jonathan, and seared scallops with chilies and avocado for me. I offered Jonathan a scallop; he gave me a piece of the meltingly delicious roast. The tension of our earlier conversation diffused. He smiled at me, enjoying his meal, and I smiled back. Both of us sure like eating. It was a pleasurable period of silence. When I had mopped up the last of the scallop juices with my bread, I resumed the conversation.

"On a different note, I have a box of photos dating from the '80s and '90s that includes some shots of what I'm pretty sure is the same land and marshy area where Bayview Preserve now sits."

"Really?" Jonathan asked in genuine surprise. "Where did you find those?"

"I have a friend whose mother was a shutterbug, and also a bird watcher. There are some great pictures of egrets on the marsh, and the view looking across the bay to Ocean City, and even the little house by the marsh. The old Donnelley house, I think."

"I know my father would love to see those," he said. "I think he would be very interested."

"I thought so, too. In fact, in one of the pictures there's a shot that must have been taken with a telephoto lens of your father and another man on the porch of the Donnelley house. Here, I have it with me," I said, pulling out the snapshot.

Jonathan actually did choke this time. "I don't see how that could be true," he coughed. "Ivory Enterprises bought that parcel from the Donnelley estate after the fire. Must be some other old guy," he said, staring at the photograph and doing his best to sound jolly. "Do you mind if I hold on to this, to show it to my father?" he said and started to slide the picture into the inside pocket of his sport coat.

"It's not my picture, so I need to hold onto it."

"I'll get it right back to you, don't worry."

"No, Jonathan. Give me the picture," I said, dropping my fork onto my plate with a clatter and narrowing my eyes. Other diners turned to stare.

"Relax, I promise I'll return it to you tomorrow, right after I see father at our morning meeting."

I glared, but he acted oblivious.

"Who is this photographer friend of yours?" he asked with strident good cheer.

I gave up the fight for the moment. "Jerry Mulvaney—you know, Mulvaney Chevrolet?" He nodded. "His mom took the photographs, and Jerry had them in a box in the attic until recently." I told him about the '72 Impala up on the roof of the dealership. "His mom was crazy about the car. She took pictures of it all the time when she was out bird watching."

"She sounds like an interesting character. Where is she these days?"

"She passed away last year."

Jonathan eased back in his chair. "Ah, I'm sorry to hear that," he said, sounding anything but. "Well, we would be very interested in taking a look at all of those pictures. Perhaps we'll talk to Jerry Mulvaney about purchasing them. We could blow a few up and frame them for our sales office."

I couldn't see how that would help sales, but then again I'm a reporter, not a PR flack. Much to the *Weekly Breeze* editor's annoyance in this case.

Jonathan tried to rest his leg against mine under the table. The spark where he touched me could have lit the tablecloth on fire. I shifted away as I reached for my wine glass.

Dinner over, Jonathan offered me a ride home, and this time I relented. I couldn't see any other choice. As we approached a plain condo complex one block away from the cement plant, I told him to pull into the parking lot. He reached smoothly across the expanse of the front seat to pull me in for a kiss. His cologne smelled rich and simple and his face was very soft and smooth. He kissed me slowly, expertly. I responded in spite of myself, opening my lips and breathing him in. I felt my heart beat faster. As he drew me closer, I put my hand on his chest, then slid my fingers into his jacket pocket and extracted the photograph. I quickly pulled away, dropped the snapshot into my bag, opened the door and jumped out. "Good night, Jonathan."

He lunged for me, his eyes glittering with fury in the dome light. I slammed the door and, without looking back, ran down the sidewalk between two condos. I turned left, hurried behind the building to the street, and walked the half-block to the cement plant.

I looked behind me and icy fear ripped through my chest. The Escalade sat idling and dark at the end of the block. Jonathan watched me hurry down the sidewalk. I shot a defiant glare at him, then opened the gate and chained it closed behind me.

8.

WAS SHAKING with nervous energy. I changed into old flannel pajamas and threw on a sweater. Then I set up my laptop and cranked some Puddle of Mudd. Times like this, a girl needs some serious '90s rock guitar. A couple of hours later, in the silence between songs, a little clank rang out on deck. I glanced out the back windows into the darkness, but saw nothing. Considering this houseboat is practically held together by clanking noises, scrapes and creaks, I hardly gave it a second thought. Music filled the room again, and I worked on, my eyes starting to get heavy and my mind wandering.

The sound of the waves against the side of the boat reminded me of an August day when I was a kid.

The summer when I was 6, my whole family left Dundalk for a week in Ocean City. One hot, hazy day, my sister Lindsey and I spent the afternoon in the ocean. I threw myself into the tiny waves that lapped the shore, letting the currents rock me gently. At first I was afraid I'd be swept out to sea by any backward movement of the water, but as the day wore on, I grew bolder. I threw myself belly-first into the surf over and over again. Lindsey had a boogie board and was riding the bigger waves. She tried to show me how to use the board, but I wasn't interested. I just wanted to belly-flop into the shallow water.

That evening, we went to Shantytown, a ramshackle collection of shops, bars, and restaurants on the west side of the Route 50 bridge. It has since been torn down and replaced by million-dollar townhouses. We were in line at McDonald's and I threw up all over the greasy floor, before I even had any food. As Atlantic Ocean water spewed from my mouth, my sister cried with embarrassment. I was allowed to have a Coke and a few French fries for dinner, and I thought that was pretty great.

The smell of smoke jolted me out of my childhood reverie. I snapped the laptop shut and shoved it in my bag along with Jerry Mulvaney's box of photographs. I slid my sock feet into wool slippers with crocheted flowers on top and threw the bag over my shoulder as I ran out on deck and toward the gangplank. The metal floor was warm. Flames leaped from the back of the boat. I reached the spot where the walkway should have been and nearly pitched into the frigid, slushy water below. The plank was gone. There was just a hole in the railing about 12 feet above the old wooden dock, which was now being showered with soot and sparks. The plank lay on the dock.

I screamed in horror into the empty winter night. But who could hear me from a pier down in the industrial section of town? I saw a set of taillights out on the road beyond the concrete plant gates, braking at a stop sign, then moving slowly out of sight. Flames began reaching out of the lower level windows. I fumbled in my bag and pulled out my cell phone. "Oh please, oh please, oh please," I said aloud, my hands trembling as I pressed the "on" button. I started to feel the warmth of the steel floor through my slippers.

Nokia, the screen artfully flashed, then gave a cheery trill. Then *AT&T* appeared, paused for effect, faded. I began to lift first one foot, then the other. *Searching for network,* the phone displayed. The hourglass tipped speculatively over and over. Glass tinkled at the front of the boat, and flames fanned into my living space.

With a growing sense of panic, I eyed the dock and the nearly frozen water below, then checked the phone again. *New voice mail,* the screen said. I punched 911. Pause. Dropped signal. Tears streamed down my face as I dialed the numbers again and hit "call." This time there was an interminable silence, and then I heard a ring. The phone rang and rang and rang nine times before the call was answered.

As I shouted that my houseboat was on fire and the gangplank was gone, and the gate was locked, the woman on the other end was all business. She kept me on the line until I could hear sirens in the distance. Then my phone dropped the call.

I took my sweater off and stood on it to protect my feet from the heat. I shivered and coughed and wept. I guessed I had about three more minutes before I had to choose between burning to death or jumping in the water and freezing to death.

Two fire trucks stopped at the gate, and some-one leaped out of the cab with a pair of bolt cutters. He opened the gate and both trucks wailed up to the dock.

Several firefighters ran onto the dock with a big ladder, which they propped where the gangplank should have been. One of them ran up the ladder like it was a set of stairs, grabbed me off the deck and carried me down. I held onto his neck with one hand and clutched my bag with the other. Through my terror a random thought entered my brain: This guy smells nice.

He cleared the dock and deposited me on solid ground. My knees buckled, and he hoisted me onto a stretcher. The stretcher was lifted into the back of the ambulance, and the nice-smelling guy jumped in. He covered me with a blanket, but my teeth wouldn't stop chattering. He warmed the stetho-scope in his palm before listening to my heart and lungs. Then he shined a flashlight in my eyes and down my throat, speaking quietly the whole time, explaining what he was going to do next, telling me everything looked fine, healthy, normal. A little bit of irritation in the throat, nothing serious. Finally, I could feel my pulse slowing and my muscles relax-ing. I drifted off to sleep before I got his name. Or number.

9.

I WOKE UP DISORIENTED, in a fog. Where was I? What was that unpleasant smell? A bowl of spackle—no, oatmeal—swam into focus, steaming on a tray at my bedside. The events of last night came rushing back. Fresh tears welled up.

Someone had tried to kill me. I had to get it together. Crying would get me nowhere. I gave myself a little talking to. "Knock it off, August," I muttered. "Nancy Drew wouldn't be crying."

Something moved at the periphery of my vision and I gasped with fear. "Hey, hey, it's okay," said a man leaning forward in the chair next to my bed. "What was that you said?"

"You scared the shit out of me! Who are you?"

"I'm Will Vernon. I'm the guy who pulled you off the boat last night. I came in with another transport, so I thought I'd check in on you."

"Oh. Hi. I'm Jamie," I croaked. The gears were shifting slowly in my head. "How long have you been sitting there?"

"I don't know. Not too long," he said. I awkwardly smoothed my hair and made sure nothing naughty was peeking out of my hospital gown. Wow. The paramedic smelled nice, and he looked good, too. His dark blond hair, in need of a cut, curled at the collar of his OCFD shirt. His eyes were bright blue.

"How are you feeling?" he asked.

"Um, I don't know. Okay I guess." I looked around blankly, disoriented and flustered by Will. Then I remembered. "I had a bag with me last night. Do you know where it is?"

Will stood up and I could see he was tall and no stranger to the gym. He opened a wardrobe door and there was my bag, sitting on the shelf along with the pajamas I had been wearing. I breathed a huge sigh of relief about my bag and about being alive. Fresh tears fell down my cheeks no matter how hard I tried to stop them.

"Don't cry, Jamie. It's okay," Will said, pushing the breakfast tray aside and patting my arm. "You're safe."

That made me cry harder. "No, I'm not safe!" I sobbed. "I'm totally not safe. My boat was torched and I don't know what I'm gonna do ..." I sobbed and coughed.

"Hey, shhh." Will leaned forward and I buried my head in his shoulder and cried until I started hiccupping. He slid onto the edge of my bed and sat, his arms around me, hugging me.

Once I had soaked the shoulder of his sweatshirt, I released Will and let out a laugh of embarrassment. "Sorry," I said, and grabbed a tissue from the side table. "So awkward. I don't even know you," I said, hiccupping again. "Well, I mean you saved my life and all, but other than that..."

"Hey, no, it's okay," he said, sitting quietly as I sniffled and pulled myself together. An orderly came in and removed the breakfast tray.

"Do you have some family or friends you can stay with until you sort things out?"

I thought about Tammy's lumpy plaid couch, about the back room of the Beach Getaway office. I thought about my miniature bank account. I imagined freaking out my sister or my parents by showing up at either of their places. Forget it. "No way,"

I said. "I can't go stay with any of my friends. I'll get their house firebombed, too!"

He gave me an odd look.

A middle-aged man in a crumpled brown suit poked his head in the door as I was about to respond. "Miz August?" he said in a friendly Eastern Shore drawl. "I'm glad you're awake. How're you feeling?"

"I've had better nights," I admitted. "Then again, I guess I've had worse. Who are you?"

"I'm Detective Francis and I'm trying to find out what happened last night out at your houseboat. Are you up for a few questions?"

"Sure, yeah," I said. Will stood and I grabbed his arm. "Please don't go yet," I whispered. Good grief, had they given me drama drugs? Will sat back down.

"Hey, Joe," he said, with a little nod.

"How you doin', Will?" said the detective, a small, quizzical smile crossing his face as he eyed my fingers around Will's wrist.

Detective Francis pulled a chair up from the other side of the room.

"Tell me what happened, Miz August," he said.

"Call me Jamie," I said. "Well, I was working at my kitchen table —"

"Working?" Detective Francis interrupted.

"I'm a reporter. I was working on a story at my laptop in the kitchen. Well, it's—it was—all one room, my houseboat, so there isn't really a separate kitchen," I said, still feeling fuzzy.

"That's fine, Jamie, so you were working on your laptop, and what time was this?" He had a slow, easy drawl, not too Southern but the edges all smoothed out. Probably good at talking people off ledges.

"I started at 9:30 or 10, worked for at least a couple of hours," I said, sliding into reporter mode, or at least trying to sound professional. Not easy with a head full of painkillers. "I heard a noise out on deck, like something hit it. Soon after that, I smelled smoke. I ran outside and saw that I couldn't get off the boat because the gangplank was gone. So I called 911, and —" I looked at Will. "And got rescued."

"Why would someone want to hurt you?" Detective Francis squinted at me, with curiosity and concern and not a little skepticism. Will was also scrutinizing me.

"Okay, here's the deal," I said, forcing myself to enunciate clearly. "The story I'm working on is going to expose a huge real estate developer, and it looks like they might be dumping raw sewage into the bay. I have to get proof of that, of course. According to my sources, they paid off Eastern Maryland College to falsify the initial environmental impact report. Plus, they got hold of the land really cheap—too cheap, which I think is really fishy, don't you? And then a couple of guys who were following Dr. Johnson stole my recorder —""

In my druggy emotional fog, I heard myself spilling all these crazy, disconnected thoughts and there didn't seem to be anything I could do to stop the flow.

The detective was looking at me with worry and amusement. He glanced at Will, who just shrugged.

"What paper do you work for?" he asked.

"*Ocean City Weekly Breeze,*" I said.

"Isn't that the free weekly that has the concert listings and, I don't know, movie reviews?"

Great. Another hater. "Yes, we have those," I said.

"And you're saying that a real estate developer attempted to kill you because of an article you're writing for the *Weekly Breeze?*"

"It's going to be a hell of an article."

He stared at me, then laughed. "Where are you going to be staying? I'll need to get back in touch with you."

"I can give you my cell phone number," I said, and rattled it off.

"Do you have family to stay with in the area?" he asked.

"I'm looking at a couple of options," I said. "I won't be leaving Ocean City."

"Okay, Jamie, we'll be in touch. If you think of anything else that might help, give a call," he said, handing over a police department business card. "Take care of yourself." He leaned across the bed to shake my hand, then shook Will's hand. "Look after her, all right?" the detective said with a friendly wink.

"Sure," Will said uncertainly.

"Wow, that went great," I said, rolling my eyes. "I don't know what kind of drugs they have given me, Will. It's Will, right?" He saved my life, and I couldn't remember his name. He nodded helpfully.

"But I can't seem to get my thoughts together before they just fall out my mouth. No wonder that detective didn't believe me. Seemed nice enough, though."

"Yeah, he's a good guy," Will said.

"And right now, I've got nothing, anyway. No proof."

I stewed in frustration. "The only way to protect myself is to finish my story and get it published.

Once the Bayview Preserve story is out in the open, then I'll feel a lot safer."

"I guess," Will said. "Unless they want revenge."

A chill went down my spine. I shuddered.

A doctor came in, checked my vital signs, shined a flashlight into my eyes, and told me I was no worse for the wear. "Take it really easy for the next few days," he said. "You've had quite a shock, and just because you are physically okay, don't just think you can go play in traffic right away."

I nodded and assured the doctor that I would not play in traffic. He had me sign some documents and gave me a prescription for a drug to help me sleep. He gave me the okay to be discharged and left the room. I tossed the sleeping pill prescription in the trash—I couldn't afford to sleep just yet—and began to get out of bed. Then I remembered I was wearing only a hospital gown.

"I don't have any clothes," I said. "Just my pajamas."

Will went to the door. "Well, put them on. I'm taking you to breakfast," he said, stepping into the corridor and closing the door behind him.

I've gone out to breakfast in worse.

A few minutes later, I emerged from the hospital room in my striped PJs, sweater, and slippers.

Will and I walked out of the hospital and into the bright morning sun.

We sat across from each other at Happy Jack's Pancake House. Will ordered buckwheat pancakes and sweet potato pancakes, sliding them onto a single plate and drenching them with maple syrup. I ordered toast and coffee. The sedative was wearing off and I couldn't eat much.

"Thanks for all your help, Will. Why are you doing this?"

"I don't know," he said with a smile. "Somebody needed to." He took a big bite of pancakes, a swig of coffee.

"Listen," he said. "After breakfast, let's get you some new clothes, then figure out where you're going to stay. You didn't have any kind of insurance or anything, did you?"

I guffawed.

"Yeah, I didn't think so. Okay, well, I have a couple of ideas. But first, let's get you out of those pajamas."

I looked at him and burst out laughing. "That's not what you meant," I said.

"That's not what I meant," he said, grinning and blushing.

After breakfast, I tried to call Tammy but got her voice mail. "Hey, girl. I had a crazy night last night. Not in a good way. Seriously. Give me a call. I need to borrow some clothes."

I checked my bank balance and we went on a $100 shopping spree at Daffodil's, which netted me two pairs of jeans (one skinny, one flared, both rhinestone-studded), a "Maryland is for Crabs" sweatshirt, a hot pink off-the-shoulder sweater, a pair of spike-heeled ankle boots, some fake Keds, and several bras and panties in various dayglo and sparkly colors.

I modeled all the clothes for him—well, not the undies. He voted thumbs down on an acrylic fisherman's sweater and a pair of green sweatpants that said "Ocean City" down one leg. I also grabbed basic toiletries and couldn't resist a couple of tubes of shimmery lip gloss.

My computer was still in my faux Gucci, and I was laden with several big plastic shopping bags. Will carried more shopping bags. It was like I was starting a new life as Rock Star Barbie. Things were looking up!

We climbed in Will's pickup, a small, dark green Toyota. The bench seat between us was piled with my loot. He turned to me, his elbows resting with a plasticky crinkle on the shopping bags. "That was the most fun I have ever had shopping," he said.

"I don't know if that means much," I said. "I can't see shopping being very high on your list of favorite things."

"Yeah, I was planning on spending the day at the track at Dover Downs," he admitted. "But this was great, too. Anyway, I like you and I want to help." I smiled a little and looked out the windshield at the grey afternoon sky.

"You have been a big help. Thank you."

"So, I was thinking. Why don't you stay at my place?"

I jerked my head around, instantly defensive. "Listen, I appreciate everything you have done for me, really, but I can't just..."

"No, listen. I've been bunking at the firehouse anyway. I have a trailer down at Sunny Shores, but I've got to clear out because they're building some new housing development. It's nothing fancy, but the power is on and the furniture is still there. You're welcome to it for a few days. What do you think?"

I reached across the shopping bags to give him a giant hug and a kiss on the cheek. He turned his head and the peck on the cheek turned into a real kiss. We kissed for several seconds before I groaned and pulled away in confusion.

"Sorry," he said.

"No, no I, uh...." I shook my head to clear it.

"That was a stupid thing for me to do, you being in such a tight spot, and I do not want you to feel like I am trying to take advantage of you because that's not what I meant at all and..."

I shut him up by kissing him. This one was slower and sweeter. The plastic shopping bags set up a racket between us. I pulled away and noticed the windows had fogged.

"It's okay," I said.

Will smiled, started the car and headed south down Coastal Highway.

Just north of 64th Street, Will pulled into Sunny Shores Trailer Park. A billboard had been constructed to block the Sunny Shores sign, saying "Coming Soon! Whispering Waters: A Family Community brought to you by Ivory Enterprises."

Gravel crackled under the wheels as he made his way down the single, straight road toward the back of the park. Almost all the trailers had already been moved, and the ground was criss-crossed with tire ruts and frozen puddles. A few trailers sat rusting and abandoned and I wondered if anyone would bother with the expense of moving them. It was kind of a spooky spot, but beggars can't be choosers.

Will pulled up to an ancient single-wide, white with a baby blue stripe. It sat at an angle just a few yards from the water's edge. Old lattice was piled next to the front stoop, and the trailer's chassis showed.

We had stopped at the grocery store, so we were each loaded with bags from Daffodil's and SuperFoods. We climbed the wooden steps to the front stoop.

Inside, boxes sat on the floor and a brown sofa faced the front door. It was centered under a picture window that looked out onto a bayside canal. A bookshelf had been emptied except for a few decks of cards and a tray of poker chips. A kitchenette spanned the front wall, with a little window over the sink. A bedroom and small bathroom took up the back half. The bed was made with a dark blue comforter and a couple of green and white-striped pillows.

"It's not much, but it keeps the rain out," Will said.

"It has about the same amount of living space as the houseboat had," I said. "And it's probably about the same age."

171

He told me to help myself to the closet and the dresser. As I unpacked my new clothes, Will put away the groceries. After a moment, I smelled onions frying in the kitchen.

"And you cook!" I exclaimed, joining him at the kitchen counter.

"Chicks dig it."

"You got that right," I said. "What are you making?"

"Just some pasta. I'll doctor up a jar of spaghetti sauce, throw in some onions and ground beef, nothing fancy. I'll eat with you before I leave for my shift."

"Your shift? Oh, that's right. I forgot about that. You have a job. And I have a job! Holy crap, do I have a job to do. I will get to work on my story tonight, check in with my editor, and, oh shit! I'll give Larry Lombardo a call, too, at the cement plant. He is probably freaking out."

What was I thinking, going shopping with a cute guy instead of letting people know I was okay? It was one thing to keep my whereabouts secret from people, but quite another to let them think I had disappeared.

I pulled out my phone and saw that I had missed four calls from Donald, my editor. Also two voice mails from Tammy. I swear my phone never rang. I hate my phone. First, I dialed the Lombardo office. Nobody answered, so I left a message for Larry telling him I was safe and I'd call him in a few days.

"Dinner!" Will called, and set a bowl of spaghetti on the table. He dealt out plates and silverware, and poured a couple of glasses of water from a jug on the counter.

"You dressed for dinner," he said, eyeing me in my new clothes. "You look great."

I blushed and said thanks, and he served me a big helping.

While we ate, he talked about his work, and I related stories about Beach Getaway and my Uncle Abe, the king of cut-rate beach rental property. I also told him about the Slomkowski family from Baltimore, who seemed to have no complaints about staying in the moldering Sunrise Paradise.

"I know that building!" Will said. "We responded to a call there last summer. A bunch of teenage Russian seasonal workers were staying on the top floor and started a fire on the roof!"

"Well, they tried. The story is, they were singing 'The roof, the roof, the roof is on fire,' and one of the comrades got a little out of control."

"That's right! Some of the trim around the top of the building caught fire, but the roof itself was asphalt, so no real harm was done."

"That building is like a bomb shelter," I said.

"Looks like one, too," Will said.

"That's where I would go if it was the end of the world."

Will smiled, then looked at his watch. "It's almost 7, and I've got to get to work. I hope you get some work done, too. You should have everything you need here. Lock the door after I leave, and don't let anyone in until I get back in the morning. Nobody knows you're here, so you should be safe."

I must have seemed apprehensive, and I was probably looking needy or helpless or some other ridiculous thing, but then he leaned across the table, placed a hand behind my neck and kissed me. And that was just fine.

"Thank you. For everything. And for saving my life."

"Just doin' my job, ma'am," he said, grabbing his fire department hat and tipping it in my direction as he put it on. He drew the curtains on the picture window and closed the blinds on the window in the front door. I locked up behind him. I cleared the table, washed the dishes, and set up my laptop, tucking my crochet-slippered feet under me. There were no more delay tactics available, so I called Donald.

"Jamie, what happened? I heard about the houseboat on the scanner last night and I've been trying to reach you ever since! Where are you? Do you need anything? Are you okay?" he charged into the conversation.

"I'm fine, I'm fine. I was in the hospital last night, but I'm okay now. I'm staying someplace safe for a few days, just until I can figure out what the hell this story is all about and get it written."

Donald fumed about my secrecy and tried to insist that the fire could not have had anything to do with the Bayview Preserve story, but his heart wasn't in it. "I wanted you to write about the color schemes and the restaurants, and look what you did!" he joked.

"I just can't figure out what I've got that is so damaging. I don't have proof of anything, just a bunch of hearsay that's either off the record or coming from a woman who regularly gets thrown out of city council meetings. And some old photos of the marshlands that used to be where Bayview Preserve is now," I said.

"Why did Jonathan Ivory make such a point that I must have been mistaken about his father being in that picture?"

"What picture?"

"Who was the other man?" I went on, oblivious to Donald. "Was it Frank Donnelley? What went on in that little house, and why did the heirs sell the land for so little? There's something going on, Donald, believe me, but I haven't figured it out yet."

"Have you figured out who the landscape architect is for Bayview Preserve, and what color schemes their spring plantings will have?" he asked. "Have you spoken to the manager of Reynaud's to learn what opening specials they'll be running in the restaurant?"

As Donald spoke, I rummaged in my bag for the old photos. My fingers touched something hard at the bottom of the bag. I pulled out a shimmery green plastic fish-shaped thumb drive. Vernette's thumb drive.

"Do you understand what I'm saying, Jamie?"

"Donald, I've got to go. I'm fine. I'll call you tomorrow," I said, and hung up despite his protests.

I plugged the thumb drive into my MacBook and watched as the new finder window displayed the contents of the drive. A folder held dozens of Excel files simply labeled with dates. The oldest was 1995. The most recent was January 17th, 2008—just a few day ago—Wednesday, the day Jonathan

Ivory confronted Vernette Johnson at Bayview Preserve.

I opened one file at random and found a spread-
sheet with numbers and scientific notations. I figured this must be Johnson's water and soil sample
data. I would need help making sense of it.

I saved the files from the thumb drive to my
computer, then remotely, by plugging my phone
into my computer for a bit of overpriced and unreliable wifi. Success. For the moment, I set aside the
question of what the heck Johnson's files meant. I
worked until about 10, stringing all my notes together into a story with holes like Swiss cheese. I
resolved to have another conversation with Fred
Western.

I massaged my neck and shoulders. In the evening's quiet, I thought I heard the gravel crunch of a
vehicle turning into the drive. I stood up to stretch
and peeked out the blinds in the living room door.
A dark sedan inched toward the trailer, its lights
off. Shit.

My flight plan was quick this time: scoop the
computer, the photos, the thumb drive, and the
notes into the purse. I stood on the couch, opened
the big window facing away from the road and
jumped out. I crouched underneath the trailer as
the car approached and parked. A pair of legs

stepped out of the driver's side door and moved quietly up the steps.

The man jimmied the door alarmingly fast. As soon as he was in the door, I crawled out from under the trailer and took off in a silent sprint across the empty expanse, toward the lights of Coastal Highway. I took cover behind the rusting hulk of a trailer about halfway between Will's place and the road. I watched as the man—where do I know him from?—was silhouetted in the lit doorway. He kicked the door in frustration, bouncing it against the outside of the trailer. He bounded down the steps and crouched to peer under the trailer, shining a flashlight around. He spotted something and reached farther under the mobile home to retrieve it. My cell phone.

He stood up and fumbled with the flashlight and the phone, finally sticking the flashlight in his coat pocket, facing up. In that light I could clearly see the face of the security guard from Ocean Mirage, the Ivory Enterprises building. He peered into the darkness.

I carefully made my way toward the road, darting behind a couple of trailers and finally reaching it. I turned south, walking quickly down the lit sidewalk, my slipper-shod feet freezing against the pavement.

Traffic was sparse. After a few minutes bright lights shone ahead. Seacrets, the largest nightclub in Ocean City, is a Jamaican-themed bayside compound. This place has everything: its own beach, hotel, five concert stages, even its own radio station, with its studio overlooking the action and its antenna lit up like some kind of low-budget Eiffel Tower. For my purposes, it was perfect because it was open for business. I stepped up the pace, my toes growing numb. If I get through this, I thought, I'm going to have these slippers bronzed and mounted. I'll hang them next to the Pulitzer.

A sign said, "Tonight! Chase Away the Winter Blues With Seacrets Freezing Bikini Contest!" I was feeling great about the lights and traffic around the club. Then a dark blue Taurus roared up behind me and skidded to an abrupt stop, causing a stretch limo to run into its trunk. The limousine's horn blasted once, then sounded continuously, the mechanism stuck. Steam poured from its hood.

The security guard jumped out of the Taurus, leaving the engine running and the door open, and sprinted after me. He seemed completely oblivious to the accident he caused. I ran at top speed, dodging the crowd of partiers making their way toward

Seacrets. A line of people waited to be carded and admitted, but I dashed up to the bouncer.

"I'm late for the bikini contest, has it started yet?" I gasped. The bouncer, a tank of a Samoan guy, looked me up and down as I heaved my chest and fanned the wide neck of my sweater in mock heat exhaustion. He exchanged glances with another, smaller guy in a Seacrets uniform shirt, who was carrying a walkie-talkie. I could hear the crowd protesting as the creepy security guard fought his way toward me.

"Please, let me in. My boyfriend is back there and he doesn't want me to enter the contest, but I've just got to get away from him and do my own thing, you know what I mean? I've got to express myself!" I said, giggling and flipping my hair.

I could hear sirens in the distance, coming this way.

"Go on in," the big guy said in a high, reedy voice. "Jeff here's gonna take you to the main stage to get you signed up. Hurry up, it's gonna start in like five minutes."

He opened the velvet rope for me, and closed it just as the Ivory security guard fought to the front of the line.

"Let me in, dammit!" he yelled as the Samoan blocked his way.

"Chill the fuck out, brah," the bouncer said. I didn't hear any more, as Jeff steered me towards the main stage—and the bikini contest.

10.

NOW I HAD DONE IT. My mind raced, trying to figure how I was going to get out of this. I thought about trying to lose myself in the crowd, but it wasn't really wall-to-wall, and the walkie-talkie guy was guiding me through the place with a hand on my back. Maybe a little lower than my back, actually.

We reached the main stage, and he herded me over to a group of women milling about in various stages of undress. Most looked fake-tanned and fake-boobed. They were shivering, clutching their arms across their chests, huddling for warmth. Some of them wearing just their bikinis, others with mini-skirts, little dresses, t-shirts. I looked down at my own getup: flowered slippers, rhinestone jeans, hot pink off-the-shoulder sweater. Underneath, I wore a pink sparkly bra with tiny matching boy shorts—and winter-white skin.

"Is there, like, a prize for this?" I asked the Seacrets guy.

"A ton of gift certificates plus two nights at the Hilton and 500 bucks to the winner, 250 for second place, and 100 for third," he said.

Oh hell yes. It was on. I sure needed a place to stay. Plus, shopping money!

I shimmied out of my jeans and shoved them in my fake Gucci, along with the flower slippers. "Where can I put this where it'll be really safe?" I asked Jeff.

"Here, I can take it," he said, starting to remove the bag from my shoulder. I grabbed his wrist in a death grip. "Where are you taking it?"

"Whoa, lady! I'm just going to put it backstage where all the other girls put their stuff."

"No. I can't let you do that," I said. "Never mind. I will hold onto it." I had an idea.

"You can't carry that big purse with you onstage when you do, you know," he gestured helplessly, "your thing."

"No? You watch me, baby," I said, touching the tip of his nose with a fingertip and turning my back on him to face my competitors.

A guy in black jeans and a black T-shirt, holding a clipboard, came up to me and took down my name and details. "What song do you want?" he asked.

"Song?"

"Yeah, what song? You're gonna dance to a song, right? What song do you want?"

"Uh..."

He was impatient, but clearly he had been through this before, probably from many seasons of herding drunken girls onstage for bikini contests. "What's your name again? Jamie?"

I nodded.

"Okay, you get Van Halen's 'Jamie's Cryin.'"

He was done, and turned away. Sweet! I love Van Halen. Everyone would agree, Van Halen is one of those majorly important bands. Not as awesome as Bon Jovi but close.

The room, which had been pulsing with dance music, suddenly went quiet. The stage went dark. The guy with the clipboard jumped onstage and welcomed the crowd to Seacrets first annual Freezing Bikini Contest.

The first woman took the stage to Joe Cocker's 'You Can Leave Your Hat On'. I stole a skittish peek toward the exit doors and almost immediately saw the creepy Ivory goon enter the hall. The colored spotlights and disco ball made it hard to focus on individual faces, but his height and oddly stiff, formal way of moving gave him away.

He scanned the crowd and I ducked behind the line of bikini girls, who were all throwing back drinks, chatting nervously, and generally not paying any attention to the jumpy girl in the sweater.

The guard began to make his way into the crowd, roughly turning women around in his search. He was starting to make a spectacle of himself, but the crowd was also getting pretty excited about the 'Leave Your Hat On' girl, who was, of course, dancing in her bikini while wearing a fedora.

There were bouncers lining the front of the floor, so I figured the scary security guy couldn't get to me while I was actually onstage. That thought calmed me a little.

The song ended, the crowd cheered, and the announcer's voice filled the room. "Ladies and gentlemen, the Island of Seacrets is a democracy, and the winner of tonight's Freezing Bikini Contest will be chosen by YOU! If you like what you see up onstage, then give it up! I want to hear you clapping, yelling, whistling, screaming, people! Make some noooooooise! The Seacrets applause-o-meter is going to measure the decibel levels in here. So vote for your favorite by shouting it out!"

The crowd roared its agreement, and the master of ceremonies called the next chilly woman to the stage. I remained behind the row of other contestants, hoping that when I got onstage, the Ivory security guard would have gone elsewhere in his search. That hope faded as the line of contestants dwindled and the guard remained in the audience, methodically scrutinizing every woman's face. Finally the second-to-last woman was called onstage and I had nobody to hide behind. I stood on the bottom step at the side of the stage, scanning the crowd. As the song was winding to a close, the Ivory thug edged through the crowd and rushed toward me. He elbowed a woman as he rushed past her, which made her spill her beer all over her shirt. She stepped in front of him, yelling and poking a sparkly manicured finger into his chest. As a Seacrets bouncer waded in and separated the two, I scooted up to the top step and waited against the wall.

"Now, ladies and gentlemen, give it up for Ocean City's own Jaaaaaamie August!"

Quickly I shrugged out of my sweater and stuffed it into my bag so I was starting out in my undies. I strutted up the stairs, swinging my purse like it was a bag of sex toys. I walked to center stage, turned my back to the audience and tipped my derriere into the spotlight as I put the bag down. As the music started, I thought, dang, this is a good song for a sexy dance!

I remember dancing to Madonna albums in the living room back in Dundalk with Lindsey. She would close her eyes when she danced, probably attempting to block out the presence of her bratty little sister. I would mimic her voguing and jump out of the way as she blindly strutted across the floor, cheeks sucked in and hips swaying wildly.

Up on the Seacrets stage, I channeled Lindsey and her bold teenage moves. Days of frustration, fear, confusion—newfound lust for my paramedic hero and lingering desire for a man who seemed to be trying to have me killed—all mixed together and I was on fire. The spotlight glossed my straight hair into shiny black liquid and warmed my skin. I sparkled and shimmied in my cheap underwear and the audience went wild.

I danced for about a minute, then grabbed my jeans out of my bag, lay on the floor and slid them up my legs, moving my hips like they were the missionary and I was the savage. The crowd roared. Then I worked it with the sweater, taking as long as possible before the pink acrylic knit dropped over my chest. As the song ended, I hoisted the bag over my shoulder and strutted offstage.

The audience went nuts. The noise level in the auditorium was deafening. I fished my slippers out and shoved them on my feet. As the announcer called for my return to the stage, I bolted out the exit, setting off the fire alarm, and raced to the front of the building and the line of waiting taxis.

"Take me to the fire station, and please hurry!" I said to the driver. The cabbie, a heavyset, dark-haired guy, was drinking a can of Slim Fast through a straw. He delicately slurped for several seconds until the can sounded empty. There was a crash and a shout at the front entrance of the club. I locked my door. "I'm trying to get away from somebody and I think he's coming," I said, surprising myself with my own calmness.

The cabbie took a long look at me in the rear-view mirror, gently put the car into drive and eased away from the curb. He made a right onto Coastal Highway, merged quickly into the left lane and cruised south. He did exactly the speed limit, which pissed me off until I realized he was catching every

---

green light. I thought at one point I saw another taxi in pursuit, but it got caught at a light and I lost sight of it.

We drove in silence and quickly reached the downtown fire house. I paid the driver well and dashed into the building.

Inside, I found the dispatcher, a chubby, sandy-haired guy with his attention focused on a steak-and-cheese sub he was eating out of a carryout box. The dispatch room had glass windows overlooking the station's garage bays. The bays were dark, but the dispatch room was lit up. I knocked on the doorframe.

"Hi, I'm looking for Will Vernon," I said.

"He's out on a call," the dispatcher said with his mouth full.

"Uh, yeah, I guess he is," I said, imagining Will responding to the accident the creepy security guard had caused.

"Is he at the traffic accident up by Seacrets?" I asked.

"Nope. Drowning," he said.

"Excuse me?"

"Body in the bay. And you are?"

"I'm a friend of his. Do you mind if I wait for him here?"

"Yeah, sure, I guess," the dispatcher said.

"One thing, though. Can I ask: Do you mind if we maybe lock the doors or something? I'm actually kind of being followed."

The dispatch guy put down the sandwich, carefully wiped the grease from his hands, rested them on his beer gut, and had a more careful look at me.

"What did you say your name was?"

"I didn't, but it's Jamie August. You know the boat that got firebombed last night? That was mine," I said.

Keeping an eye on me, the dispatcher heaved himself out of his chair, lumbered to the door and locked it. Then he disappeared down a hallway. A moment later he returned. "Okay, the doors are all locked, so nobody's getting in." He looked at me and narrowed his eyes.

"I wasn't out on last night's call, but don't I know you from somewhere?"

I looked more closely at him. He did ring a bell, but I couldn't place him.

"I don't know. What's your name?"

"Barry."

"Hmm. I don't know, Barry, but it's a small town."

He continued to look at me, then a slimy smile spread across his face.

191

"Millie's."

"Millie's? What's that?"

"It's the bar where you were drinking last week. Drinking and some other things."

"Oh man. You were there?"

"'Fraid so. I was your bartender."

I covered my face with my hands. "Not one of my best nights."

"Yeah, well, shit happens. I gotta say, you sure did get friendly with that guy."

"Right. Shit happens, like you say."

"That guy? He's always getting lucky in my bar. Different chick every time. You know that, right? Real douchebag."

"I know it now. Didn't know it then."

"Sure. But you say you're Will's friend?" He looked at me skeptically.

"Oh god, Barry, you're a bartender," I said, throwing myself on his mercy. "I'm sure you've seen it all. That was a stupid thing I did last week, hooking up with Jo—with that guy, but it was before I knew Will. There's a big difference."

"Yep. Will's a good guy. I'd hate to see him get hurt."

I sighed in regret and blind exhaustion. "I don't want to hurt Will."

"He hasn't really gotten out a lot since Cindy."

"Cindy?"

"His ex-wife."

"Oh." I didn't even know Will had an ex-wife. Come to think of it, I didn't know much about Will Vernon. I was kind of hoping to change that. "Well."

"Yup, she left him and took everything they had. Not like they had much, but still."

"Seriously? That sucks."

"Yeah, she was always givin' him shit. Didn't like him hanging out with his friends. Didn't like him playing a little poker on duty night. You think that's some kind of a problem, a man spending a little time with his friends?" His tone was accusing and he scrutinized me. He was itching to get a rise out of me. His fat, meaty fingers gripped his sandwich. I knew that if I pissed this guy off, I'd be out on the sidewalk.

"Hey, everybody's gotta have a hobby," I said. "Listen, I cannot tell you how wiped out I am. So, thank you for letting me hang out here. I think I'll just..."

I sat heavily on a beat-up Naugahyde sofa in the truck bay. Barry gave me a long, hard look, then took another messy bite of his sub.

A full ashtray sat on the end table next to the sofa. The smell of stale smoke was oddly comforting. The silence stretched out for several minutes and I could feel the dispatcher's bad attitude dissipating.

Then the radio crackled to life.

A voice announced a car fire in Salisbury. A few minutes later a call came in about smoke at a residence in Ocean Pines. The traffic sounds on Coastal Highway were soothing, and the couch was comfy. I put my feet up. The radio announced new emergencies every few minutes, the traffic sounds lulled me, the couch was warm and soft, and I was so very, very tired...

The sound of the bay doors opening and the glare of headlights as the ambulance nosed into the garage woke me from a deep, dreamless sleep. I uncurled from the couch and watched as the truck moved into place. Will and another guy in dark blue cargo pants and OCFD jacket jumped out of the cab. The driver went around to the side and plugged a power cable into the boxy ambulance, while Will dashed from the passenger door over to me.

"What are you doing here, Jamie? What happened?" he asked as I threw my arms around his neck and held onto him shamelessly.

"Did you hear about the accident up by Seacrets?" I asked into his collar.

"I know a call went out for a car accident up there, and another one for a trailer on fire. Wait. A trailer. Oh no. My trailer?"

He pulled me away and looked at me.

His face registered disbelief, followed by anger and, oddly, guilt? Regret? Oh god, I thought. Because of me, that crazy guy burned down his trailer. He's probably sorry he ever met me.

Then his eyes refocused on my face and his expression turned to relief. He put his hand to my head and tucked it back into the crook of his neck. We stood there for a moment as the other firefighters and medics hustled around us.

"He came after me again. He also burned down your trailer? I didn't know he did that. I saw him coming and got out. I'm sorry. I'm sorry. I'm sorry," I said as he shushed me.

"I'm sorry too, Jamie. I'm so sorry. I'm really glad you didn't get hurt." A few moments later he said, "Well, I guess we better get up there and see what happened."

We jumped into an OCFD work truck and sped up Coastal Highway to the accident at Seacrets. On the way, I told him about the Taurus with no lights coming toward the trailer, and how I managed to sneak out. I described the scene when the security guard saw me on the street and slammed on his brakes, causing the accident. And I told him I ducked into Seacrets, and then grabbed a cab. I left out the part about the bikini contest because, really, how was that relevant?

We arrived as a tow truck was hitching up to the charred remains of the limousine. We parked in the Seacrets parking lot closest to the street, next to a black Ford Mustang, and got out.

I was wrapped up in a heavy OCFD jacket, feeling warm except for my feet, which were still protected only by slippers. We walked over to the police working the scene. "Hey, Joe," Will said, shaking hands with the same detective who had stopped into my hospital room.

"Hello, Detective Francis," I said, and he eyed me curiously.

"Joe, you're going to want to talk to Jamie about this situation," Will said. "As it happens, she was staying in the trailer that caught fire up at Sunny Shores. That was my house."

Francis did a double-take and turned to me.

"I saw the guy and I know who he is," I said. "And that'll probably go a long way toward explaining who firebombed my houseboat."

Francis whistled. "You really pissed somebody off."

Just then, the Freezing Bikini Contest announcer walked to the Mustang next to the OCFD truck. He was checking out the scene of the accident and caught sight of me. He glanced down at my feet in the slippers. Then he broke into a grin, waved, and shouted, "Hey! Jamie August! You didn't collect your prize money. Hang on. I'll go get it." He turned and jogged back to the entrance of Seacrets.

"Oh, hi!" I hollered, grinning sheepishly and waving back.

Will and Detective Francis turned to look at me.

"I, uh... It seems I won the Freezing Bikini Contest at Seacrets tonight. I ducked in there to get away from the guy who was chasing me, and, well, it just sort of worked out that way."

"You did what?" Will said, taking a step back and looking me up and down.

"I had to get away from the guy, and it worked!" I said, feeling embarrassed.

The announcer dashed across the lot, handed me an envelope stuffed with cash and gift certificates, and shook my hand. "Congratulations!" he said. "I don't know why you ran away, but it made the audience love you even more."

"You see? He couldn't get to me while I was on-stage, then I escaped out the stage door."

"You're amazing," Will said, his mouth hanging open.

I looked down at the pavement and grinned.

Half an hour later, Will and I were wedged into Detective Francis's cubicle at the police station. All three of us were drinking terrible coffee. It wasn't doing much to keep me awake; it was just opening up a hole in my gut. My stomach hurt, my head hurt and my eyelids weighed about 10 pounds each.

"Okay, Jamie, so if I understand you, you're telling me that the security guard from Ocean Mirage broke into Will's trailer while you were hiding under it."

"Ocean Mirage?" Will asked.

"That's the building where Ivory Enterprises has its offices," I said.

"You with us?" the detective said to Will, testy at the interruption. Will nodded, and Francis turned back to me. "Okay. You managed to get away without him seeing you, then he set the place on fire."

"I don't know for sure that he set the fire, but I can tell you that he broke in there looking for me."

"Right, okay, that's fine," he said. "Later, he spotted you on Coastal Highway and slammed on his brakes, which caused the limousine behind him to collide with his vehicle. Then he jumped out to chase you. Why would he do all that?"

His friendly drawl was starting to take on an edge. He was trying to buy into the concept but was struggling.

"Okay, listen, here's the thing," I said, running my hands over my face and through my hair in exhaustion. "I'm a reporter for the *Weekly Breeze* and I'm putting together a story about Bayview Preserve —"

"Oh, yeah, fancy place! I hear they've got some kind of singing fountain or something," Detective Francis said.

"Yeah, something like that," I said. "So, I found out that Ivory Enterprises bribed Eastern Maryland College to falsify their EIR —"

"What's an EIR?"

"Environmental Impact Report."

"Oh. Okay, go on."

"So they filled in a bunch of marshland, which destroyed the last breeding ground for blue crabs in Assawoman Bay."

"What?"

"And now that people are moving into the place, traces of raw sewage are showing up in the water."

"Where did you get all this?"

"I know, I know, it's crazy, and I can't prove it yet —"

Francis scowled and leaned back in his chair, which caused it to creak. The friendly cop routine was fading. "You're out of your mind. You can't just throw around accusations like that! What paper did you say you're with?"

"Uh, the *Weekly Breeze*."

"Oh, right. The *Weekly Breeze*. It's where I look first for hard-hitting news."

"You don't have to be snide."

He tipped his chair forward and placed his palms on the desk. "What makes you think you can print that kind of craziness? Just because nobody reads the *Weekly Breeze* doesn't mean you can print whatever you want in it. What kind of liberal agenda have you got going on down there?" Why did I ever think Detective Francis was a nice guy?

"Ivory Enterprises must be worried I'm onto something, don't you think? Considering they tried to kill me, twice," I reminded him. "I don't have the evidence right now, but I'm getting close. Ivory Enterprises somehow got hold of that property for only $75,000. Then they paid off Eastern Maryland for the EIR. Then they harassed Vernette Johnson, the one scientist who tried to stand up to them, until she lost her job and all her credibility. Now I've got some data and pictures they seem to want really bad, and I'm sniffing around with my 'liberal agenda,' asking questions that are making them nervous."

Will put a cautionary hand on my knee, but I was on a roll. "I tried to tell you yesterday morning, but you didn't want to hear it. Kind of like you don't want to hear it now. You see what I'm saying?"

Detective Francis fumed. "You should have given me all of this yesterday. You withheld information from the police. You put yourself in danger, as well as Will here, and you put Ocean City's motorists in danger —"

"Excuse me? I did what?" I stood up and leaned across the desk, my hot pink sweater falling off one shoulder to reveal a sparkly strap. Maybe not my most intimidating look. "Some asshole lights Will's trailer on fire, then chases me down Coastal Highway and causes a car accident and this is my fault how?"

Will jumped in. "Jamie, maybe you should —"

"Yes? I should do what, exactly, Will?"

All three of us were facing off in Francis's cubicle when another officer popped his head in.

"'Scuse me, Joe. Can I see you for a minute?"

Francis raised an accusing finger at me. "At this moment, I don't know what information you are still withholding from this investigation. You are not to leave this office."

He stepped out. A door slammed down the hall.

I stood up and paced—or tried to, but I could only take a step and a half in each direction. My anger hung in the air. Will looked down, silent. He seemed to be trying to melt into the floor.

A moment later, the detective reappeared, looking pale. "We've got an ID on that drowning in the bay. It was Vernette Johnson."

11.

"NO!" I WAILED, my head in my hands.

"Oh, no," Will said. "That was the call I worked tonight."

I looked bleakly at the detective. "I met Vernette at Piezano's the day my houseboat got hit. She ran off because two guys came in and she said they were following her. Then they tried to steal my stuff."

"That *is* unusual," he said.

"But it looked like she drowned," Will said. "I tried to revive her, but she was already gone." Exhausted frustration washed over his face.

"If she drowned, it's because someone drowned her," I said. "Vernette Johnson did not go for a therapeutic wintertime swim."

"There's no use in speculating at this point," Francis said. "An autopsy will be done and we'll know more. Meanwhile, let's go over that meeting you had with her again. You met with her when?"

"Friday at lunch."

"You said a couple of guys came into the pizza place and tried to steal your purse?"

"No, it wasn't like that. Two men came into Piezano's. My back was to the door, but I saw Vernette react to them as soon as they came in. She said, 'They found me,' or something like that, and she grabbed me and marched me off to the women's room. She went out the bathroom window and tried to get me to follow her, but I wouldn't. A minute later, or not even a minute, I went back out to the dining room and the guys were gone. Luigi— the owner of Piezano's—was there and said he had come in and found those two making a grab for my stuff."

"But Luigi stopped them?"

"He ran them out, but they took my voice recorder. That had a recording of everything Vernette told me."

"Which was?"

"Oh, so now you're interested in my story?" I said with equal parts exhaustion and sarcasm.

"I am asking you to provide information that might be useful in a possible murder investigation, Miss August. I'd watch that mouth if I was you."

I pulled up short. "Excuse me?"

"Are you accusing her of something?" Will asked incredulously.

"I'm saying I need to know everything Miss August knows that might be relevant to this investigation, and I need it right now and without that attitude. Am I making myself clear?"

"Do I need a lawyer?" I said, turning to Will.

"For God's sake, Joe, can you lay off just a little? Someone has tried to kill Jamie two nights in a row. She has had no real sleep in 48 hours, and has been running full-out to try and put together the facts —"

"She had time to enter a bikini contest," Detective Francis observed.

"This is true," Will said, relenting.

I sighed with frustration and flopped in my chair.

"Okay, look. She's with me," Will said, putting his arm around me. "I will take care of her. Just let me take her with me back to the fire station for a few hours of sleep. She'll be as safe there as any place I can think of, and we'll come back in the morning when we can all be more civil."

"I'm civil," I said.

Will and the detective both glared at me.

"I'm giving her a break because I know you," he said, then leaned across the desk and glared at Will. "You bring her back here first thing tomorrow morning, or I'm coming after both of you."

Will squeezed my shoulder tight.

"What am I, a side of beef?" I said, shrugging Will's arm aside. "You will not talk about me as if I am an inanimate object when I am sitting in front of you."

The detective's face reddened with anger. Will moved away from me and crossed his arms.

"I will go with Will and get some sleep. When I wake up, I will go somewhere and get a decent breakfast. Then I will return here and I will tell you everything I tried to tell you yesterday morning in the hospital."

With that, I stood up, pushed the pink sweater up on my shoulder and walked out. Will followed.

"Thanks, Will, for taking me with you. I am grateful for everything you're doing for me," I said, the adrenaline seeping from my body. Will was silent behind the wheel.

"What?" I said.

"Nothing," Will said.

"Wait, are you mad at me because of that side of beef thing?"

"No, Jamie, I'm just tired. It's been a long night. Can I give you a piece of advice, though? Don't get snarky when you're being questioned by a police detective about a possible homicide."

"You were there! You heard what the man said! He insulted me, he insulted my profession."

"He insulted the *Weekly Breeze*. Come on, Jamie. The man has a point."

I looked at him with fresh eyes.

"I tried to tell him what was going on while I was in the hospital!"

"Yeah, but you were high as a kite."

"Everything I said was true," I retorted. "He wasn't interested. And he still doesn't believe my story could possibly mean anything important, that Ivory Enterprises could possibly have so much to hide that they're willing to kill to keep this story from getting published."

Will pulled into the fire station lot.

"You really think they're trying to kill you because of the story?"

I got out of the truck and hoisted my bag on my shoulder. I stared at him. "You don't believe me either."

"No, that's not —" Will flapped his arms in exasperation.

I saw the headlights of a bus coming down Coastal Highway.

"Whatever. Thanks again for your help," I said, my stomach feeling like lead. I walked across the lot toward the street.

"Wait! Where are you going?"

I kept walking. The bus stop was right in front of the fire station.

"What are you doing? Seriously, you have to stay here!"

I turned to face him as the bus pulled up to the curb.

"No, I don't." I got on the bus, the door hissed closed, and set out into the night.

My fifth-grade teacher look-alike, Mrs. Cod, was driving. One other person was on the bus, a teenage boy who looked like he was about to hurl whatever booze he had been drinking. He slumped against a window, eyes half open, unfocused.

I took a seat at the back. My head hurt, my stomach was queasy from stress and fear, and tears were forming. I willed myself not to cry: I couldn't spare the energy and didn't want to inflame the headache. I sat gingerly, stretching my legs across the long rear seat, leaning back and closing my eyes. Just for a minute, I'll rest here, I thought. I'm safe. Mrs. Cod won't let them get me. I'm safe. I'm safe.

When I woke up, the sun was streaming in the windows. I struggled to a seated position and saw that the bus had just made its turnaround at the Delaware line and was headed south on Coastal Highway. Who knows how many complete Ocean City loops I had made.

I hit the bell to get off at the stop near the *Weekly Breeze*. As the bus slowed to a stop, I fished my office keys out and had them in my hand. I was off the bus, across the pavement and inside the office in 30 seconds. I locked the door behind me and retreated to the shadowy darkness.

In the kitchenette, I was momentarily confused because it smelled like someone was baking sugar cookies. Then I spotted one of those plug-in air fresheners, Donald's latest office fragrance craze. He used to burn scented candles, but that ended when he caught his sleeve on fire with a cinnamon pillar on a late-night deadline crunch.

I put on a pot of Donald's vanilla almond cream coffee, thinking I'd much rather have that as an ice cream flavor. It was either that or mocha amaretto. My teeth ached at the thought.

The microwave clock showed 6:15. After doing a quick face-and-armpit wash at the sink, I raided the refrigerator, pulling out a carton of Chinese leftovers that didn't have any visible mold. I put up a little note apologizing for the theft, because that really sucks, having your food stolen out of the office fridge.

I carried this strange feast over to my desk, set up the laptop, pulled out the photographs and the thumb drive, and sunk into thought.

Why was the Ocean Mirage security guard—obviously a hired thug for Ivory Enterprises—so crazed and out to get me? I mean, there's job satisfaction, sure, but last night's display seemed a little excessive for someone who was simply hired to take me out.

Then I remembered that the trailer park was slated for new development and I wondered if Will's trailer fire had conveniently pushed forward the construction schedule.

I tapped on the keyboard, adding to my already lengthy story the death of Vernette Johnson and speculation about the trailer park. What I guessed the data on the thumb drive would show needed to be discussed with the boozy Fred Western, presuming he was still willing to help.

I worked until 7:30, then emailed my story-in-progress to Donald, along with a lengthy note about what research I still intended to do. I also told him my cell phone had been stolen. I scanned the photographs and sent them to myself and to Donald.

All this efficiency was wearing me out. That and my newly hazardous lifestyle. I put my feet up on the desk and closed my eyes for a minute. When I re-opened them, they rested on a big wall map of Ocean City. I let my gaze soften and noted a spot on the map for the cement factory, north of the inlet. My home no longer. My eyes drifted slightly south, to the inlet, and rested on the square inch I estimated to be Charlie's Charters, across the water and down a bit from the cement plant. Both waterfront. Both a little ragged. Both owned by members of the same family. Both getting the shakedown from Ivory Enterprises. Lights flickered on in my brain.

The clock read 7:45, too early to make phone calls. I grabbed a copy of the latest Salisbury *Daily Times* from the stack of recent local papers and put my feet up as I read their coverage of Mulvaney's party. It's good to study the competition. About five paragraphs down, the article quoted Jerry Mulvaney: "My momma loved that Impala more than she loved me. Even had a name for it. She called that car Jeanine."

Jeanine.

The newspaper fluttered to the floor as I cursed Jerry Mulvaney and his supposed "exclusive" with me. I lunged for the telephone.

"Tammy, it's Jamie," I said, my voice gravelly.

"Jamie?" Tammy said, groggy with sleep. "What time is it?"

"Uh, it's a little before 8 o'clock. Sorry to wake you."

"Eight? But it's Sunday! You're not supposed to call anybody before 9 a.m. and after 9 p.m., especially on Sunday. Didn't anybody ever tell you that?"

"I'm sorry, Tammy, but I gotta tell you, it has been one hell of a weekend and I could really use your help."

I heard the phone jumble around for a second, then Tammy's voice became more clear and awake.

"Actually, I've been trying to call you but you haven't been picking up on your cell. What's going on?"

I quickly gave her the highlights, including the fact that a murderous arsonist stole my cell phone. She punctuated my account with:

"No way... Get out!... Oh my god oh my god, you must have been so scared!... Seriously, why are firemen always so hot?... Nuh-uh, the limo plowed right into the back of the dude's car?... You fuckin' won the Freezing Bikini Contest? Damn!... Oh my God, no! And they think you *killed* Vernette Johnson? That's crazy!"

I told her about walking away from Will last night after his comment in the parking lot. "He said, 'Do you think it's the story or do you think it's something else?' And I was like, yes! It's the goddamn story! Seriously! I know it's just the *Weekly Breeze*, but it's going to blow them out of the water!"

Tammy was silent for a beat. "Jamie," she said. "He's right, you know."

"Oh, what the fuck, not you, too?" I said, one hand to the phone receiver at my ear, the other in the air.

"No, no. What if they're trying to kill you because of something you have? Or something they think you have? Not necessarily the article you're writing. Could be they don't care about the story

213

because it's just the *Weekly Breeze* and because they figure Vernette Johnson has said it all before."

I thought about this for a second. The Chinese food sat like a stone in my belly. I sincerely regretted walking away from Will, because once Tammy said that, I knew she could be right. Maybe Will believed me. And I had gone and done the drama queen thing. For the umpteenth time, I felt my nose get congested and my brow ache with tears that I would not let leak out.

"I guess I can see what you mean. Damn." I blew out an exhausted sigh. Well, nothing to be done now except move forward.

"I'm sorry, hon," she finally said. "I think you'll be able to straighten it out. Nothing a little love won't fix." Spoken by a woman who's got somebody.

"Hey, I need to give you something," she continued. "I did some more research after you left the library the other day, and I printed out an article for you. It's about the Donnelley house fire."

"Thanks, Tammy. Maybe I could get it from you this morning. I was wondering if we could run out to Salisbury real quick," I said. "I need to go back to that Chevy dealership."

"Sure, of course, hon, whatever you need. But like I keep saying, it's Sunday. Aren't car dealerships closed on Sundays?"

"Yes," I said. "But Vernette's disk is in the Impala."

"Oh." She was silent for a moment. "I probably don't even want to know what we're gonna do," Tammy said amiably. I love this woman. "Why don't you come over here for some breakfast first."

"No, I'm not coming anywhere near your house. What if they're following me? I'm at the *Weekly Breeze* office. Come and get me here. Make sure nobody's on your tail and pull in behind the building. I'll come out the back way."

"I can try to make sure nobody's tailing me, but how am I going to shake them if they are? There's only one road between here and there."

"Well, work with what you've got," I said, and hung up.

I sat and stared at the phone, my head a fuzzy mess of questions. How can I keep from getting killed? How can I make things right with Will? How am I going to get onto the roof of that Chevy dealership on a Sunday morning?

I hadn't the slightest idea how to keep from getting killed, so I put that one on the back burner. And I figured the roof thing would resolve itself.

My love life, as usual, was the biggest conundrum. Should I call Will and try to set things right? He probably thought I was a nutcase. I wanted to call him, but then I thought about how he was homeless too, since getting mixed up with me. I needed Tammy's help to dig myself out of this hole. I only needed Will because I had the hots for him. Not an acceptable reason to put him at further risk. Plus, I remembered that just 48 hours ago I had the hots for a guy who was now likely trying to kill me. My dating instincts needed some fine-tuning.

When Tammy's car pulled into the back lot of the strip mall, I got in after determining nobody had spotted me. It was a bright, cold, and quiet morning.

Tammy leaned across the center console and gave me a huge hug. "I am so glad you're okay! You sure you want to keep this up? Because, you know, I can just drive you all the way to Dundalk right now, if you want."

I gave her a little squeeze and a tired laugh. "It's tempting, you know, I could just go back home to my mom. But no, it's good. I'm getting close to being finished with this damn thing. Once I publish the article and turn everything over to the police, it'll all be over, right?"

"I don't know," she said. "Hey, here's the article I told you about." She pulled out a copy.

"Maybe you can use this. It's kind of odd. I went back in the microfiche and looked at the newspapers around the time that the Donnelley property was sold. On the night of July 16, 1995, the house burned down, right? They found Frank Donnelley dead in the house. And get this: He had been shot before he burned to death."

"Oh my God."

"And get this: Donnelley had a son, and the son was never found."

"A son? Seriously?"

"Yeah, he was 14 at the time. Maybe the kid died in the fire, too, but they didn't find him. Maybe the kid shot the dad and took off."

"Wow. What was that date again?"

She repeated it.

I rummaged around and pulled snapshots out of my bag. "Jerry Mulvaney gave me some old pictures," I said. "His mom—the one who owned the Impala—used to drive around on Sunday afternoons and photograph the bay. The lady must have had a serious telephoto lens. Vernette knew her, and that's how the floppy disk ended up being hidden in the car. I hope." I showed Tammy the picture of Grandma Mulvaney and Vernette on the front porch. Tammy squinted at it. "Huh. Okay."

"And here's one she took of the Donnelley house." I showed Tammy the picture of the two men arguing in front of the house. My breath caught as I looked at the date stamp on the photograph: July 16, 1995.

"Tammy, this picture was taken the day of the fire."

"Duuuude..."

"You are so eloquent."

Tammy grinned. "What if the two men argued, Donnelley told Ivory to get out, and Ivory came back and set the place on fire?"

"Maybe Ivory shot Donnelley, then came back later and burned the place."

"Maybe. Anyway, the Ivory family sure seems to be connected to a lot of places that catch fire."

I rubbed my hands together, the car heater not really keeping them warm, even with the motor running.

"All right, let's get going."

When we reached the dealership, Tammy pulled in behind a row of "Previously Owned" Chevys, out of sight from the road. "How're we gonna do this?"

Tammy asked, as we peered at the Impala—Jeanine—high above us.

I blew out a breath. It was an awfully long way up there, and the dealership was closed and dark. "I don't know. Let's see what it looks like around back."

We dashed around the building. As we rounded a corner, we let out a whoop. A narrow metal ladder was bolted to the concrete wall. About 10 feet from the bottom, the ladder folded against itself with a fire-escape-type hinge. "I knew it!" I shouted, which was completely untrue.

"I gotta get up on your shoulders," I said. Without looking at her, I began pushing down on Tammy's shoulder.

"Hey! How come you get to stand on my shoulders? Maybe I should stand on your shoulders."

"How much do you weigh?" I asked tersely.

"Bitch. How much do *you* weigh?"

We looked at each other with narrowed eyes. Tammy broke eye contact. "Fuck you," she said, and bent her slightly larger frame down. I smirked.

I eased up onto Tammy's shoulders and as she straightened to her full height, I walked my hands up the wall. I stretched as high as I could go, and my fingers grazed the bottom rung of the ladder.

"Just a little higher!" I squeaked. "Stand on your tiptoes!"

Tammy grunted and I felt an inch or two more of the rung against my fingertips. I made a desperate lunge, grabbed hold, then pulled up so I was standing on Tammy's shoulders. It was easy to clamber up the ladder and climb high enough to release the swing arm. The folded-up portion of the ladder lowered on rusty springs with a deafening screech. Tammy reached for the bottom, pulled it down, then began climbing behind me.

The metal was flaky with rust and the palms of my pink gloves were turning a dirty orange. When my head cleared the top of the wall, cold wind hit me in the face.

"Holy crap, it's cold! That's it! I gotta get out of Maryland. It's not safe here. People try to kill you here and you can freeze to death."

"No, Jamie, people just try to kill you here, and it's not so cold if you stay off rooftops in the middle of the winter," Tammy said with her usual cool. "Hurry up! My hands are getting numb. And you totally owe me a manicure."

I hoisted myself over the top of the wall and crossed the pebbled surface to the Impala. I opened the driver's side door—weak-kneed with relief to find it unlocked—and looked around the car's immaculate interior. I popped the glove box and found nothing but the owner's manual. I flipped through the stiff-covered book and came up empty.

As I was starting to look under the floor mats, Tammy approached, her hair whipping like a flag in the wind. Traffic was light on Route 50, but one car honked as it passed. The roof jutted out almost over the roadway, so this was no stealth operation.

"Pop the trunk," Tammy said. She searched the trunk for a few minutes then slammed it shut. Tammy came back to the driver's side door, leaning in to say she found nothing, her backside pointing toward the westbound lanes.

When a car honked as it blew past, Tammy wiggled her butt in response. "I've looked all through here, and I just can't believe there's not some kind of disk somewhere," I said in frustration.

"Let me have a look in there," Tammy said. "You check under the hood."

"Are you kidding?"

"We haven't found it anywhere else, have we? Anyway, I'm freezing. Let me in."

Tammy got in and shut the door as I climbed out. A second later the hood unlatched with a heavy click. I swung up the hood prop, and leaned in, my ass hanging out in the breeze. I absentmindedly waved as another car honked. I checked for anything under the hood, then began checking the engine compartment for anything unusual. Of course, not knowing the first thing about cars, I have no idea what that means.

I heard a police siren in the distance and looked up just as a Maryland State Trooper was stopping to turn into the dealership. At the same moment, Tammy opened the driver's door and waved an old-style floppy disk, saying, "I got it!"

"Oh, thank God," I said. Tammy handed me the disk, and I stuffed it into the inner pocket of my coat. "Now wave, Tammy."

"What?"

"Come on. Parade wave, big smile for all the motorists out on Route 50."

Tammy grinned and gave a halfhearted wave as she eyed me quizzically. I dropped the Impala's hood then stood next to her, smiling and waving at the highway. Then she saw the green and tan police car coming to a halt below us. "Oh, crap."

"Don't worry," I said.

"I'm getting more worried by the minute," she said, but got a little more theatrical with the smiling and waving.

More cars were honking as the trooper got out of his car. He stood on the blacktop, feet apart, arms akimbo, and gazed up at us. "Ladies! What on earth are you doing?" he hollered.

"Crazy, right?" I said with a merry laugh. "That Jerry Mulvaney! First he puts a car on the roof, now here we are up here waving at traffic!"

"Mulvaney hired you to stand on the roof and wave?"

"Sounds a little nutty, doesn't it?" I concurred, not answering him. "Sure seems like it's working, though." I blew a kiss at an eastbound pickup truck and got an extended honk and a holler.

"All right now, that's enough for today," the cop said. "You're going to have to come down from there. How did you get up there, anyway?"

"Glad to," Tammy said. "It's cold up here. We'll be right down." We scooted away before the officer could get more details.

We climbed down and went back to the front parking lot, where the trooper was, unfortunately, waiting.

"Ma'am, when I first drove up, I noticed you were looking under the hood of that car," he said. "Now, why were you doing that?"

I paused, my brain spinning. Why would I be looking under the hood? Um. I opened my mouth.

"Ohhhh, honey," Tammy breathed. "That's a '72 Impala with the original Turbo engine up there! Of course she was looking under the hood. Wouldn't you?"

"Really? Oh, man. Is it the Turbo-Jet 400 or the Mark IV 454?"

She leveled a steady gaze at the cop, licked her lips, then her eyes shifted up to the car. "That is a factory original Mark IV with the four-barrel carburetor cranking out 270 horsepower off the line!"

The officer tore his gaze from Tammy to look at the car. "Sweet."

"The car is cherry. I can't believe he put it up there on the roof."

"Yeah, I'm with ya there."

Tammy and the officer spent a few more minutes saying sexy things about the Impala, then I started stamping my feet to fight the cold.

"All right, you ladies should go get yourselves some coffee and warm up."

"We sure will, officer. Thank you so much," Tammy said. I smiled and waved and we beat it back to the car and took off.

"I need a drink," Tammy said.

"How do you know all that stuff about cars?"

"Owners manual. That's where I found the disk."

"You are, like, Wonder Woman or something," I said, awestruck. "And where'd you find the disk? I flipped all the way through the manual!"

"The back of the book had a false binding and the disk was hidden inside."

"Amazing. You are amazing."

"I'm a librarian. I know stuff."

"All right, then. What're you drinking?"

We rolled back to Ocean City and went to Tequila Mockingbird in a North OC strip mall, where I ordered a double margarita on the rocks. Tammy threw back a couple of shots. It was not yet noon, but this was one of those days.

On the drive back, Tammy suggested we look for an old computer in the library storage room.

"I hope you have some kind of relic that can read this," I said, putting the disk on the heavily varnished wood bar and examining it. It was a 5 1/4" disk and it actually was a little bit floppy. It had a typed label: "BP Final Report + Appendices." I wondered if the data had survived the years.

Tammy took the alleys for most of the way to the library and parked in one of the spots under the building. We scanned the lot, saw no movement, and ducked into the building, Tammy's ring of keys clinking softly against the glass door.

The wintry sunlight shining through the windows was bright enough to keep the lights off as we made our way to a storeroom at the back of the main reading area.

Old chairs and tables filled the room, along with dusty overhead projectors, file boxes, old card catalog cabinets. In the back corner, a metal shelving unit held old computers and computer parts.

"Good thing we're not digging through the storeroom in the old building," Tammy said. "That place dates back 50 years."

We poked around and found on a high shelf an old IBM computer with a floppy drive slot. Tammy dragged over a heavy, plaid-upholstered chair to stand on and pulled the computer down with a grunt. She handed it to me, and I staggered under its weight. We had cleared space on a metal table and I put it there, in front of a huge cathode ray tube monitor. Tammy blew dust off a keyboard, and expertly plugged the components together. She said a little prayer as she plugged the power cord in and hit the power switches on the computer and the monitor.

The machine made oddly comforting clicks and groans. Who knew I'd have a memory of those antiquated computer startup noises filed away in my brain under "sentimental"? A moment later, a little white cursor blinked brightly on the black screen.

"Wow," Tammy said. "I haven't seen one of those since I was a kid."

"Yeah. Crazy."

"Go on, stick the disk in and see what happens," Tammy said.

I held my breath as I turned the toggle on the floppy drive and slid the disk in. The computer made more noises, then a menu of text scrolled up on the screen.

"Oh my God, it works."

There was a series of files called BP_O2_DATA, followed by dates: 08-04-96, 09-04-96, 10-04-96.

"Bingo."

I opened a file called BP_ENV_IMP_REPORT_FINAL, and scanned through pages of the original environmental survey, written by Fred Western and Vernette Johnson. It was, as she and Fred had both said, an assessment of the marshlands as an extraordinarily diverse wetlands, with osprey and crabs breeding there, and healthy levels of oxygenation. The conclusion section argued passionately—too passionately, considering the dry, scientific tone of the rest of the document—against altering the marshlands in any way.

"I need a copy of this," I said. We looked all over the storeroom for a compatible printer, but came up empty-handed.

I stared at the screen, at this report that changed everything, and had an idea.

"Tammy, I need one more thing."

At the front entrance to the police station, I banged on the door with my foot while struggling to hold onto the heavy IBM. Tammy sagged under the weight of the monitor. Power cords snaked out from both of our faux designer purses.

A uniformed officer opened the door, flustered, and helped us set the equipment on the front counter. I asked for Detective Francis.

The officer made a quick call, then escorted us and our electronics down a corridor and to a small room painted institutional green. He closed the door, and Tammy said, "Check it out! I've never been in an interrogation room!"

We put the computer on the table. "If they lock me up, Dustin's gonna kill me," Tammy said. "We've got monster-truck rally tickets for next weekend."

"What are they gonna lock you up for?"

"Aiding and abetting. Stealing library property."

I rolled my eyes and we sat at either side of the table where the bad guys get handcuffed when they're being sweated for confessions. I started sweating a little.

A few minutes later, Detective Francis opened the door. He had bags under his eyes and, like me, was wearing yesterday's clothes. And he was steaming mad.

"Jamie August, you are under arrest," he shouted.

I gasped. "But —"

"Seems that's the only way I can be sure you won't run off and do something else stupid."

Well, that just wasn't fair.

"You gave me your word that you would go to the fire house with Will, with whom—in whom—I placed full responsibility for your safety, and who promised to return you here this morning, but who was unable to do so because you did a runner." He was getting further steamed by his own complicated grammar. "Which, as you would surely be aware, if you stopped for one second to think about it, caused Will and, I might add, the entire fire station, to panic, and caused me to wonder where the hell you might have felt the need to run off to and what you might have been doing, and..." He stopped, looked quizzically at Tammy and at the relic computer and monitor. "Who's this?" he asked. "What's this?"

In my coldest, most formal voice I said, "Detective Francis, I'd like you to meet Tammy Wayne, Worcester County Public Library System. Tammy, this is Detective Francis."

"Pleased to meet you," she said with a professional smile, extending a hand, her hot-pink manicure looking a little rough.

"And this is a computer that can read a floppy disk," I said. "And this —" I pulled the floppy disk out with a flourish—"is the floppy disk that Vernette Johnson gave to her friend and neighbor, Mrs. Mulvaney, mother of Jerry Mulvaney of Mulvaney Chevrolet. It has on it the original version of the environmental report for Bayview Preserve, stating in no uncertain terms that the place was crawling with crabs and ospreys and should never have been built on."

I laid the floppy disk on the table.

Some of the steam seemed to go out of Detective Francis.

"That's some very interesting history, but couldn't you have just brought me a copy?" he said.

"No printer," Tammy and I said in unison.

"Oh," the detective sighed. "Hang on."

He left the room and returned a moment later with an officer who looked to be about 17.

"Andy, take this computer equipment here —" he pointed to the IBM, and Andy guffawed. "See if you can find an older printer that'll work with it. Then take this," he picked up the floppy disk, "and print out everything on it."

I jumped up and grabbed the disk out of the detective's hand. "No! I mean, please don't take that," I said, as meekly as I could manage. "I don't know what I'll do if anything happens to that disk. It's the only proof I have of everything that Vernette Johnson told me."

"And, uh, I have no idea how to work one of these things," Andy said.

Francis scowled. "Okay, you," he said, pointing to Tammy. "Go down to the basement with Andy and try to get a printout of this thing, okay?" She nodded, and I handed Tammy the disk, and the thumb drive. She and Andy would have to return to the 20th century to print out that information for Detective Francis. "You," he swung his pointing finger in my direction, "come with me."

I followed the detective down the hall to his cubicle. Will was sitting inside, looking a lot worse for wear.

"I'm sorry, Will."

He stood up and I hugged him.

"It's okay," he said. I held on, and after a moment I felt his arms go around me.

"Ah, fer crissake. Knock off the Harlequin Romance crap," Francis bellowed.

Will and I separated and sat down in the two battered office chairs across from Francis's desk.

I told Will about the disk, then I told them both about the thumb drive I found at the bottom of my purse, and the data on it that started 12 years ago and ended last week.

"So Vernette Johnson wasn't a wack job after all," Will said.

"Oh, she was kind of wacky," I said. "But she wasn't lying about Bayview Preserve."

"All right, all right," Francis said. "So we've got a mystery computer disk from the past that seems to confirm Johnson's story about the false environmental study, and a mystery thumb drive from the present showing I don't even know what. But why would they kill Johnson now, all these years later, and *after* she had spoken to you?"

"I don't know. But I do have another interesting piece of information," I said, and told them about the fire at the Donnelley house on the day Bernard Ivory was there arguing with another man, maybe Donnelley himself. I showed them the picture.

Just then, Tammy and Andy came to the cubicle, wheeling the old computer on a cart. Andy handed Detective Francis a dot-matrix printout. "We did it!" Andy said. He gave the disk back to me.

"May I please have a copy?" I asked. Francis grimaced, nodded, and handed the printout to Andy, who headed off to the copy machine.

Tammy was giving Will an appraising look. "Tammy, this is Will," I said. "Will, this is my best friend, Tammy." Tammy grinned at me, then at Will, and extended her hand for a shake. Will nodded and shook her hand.

I spent the next hour telling and retelling the whole story, as I knew it, to Francis. Then I asked if funeral arrangements had been made for Vernette, and he said no. They were still trying to locate relatives, and hadn't released her name.

I also let him know the security guard had my cell phone, which I had dropped under the trailer. He wrote down the number.

"And where were you last night?" Francis finally got around to this. He planted his elbows on his desk and glared at me through his eyebrows.

"I fell asleep on the bus."

"The bus?"

"I love the bus," I said. The detective mumbled to himself and rested his forehead in his palms.

233

"All right, Jamie. Where will you be staying now?" he asked.

I pulled out the envelope of bikini contest prizes and fished out a gift certificate. "The Hilton!"

12.

OUTSIDE THE STATION Will and I agreed to meet up later at the Hilton. To be safe, I would check in under his name. Tammy dropped me at the *Weekly Breeze*.

Donald jumped up and enveloped me in a hug. "Jamie! Thank God you're okay!" When I hugged him back, he pulled away. "You smell awful."

"Hey, thanks, great" I said, stepping back and crossing my arms to try to hold the stink of three action-packed days inside my coat.

Donald sized up my sorry state. "That's it," he said. "You're coming with me. We're going back to my place and Wesley can put together some lunch, since you ate mine."

"That was your Chinese? Sorry."

"Mmm, hmm. I got your story notes. I'm not letting you out of my sight until we go through the whole thing."

The thought of a hot shower and a home-cooked meal at Donald and Wesley's was intoxicating. "Okay," I said. "Let's go. I can tell you about even more stuff that has happened since I filed my story."

As we drove, I filled him in on the morning, about my adventures on the dealership rooftop and the hidden floppy disk. I outlined the possibility Ivory Enterprises was already stalking its next prey: the Lombardo family with its two waterfront properties. Plus I mentioned that the *Weekly Breeze's* star reporter nearly ended up in the slammer for obstructing justice. Or something.

When we arrived at the door, Wesley took control. He looked like the owner of an Italian deli, short and round with dark, curly hair. The sleeves of his creamy white sweater were pushed up on his forearms and he had a bit of flour on his cheek. He shooed me off to the palatial guest suite, where he told me to leave my dirty clothes for him to throw in the washing machine. Donald called down the hallway, "Don't spoil her or she'll never leave."

"Jamie, you can stay here as long as you want," Wesley said, chuckling. "I'll get some lunch together and you come out to the kitchen when you're cleaned up."

I stood under the rainfall shower until I was wrinkled like a raisin. Then I wrapped up in a fluffy white robe and padded out to the kitchen. We sat at the kitchen table eating spinach and goat cheese omelets and drinking fresh-squeezed orange juice and cappuccinos. I wished I could afford to eat like this every day.

After lunch, Donald and I sat in his home office and reviewed my story. He admitted this was breaking news and not a *Beach 'n' Bay Lifestyle* feature. We agreed I needed to track down Fred Western and get him to make sense of Johnson's notes.

Wesley came in carrying a folded pile of my clothes: rhinestone-studded jeans, acrylic sweater and sparkly underwear. The sweater was pilled and the undies unraveling. We gazed at them.

"Those are the only clothes I own," I said, breaking the silence. "I have to go shopping today. But hey, I have a gift certificate!"

"A gift certificate for where?" Donald asked.

"South Moon Under."

"I'm going with you."

"No, really, you don't need —"

"Jamie. South Moon Under sells clothing made of natural fibers. You don't have much experience with that sort of thing. I can help."

I kicked his shin with my bare foot.

Wesley snorted. "Donald! Don't talk to Jamie like that!"

"He can't help it," I said. "I didn't used to dress quite so ghetto, but now it's like a hobby. I do it just to mess with him."

"I believe it," Donald said. "You're going to put me in an early grave."

I put on my sparkly, threadbare clothes, and then Donald drove us to South Moon Under, where I replaced my wardrobe again with designer labels and rich, deep colors in wool, cotton, and cashmere.

Donald fed me a stream of items over the dressing room door and I paraded each outfit before his critical eye. At one point he told me I should not chew gum while wearing expensive clothes because it ruined my newfound veneer of respectability. I stuck a second piece in my mouth. Then I reflected on how profitable it was to shake my moneymaker and told Donald I was considering leaving journalism to become an exotic dancer. He tried to make me promise, but I refused.

Donald and I pulled up to the Hilton, and I gave him a peck on the cheek and he squeezed me in a quick hug. "Don't get killed, Jamie," he said. "All those nice clothes would just go to waste."

"I love you, Donald!" I called as he pulled away. I was loaded down with shopping bags and the faux Gucci. A doorman held the glass doors open. Will was waiting inside.

I dropped my stuff to hug him. He was chilly. "Who was that?"

"Oh, that was my editor, Donald. I wish I had known you were right here. I would have introduced you."

"Is that why you wish you had known I was here?" he asked peevishly.

"Well, uh, yes." I looked at him quizzically. "What are you talking about?"

"You seem to have an excellent relationship with your boss," he said.

"Sure, yeah, I do. But what's the problem?" Then it hit me. "Ahhhh! I understand. Do you think that Donald and I —"

"Forget it, Jamie. Don't worry about it," he said.

I laughed. "No, no, no! Will, Donald is —"

"Stop it, Jamie. You don't owe me any explanations. You don't owe me anything." As I started to

239

protest, he put his hands on my shoulders and kissed me. He smelled like beer. "Stop. Let's go get you checked in."

I was simultaneously annoyed and amused. I figured Barry the firefighter/bartender had given him the lowdown on my trashy hookup last week. Now it seemed Will was not going to let the truth get in the way of his preconceived notions.

He picked up some of my bags, and we walked up the flight of marble stairs to the lobby.

We checked in under Will's name to keep my name out of the Hilton's system. Better paranoid than dead, I always say. The dark-haired, elegant woman at reception smiled at Will and let her fingers graze his when she took his credit card. I handed her my Hilton gift certificate, which had my name in calligraphy. She arched one beautifully shaped brow and looked up at me through long, dark lashes. "Jamie August. Ah, you won the Seacrets contest, yes?" she said, sounding like Russian aristocracy.

"You bet," I said, winked and popped a bubble. So much for anonymity. Will looked away, his face flushed.

"Congratulations," she said, then turned a dazzling, enigmatic smile toward Will.

She handed Will a key card and we took the elevator to the seventh floor. The suite had a seating area, small kitchen and a bedroom beyond, with a view of the sea.

I dumped my stuff on the sofa, then locked my computer in the hotel safe with Vernette's thumb drive, the floppy disk, and the photos. I went through to the bedroom and opened the drapes to the view and the sun. I fiddled with the sheers, opening them partway, adjusting the plastic pulls. I was bustling around acting busy and sensible.

Will opened the mini-bar and took out a mini-bottle of Jack Daniels. As I walked into the kitchen, he cracked it open and downed it.

"Dang. A little thirsty, were you?"

"Yes. Do you want some water?" Will asked, holding up a liter bottle.

"Sure, yeah," I said. "Are you okay?"

He poured two glasses and handed me one. He watched me take a sip, then pulled me into an embrace. The glass tipped as my arm encircled his neck, spilling water down his back.

He jumped back with the shock of cold and I squealed. "OhmyGod, I'm so sorry!" I put the glass on the counter and covered my face in mock horror.

"It's okay," he said, and pulled off his shirt. His chest was ripped, seriously cut, probably from daily workouts at the fire station. He looked at me with an intensity that wiped the smile off my face, then he came at me, scrambling to get his hands inside my clothes. His skin was hot. He smelled warm, clean.

Lust easily won out over the little voice inside my head telling me to stop. He backed me through the bedroom door. I fumbled with his belt buckle, playing right into the trashy ho role he had clearly cast me in. I didn't care. He made several attempts to unhook my sparkly bra, and I finally pulled it off over my head. The trail of clothing continued to the king-size, pillow-top bed. His hands raked my body.

"You shouldn't have left me last night."

"I know," I managed.

I ran my fingers through his hair as his head moved to my breast and he kissed me, gripped my body with his strong hands, bit me. I watched us in the mirror over the dresser, feeling overwhelmed.

"I can't protect you if I don't know where you are."

He opened my legs and I watched as his kisses trailed south, his head moving between my thighs. I wasn't so sure I liked the idea of him protecting me, but I forgot about that as his tongue dipped into me and I gasped with pleasure.

We went at it for hours with a ferocity like locked battle. I finally drifted into a troubled sleep. It felt more like the end of something than the beginning.

As light faded from the sky, I woke in a tangle of 1,000-thread count sheets, feather pillows, and duvets. I heard the shower and leaned back against the headboard, my body wrung out.

Will came out a moment later, towel wrapped around his waist, his damp hair spiky from a towel drying. He leaned over the bed to kiss me. I pulled him back into the sheets by the edge of the towel, which came off in my hand. I dropped it on the floor as Will kissed me again, and I leaned in to him.

"This place has an excellent shower," he said.

"You think I need a shower?"

"Take a shower, baby."

I smacked his butt as he stood to let me out of bed. I padded across the carpet to the bathroom, steamy from Will's shower, and turned on the water. I looked back as Will swept plastic condom wrappers from the bedside table into the trash can and took the water glass into the kitchen. His body was long and angular and, unlike earlier, he was now completely calm. Efficient.

He caught my eye, then his eyes traveled downward and he gave me a dirty smile. I was blushing as I stepped into the shower.

When I came out 15 minutes later, redolent of upscale hotel soap and wrapped in a thick terry robe, Will was sitting in bed wearing plaid boxers, remote control in hand, football on the wall-mounted flat-screen TV.

I tucked in next to him to watch the Redskins against the Cowboys. I knew the game was causing gridlock on the Capital Beltway and I was happy to be nowhere near there. I tried to snuggle close, but the game had him tied in knots.

"You're quite the 'Skins fan," I said.

"Yeah. I got a little riding on this game," he said.

"A gambling man, are you?" I asked, arching an eyebrow.

"Nothing serious," he said, seeming not to appreciate the distraction of me next to him.

I slid away from him on the bed, a little sullen. But the Redskins sent the Cowboys home crying, so I couldn't stay too upset.

About 7:30, Will left, after extracting a promise that I would not leave the hotel room without letting him know. "Please let me keep you safe," he said.

I felt sort of relieved to have him out of there. Some women love to feel like they are being protected by a strong man, but I felt smothered. I ordered room service and called it an early evening.

I slept fitfully, dreaming that I was drowning in a giant bed that was actually a bottomless pool. Will kept throwing me an anchor, but it hit me on the head, over and over, and pushed me deeper. When I finally dragged myself out of bed in the morning, I felt disoriented. Some people have dreams that are full of complex symbolism. Not me. I get hit over the head with an anchor. I think my subconscious knows I need all the help I can get.

Room service breakfast brightened my mood. Anything served under a shiny silver dome tastes delicious. Lounging in a plush hotel robe, I called the answering service for Beach Getaway and told them to keep answering the phones. In effect, I was calling in sick. Darlene, the lady I usually talk to from the answering service, told me that the Slomkowski family was extending their stay at Sunrise Paradise for another week. "Such a nice, friendly man," she said. The grouchy grunter? Maybe the guy's personality was changing because of asbestos poisoning or mold inhalation.

Next I called Professor Fred Western on his cell, and got a chilly initial reception.

"I told you everything I know already," he said. "Why are you calling me again? I took a huge risk talking to you in the first place."

"I appreciate that, Fred, and I know what you're saying is true. Vernette Johnson was found dead two nights ago."

"I heard about it. It's awful."

"Vernette talked to me the day she died. We were in Piezano's and she ran off when two men came into the restaurant. I guess they caught up with her. I know you cared about her, and I'm sorry."

He was silent. Finally he said, "Yeah."

"I've got a couple of things I'd like to show you. A couple of old photographs, for one. Also, I have come across an old floppy disk I believe she gave to a friend for safekeeping. I've looked at what's on it and I believe it is your original report and supporting data. I'd like you to take a look and verify it."

"Seriously? Where? How..." he stopped himself. "Doesn't matter anyway. What would be the point? She's dead."

"Fred, the last time we talked you said you'd be willing to take a look at any data I found."

"And now Vernette's dead. You see? I can't help you."

"The point is, if Ivory Enterprises did everything you said they did, everything Vernette said they did, now is finally your chance to expose them and make them pay."

"You are overlooking one thing, Jamie."

"What's that?"

"Bayview Preserve is built. It's too late. It's all too late. What's the point of any of this?"

"I know it's too late for Vernette and it's probably too late for the bay, but wouldn't it be nice if Ivory Enterprises—and your boss—at least had to pay for their crimes? Jail time, huge fines and bankruptcy won't bring Vernette back, and it won't bring the marshlands back, but it will keep Ivory Enterprises from doing it again. And I think they are planning on doing it again," I said.

"Okay, Jamie, what do you want?"

"Meet me today. Tell me if this is the real report. Explain Vernette's data."

There was a pause. "Hello?"

"Don't do this," he said.

"Fred, how am I gonna stop doing this? I no longer have a choice. Ivory Enterprises tried to kill me—twice. So I'm pretty well backed into a corner, wouldn't you say?"

"Well, I —"

"The only way I am going to save my own ass is to get this story published. Once it hits the newsstands, Ivory Enterprises is screwed. If anything happened to me after that, they'd be the first people the cops would look at."

"What if you're wrong?"

"Look, Fred. Before they started coming after me, I had nothing. All I had was a bunch of hearsay—and one off-the-record conversation with you. And if things looked suspicious before, Vernette's death makes everything clear. Ivory Enterprises will stop at nothing to keep this story from going public, but I've got to tell it to save my own life. And you're the only one who can help me with Vernette's notes. Please help me. If you don't care about me, then do it for Vernette. She lost her life because of Bayview Preserve. You owe this to her."

I could hear Fred's breath coming in short sobs. "Okay, uh, I'll have to see. I'll call you back in a moment. Where are you?"

I looked down at the bedside phone and gave him the number.

"Where are you, Jamie?"

"It doesn't matter, really. Does it, Fred?" I hung up. I fought off a feeling of dread. I knew I probably shouldn't trust Fred in the state he was in, but he was the key to transcribing the data on the thumb drive and disk. And I couldn't help but feel that he wasn't really a bad guy. Just a weak guy.

A few minutes later, the phone rang. "Hello?"

"Jamie? It's Fred Western. Okay, I will meet with you and only you, 2:30, at the Exxon station on 50 west of Salisbury."

"No, you come to the Ocean City Public Library. We can look at everything there."

"I don't have the time to do that. I'm crazy to meet with you at all. If you want to see me, you have to come here."

"Why the Exxon station?"

"Just a precaution. We'll go on from there."

I didn't like it, but I agreed.

Staying true to my word, I called Will and told him about the meeting. I told him I couldn't take him with me, but I sure could use his truck. He said he was on his way.

The shopping bags were on the floor where I had dropped them. I pulled out a pair of skinny charcoal corduroys and a loose-knit wool sweater of purple, mauve and grey, with a silky T-shirt to go underneath. Then I chose a lacy black bra and matching G-string. These days, I never know when my undies might be on display. It felt great to put on some high-quality stuff for a change.

About half an hour later, Will knocked, then let himself in as I was finishing the last of the coffee.

"Hi Jamie."

"Good morning," I said, standing to give him a kiss. He kissed me gently and looked at me with an expression that could have been tenderness, could have been wistfulness, or perhaps regret. That fog of weirdness from last night began to creep into the room.

"You look beautiful," he said. "Somehow different."

"Hey, thanks! Expensive new clothes."

"Is that all?"

"What's going on with you? Are you okay?" I looked into his clear blue eyes, and he flashed an easy smile and kissed me again.

"Of course I'm okay. Just a little tired from last night's shift."

"Right. Man, I don't know when you get any sleep."

"I haven't gotten much lately. You keep me busy."

"Yeah, sorry about that."

He put a heavy arm around me and drew me in for a hug, then said, "I don't like you going out there to meet this professor guy by yourself."

"It's not Fred Western I'm worried about," I said, waving my hand dismissively. "I think he's trying to do the right thing. He's basically a good guy. I just keep thinking Ivory Enterprises' people will spot me as soon as I hit the street. It feels like they always know where I am."

Will gazed out the window at the clouds and the steely light flickering off the ocean. "Yeah, it is weird," he said. "Well, are you ready to do this thing?"

I grabbed my bag, double-checking for the printed copies of Vernette's notes, and we left the room. I listened to make sure the door latched.

After dropping him at the burned-out shell of his trailer to meet with an insurance adjuster, I lurched off in Will's pickup. It was a nerve-wracking drive to Salisbury. It had been years since I had driven a stick shift, but fortunately it was mostly smooth, empty highway driving. I took the bypass around Salisbury and a few miles later I saw the Exxon station. I rolled up to a gas pump. I didn't see any other cars in the lot, so I took a few minutes to fill Will's tank. Low clouds spread across the winter sky like a wet, grey blanket.

Inside the mini-mart, Fred was in the candy aisle, flushed and unsteady, wearing a frayed brown sweater with leather elbow patches. I walked toward him and he silenced me with a look. As I walked past him, I caught a boozy whiff.

When I paid for the gas, the cashier gave me a funny look. Fred got in line behind me with a package of Twizzlers. The cashier handed me a receipt, staring hard. I looked at him quizzically, then realized that Tom, the guy who got fired at Bayview Preserve for watching the pre-game show while Vernette Johnson took her samples. I gave him a quick nod, then lowered my eyes and turned toward the door. When I was between Fred and the cashier, Fred stuffed a note into my hand. I didn't look at him, but returned to the truck. There I read the note. The note said, "Follow me." How clever. I never would have thought to follow. Jesus!

Fred came out and walked around to the side of the station. A moment later, he drove around the corner in an old brown Camry. He turned west on 50 and I followed.

My brain was humming along efficiently, brightly, like a soda machine outside a motel in the middle of the night. Facts and snippets of conversation were lining up in my mind, becoming sentences and paragraphs for my story.

Suddenly, one fragment caused everything else to fade. The police had not released Vernette's name yet. How had Fred known she was dead? The hairs stood up on the back of my neck.

In Cambridge we crossed the Choptank River and shortly the Camry's brake lights came on. I slowed and watched Fred turn into a driveway and through a windbreak of evergreens. I debated whether to follow or get the heck out of there. My curiosity overcame my common sense and I made the turn.

We drove to the side of a long, one-story brick house, to a three-car garage. Fred parked in front of one of the garage doors. He walked to my window and I hit the button to roll it down. Cold wind was picking up, lifting his hair to expose the beginnings of a combover.

"Park over there." He pointed to the edge of the turnaround. I leaned out the window.

"Fred? Whose house is this?"

Fred paused for a moment. "It belongs to a friend. It's okay. We're safe here."

"Who is this friend?"

"Just a colleague, okay? Now come on in. You can leave the car right here." He began to open the truck door.

I pulled it shut again and locked it. "No, Fred, what's going on here? Don't touch the door."

He made a show of backing up and showing me both hands. "Sorry! It's just, it's cold out here and I want to get this over with."

"Whose house is this?"

He faltered. "It's ... well, I thought the best thing to do in the circumstances was to talk to Paul Saunders about the situation, and —"

"This is Saunders' house? What were you thinking?"

"He was going to find out everything soon enough, so the best thing was to bring him on board, get his version of events. He was surprisingly agreeable and suggested that we get together here, where it's safe and private, and talk about everything."

"I don't think so," I said. "Saunders is going to get fired and arrested when this story comes out. I'm not going in his house."

"There's more to the story than you know, Jamie. You need to hear every side of it. Don't worry. I promise you, you're going to be pleased." I looked at his eyes, bright with adrenaline, the broken blood vessels around his nose, the fraying sweater. Clearly, he had made another bad professional choice.

"Sorry, Fred. Tell Paul Saunders that I'd love to hear his side of the story, but in a public location of my choosing."

"Jamie —" he approached the car again.

Just then a door opened at the side of the garage and Paul Saunders stepped out.

He plastered on a jovial smile and walked toward me, hand extended to shake mine. He wore crisp, dark slacks and a sky blue cashmere sweater over a pale yellow button-down. The Miss Manners cortex of my brain kicked in, and I reached through the driver's side window to shake Saunders' hand. His hand closed around mine in a firm grip. In one smooth motion he stepped in, unlocked the door with his left hand, opened it, then stepped backward and pulled me toward him.

The truck lurched and stalled as my feet came off the pedals. Like a big brown bear, Fred moved in to hoist me over his shoulder. I squeezed Saunders' hand tighter and grabbed it with my left hand as Fred tried to pull me away from the truck, giving his wrist a sharp twist. He cried out in pain when I banged it against the window frame. Fred swung around and cracked my forehead against the top of the door. I saw stars and let go of Saunders' hand.

I had a vague sensation of being hauled through the door next to the garage just as the sky opened with a torrent of freezing rain.

Some time later—minutes, it seemed, not hours—I realized my head was resting on a velvet cushion. I opened my eyes and blinked in the grey light pouring through the bay window of Saunders' living room. My head thundered. I became aware of the two men sitting in wing-back chairs facing me, a drop-leaf maple coffee table between us. On the table was a hand towel, peach with embroidered flowers, and a fine china bowl edged in gold containing a Ziploc bag filled with ice cubes. The bowl was sitting on a wooden trivet. A bottle of Advil sat next to the bowl, and a small glass of water.

The men held highball glasses with amber liquid and melting ice cubes.

I slowly sat up. Pain shot through my head.

"Ms. August, I deeply regret that it took such extreme measures to persuade you to come inside," Saunders said. "I've brought you some ice and some pain reliever. Please help yourself."

As my vision began to clear, pain focused on my forehead. It hurt like a bitch, but I wasn't feeling nauseated. My stomach fluttered with fear, but I didn't think I had a concussion.

I slowly reached for the baggie of ice, wrapped it in the towel, and gingerly touched it to my head. The pain sent sparks through my field of vision and I could feel heat radiating from a goose-egg above my right eye.

I desperately wanted to swallow a couple of Advil with that water, but I didn't trust either.

The two watched me intently. I saw that Saunders pressed an identical towel-covered ice bag against his right wrist.

"Are you going to kill me, too?" I said.

"*Kill* you?" Saunders said in mock horror, genteelly crossing one knee over the other. "I have never killed anyone in my life and certainly don't intend to start with you, my dear."

I arched my eyebrows and leaned back on the plush, bottle-green sofa. "You don't have to get your own hands dirty to kill someone," I said. "You had Vernette Johnson killed, didn't you?"

"Certainly not," he said in a surprisingly sincere display of shock.

"It was either you or one of the fine members of the Ivory family, but in the end it doesn't matter because you are all covering up the same filthy secrets."

257

Fred crossed the room to an inlaid-wood wet bar in the corner. He made himself another bourbon on the rocks.

Saunders glanced at him, then turned back to me. "You see, there's where you're wrong," he said, his face illuminated and his manner that of a professor explaining an interesting distinction to a bright student. "You have no proof of any wrongdoing with regard to the Bayview Preserve environmental impact report. You have no witnesses, no facts, nothing. Here's what you have: an unfortunate but off-the-record interview with my colleague here"—he nodded to Fred, who was busy pouring bourbon down his throat—"plus the ravings of an unhinged—and now deceased—former adjunct professor, and a computer disk of uncertain origin containing unverifiable data."

His expression turned from scholarly detachment into something much more sinister. "If you weave all of these fantasies into a story and print it, if your arts and entertainment freebie would actually print your story, you—and it —will be sued for slander, and you and your children and your children's children will be paying for that mistake with every dollar they make until they die of natural causes. Do you understand? You have nothing."

"Libel."

"I beg your pardon?"

"You'll sue my great-grandchildren for libel. Slander is spoken. Libel is written, so that's the word you're looking for."

Saunders face turned nearly purple. I kept going.

"I guess your cronies at Ivory Enterprises didn't bring you up to speed on everything. Not surprising. For example, there's the matter of the photographs I have in my possession. Particularly one that places Bernard Ivory at the old Donnelley house on the day it burned to the ground with Frank Donnelley in it."

Saunders' expression shifted from fury to calculated interest. My head pounded so hard that just the weight of his gaze was painful.

"No, in fact I did not know about any such photographs. Or the fact that Bernard was even acquainted with Donnelley."

"He seems to leave a trail of destruction wherever he goes," I said. "A birdwatcher with a telephoto lens took the picture, then dropped it in a shoebox for 20 years. Now it has resurfaced, date stamp and all, and Jonathan Ivory nearly fell off his chair when I showed it to him."

"Jonathan Ivory, yes," Saunders said. "You and he have been seen together quite a bit lately. Curious. It does make me wonder. Are you fucking him for information, despite all your morally superior instincts?"

His eyes glinted with malice. I started to jump up from the sofa, the better to poke Saunders' eyes out, but the movement caused a sharp pain in my head and I sank back into the sofa and groaned.

The wind howled outside the bay window and sleet pelted the glass. Fred took a final swig of his drink and put the glass down on the table between the two chairs. Saunders moved the glass onto a coaster painted with a mallard.

"I do not see how this photograph you've gotten your hands on is anything other than a coincidence, and my guess is that you're just having some good fun with the pretty Jonathan Ivory. I can understand what a good career move this story would be for a budding, ambulance-chasing reporter. Quite a thrilling exposé. If you had your eye on a career with the *Weekly World News*, this would be a great press clipping," he said with an indulgent chuckle. I crossed my legs and stretched my left arm across the back of the sofa, as though I have these kinds of meetings all the time. My right hand pressed the ice bag to my forehead.

"You gentlemen also should be aware that Vernette Johnson left a thumb drive with me before she was *murdered*," I said. "She had been collecting and analyzing water and soil samples at Bayview Preserve every month since that ill-fated environmental survey in 1996. I saw her at Bayview Preserve last week, the day she took her last sample. Ever."

Fred picked up his glass with a clumsy tinkle and walked to the bar. Saunders' face registered annoyance.

"As I have already made clear, Dr. Western and I had nothing to do with Vernette's unfortunate demise. We do not support violence. We are scientists, not thugs."

"Is that so?" I said, shifting the ice on my forehead.

"Yes, and we invited you here to make you an offer that demonstrates exactly that sentiment. Regardless of the unbelievably far-fetched nature of your little story, my colleagues and I would prefer that you refrain from publishing it. We thought some sort of agreement might be in order. Something to compensate you for the work you've done, the time and energy you have spent on this project."

"Oh really? What sort of compensation did you think would be appropriate to cover three attempts on my life in three days?"

"Three?" Saunders asked. "Oh, I see. You're in-cluding today's little misunderstanding in that count."

"At minimum, today counts as false imprison-ment, maybe even kidnapping," I said, gazing at him dispassionately.

"I can see that it has been a harrowing time for you these past few days. I assure you that, although I was not responsible for those unfortunate inci-dents, I am in a position to secure your safety if we can come to an agreement."

"So you brought me here to try and bribe me?"

"It's such an unkind term," he said.

"Whatever. I'm all ears."

Fred belched. "Excuse me," he murmured, pull-ing at a thread on an elbow patch. Saunders shifted in his chair, careful with his wrenched wrist.

"Fred, why don't you go and make us some cof-fee?" he said. "You'll find everything next to the coffeemaker in the kitchen."

Fred was unsteady as he walked to the kitchen.

Saunders leaned forward. "I am prepared to of-fer you $1,000 for your troubles in exchange for the disk and thumb drive, the photograph you men-tioned, and your complete silence about this unfor-tunate misunderstanding."

I snorted. "A thousand bucks? In the last 72 hours, you clowns have torched the houseboat that was my home, along with all of my possessions, then the trailer where I was staying. One thousand dollars won't begin to cover the actual cost of the damage that has been done, let alone buy my silence. Get real."

"How much did you have in mind?"

"Fifty thousand," I said without missing a beat. Dang! I need to get clocked on the head more often.

Saunders chuckled. "My dear, we are university professors, not stock brokers."

"You're a university professor who got bought. How much did you cost?"

"A much more complicated arrangement, I assure you, and one that benefited all parties, including a perpetually cash-strapped research department."

"I don't give a damn about that," I said. "Fifty thousand dollars will make this go away for you."

"Ten."

"You're not listening to me." I dropped the now soggy compress onto the coffee table with a splat. Adrenaline and the stars in my head were making me feel reckless. "You've got my price. We need to wrap this up, because I should have been back in

Ocean City a long time ago with my friend's truck. My friend is the medic who tried to save Vernette Johnson. He's also the guy who rescued me from the burning houseboat. Oh, and that trailer that went up in smoke? That was his. I cannot tell you how pissed off he's going to be if I don't get back soon. I'm guessing the entire OC fire department and half the police force will be crawling up your ass looking for me if we don't hurry up."

"I can't just spit out money on demand. Ten thousand, cash."

"Right now?"

"We can offer you $10,000 cash today."

"If you give me ten grand right now, then we have a deal."

"Excellent," he said. "You have the materials with you? We could not seem to locate them."

"You searched my stuff?" I asked.

Saunders raised his eyebrows and looked at me as if to say, of course we searched your stuff, you idiot.

"Why on earth would I carry around those originals?" I asked, pulling a similarly contemptuous expression.

"Where are they?"

"They're locked up safe in Ocean City."

Saunders looked annoyed but resigned to another inconvenience. "Very well. Dr. Western will
deliver the funds to you when we have received the
disk and verified its contents, plus the photograph."

I stood up, fought to hide any sign of unsteadi-
ness, and held out my hand, wiggling my fingers.
"My keys, please. This conversation is ridiculous,
and it's over."

Saunders stood, too, wincing as his wrist grazed
the arm of his chair. "Okay, how's this?" he said.
"Fred follows you to Ocean City, you give him the
disk and other materials, and the two of you conclude the transaction there."

"I hand him the disk, the thumb drive and the
photo and he hands me $10,000 cash, right?"

"Correct. And further, you remain silent about
the, er, provenance of Bayview Preserve, and—well,
you remain alive."

"Where's the cash?"

"We have already arranged for it."

"You were planning to bribe me all along?"

"Let's just say that Dr. Western and I have been
having some philosophical differences with our
colleagues at Ivory Enterprises. We feel that finan-
cial incentives generally work better than violence
and are, in the long run, more cost effective. Plus,

Alan's methods were not meeting with much success in your case."

"True enough. So the crazy security guard's name is Alan?"

Saunders paled at this slip. "Uh, I'm not sure I, ah..." Western returned to the living room just then and Saunders turned his attention fully to the three mugs of coffee Fred was balancing. He set them on the coffee table, sloshing liquid on the varnished wood.

"Sorry," he said.

Each of us took a mug and Saunders held his up in a mock toast. "Here's to a mutually beneficial business arrangement," he said, and took a swig. Fred slurped. I raised the mug but did not let the coffee touch my lips.

It was sleeting as we stood in the driveway, the asphalt treacherous with black ice. The late afternoon sky was darkening. Fred was subdued as he loaded a black duffel into the trunk of his Camry.

"Where in Ocean City are you storing the materials?"

"The firehouse," I said. It was as good an answer as any.

I jumped into the truck, nervous about the prospect of driving through an ice storm in a stick shift with no weight in the open bed. With a crushing headache. I noted that my bag was still in the truck, though it was now on the seat and I had left it on the floor.

I rolled carefully down the driveway, followed by a possibly drunk and definitely unhinged marine biologist who was tailing me too closely. This didn't look promising. I kept reminding myself that all I had to do was get to the firehouse and I would be safe. If they thought they could buy my silence, they had another thing comin'. Just like the Judas Priest song says.

13.

WHEN WE PULLED into the firehouse lot, I heaved a huge sigh of relief. I jumped from the truck and Fred rolled down his passenger window.

"Come inside and I'll give you the stuff," I yelled, sleet pounding my uncovered head.

"I'm not going in there," Fred said. "You bring everything out and we'll do the exchange here."

I looked at the dark sky and back at him.

"Suit yourself, but I'm not doing this solo. You're just going to piss off the whole duty crew 'cause they're going to get wet standing out here to make sure you don't do anything else stupid."

"No," he said. "You have to do this alone."

"No deal," I said. "You can read about it—including today's assault and attempt at bribery—in the paper."

Fred suddenly opened his car door, which emitted a sharp squeal, and stood. Was that the glint of a gun in his hand? The freezing rain was sharp and relentless, and I couldn't tell if he was pointing a gun at me, or just making an angry gesture. Taking no chances, I dropped to the ground and rolled under the truck to the other side, sloshing through a half-frozen, greasy puddle. I opened the passenger door and crawled in, trying to keep my head low. I laid on the horn and waited for the windshield to explode in a thousand fragments.

No gunshot came, but a second later I heard the Camry's door squeak shut and the engine start. Fred was trying to get away. I started the truck, threw it into reverse and cut the wheel sharply. The Camry crashed into the side of the truck.

A half dozen firefighters streamed from the building.

Fred bailed out and sprinted down the street. One firefighter took off after him, slipped on a patch of ice, and went down. Two others dashed over to tend to him, while the rest, including Will, rushed to the truck to see about me.

"He has a gun!" I shouted. "I think he has gun." Did he have a gun, or was it just a trick of light in the heavy storm? I was rattled but not hurt from the impact of the crash. The guys insisted on taking me inside and checking the bump on my head, which they assumed had just happened.

I rolled the truck back into the parking space, pulled out my bag and locked up. The damage was minimal to the side of the truck. I eyed the Camry, with its driver's door wide open. The duffel —of cash?— had to be in the trunk. Five or six firefighters were milling around.

Will was beside himself. He was so sweet it made me a little nervous. He walked me inside, talking the whole time. "When you didn't come back to the trailer park, I knew something was wrong. I knew something had happened. I didn't know where to go, though. I didn't know what to do," he said, running a hand through his hair. "I called a buddy in Salisbury and he cruised past the Exxon, but you weren't there. The cashier said he saw you and some guy who was acting weird and smelled like he'd been drinking, but he didn't know which way you had gone. Oh God, I'm so glad you're okay."

"Will, you are the kindest man," I said. "Especially considering in the three days you've known me, everything you own has been either destroyed or at least dented up."

He kissed my forehead on the side without the goose egg. "Don't worry about that," he said. "Don't even think about it. Anyway, I came out ahead on the trailer fire. I'll get enough to put some money down on a nice condo."

"Really? That's great!" And so very strange. Since when can you get a nice condo for the price of an old trailer?

Will brought me an OCFD sweatshirt and an old pair of sweatpants. I changed out of my wet, greasy clothes. We sat on the couch in the truck bay and another medic brought me a cup of coffee. I settled into the comfort and safety of the station.

"What happened?" Will asked, once my teeth stopped chattering.

I recounted my meeting with the evil Dr. Saunders and his hapless minion Fred. I told Will they had tried to bribe me for the original files, the photograph, and my silence. I didn't mention the 10 grand in the trunk of the Camry, because I was still trying to figure out what to do about it.

Larcenous thoughts crowded my head. Ten thousand dollars could buy a lot of skinny jeans and Ugg boots. Ten grand could put a roof over my head—for months. If Will didn't know about the bag of cash, he couldn't talk me out of doing bad things. And he couldn't tell Detective Francis.

The duty crew was setting up for a poker game, and Will went over to help after making sure I was warm. The cards were soon dealt and all eyes were on the game table, glowing under the truck bay lights. Will glanced my way a couple of times and I smiled as I snuggled down into the cushions.

As soon as everyone's attention was locked onto the game, I wrapped myself in Will's heavy coat, and slipped out to the parking lot.

The sleet had slowed to freezing drizzle. I looked around for any sign of Fred. Way down at the other end of the block, I thought I saw a man heading my way on foot. I quickened my pace. The Camry's door squeaked as I opened it and leaned in to pull the trunk latch. The trunk lid popped open, and I grabbed the duffel.

The man was running toward me.

I beat a hasty retreat into the station and went to the women's room and locked the door. I set the bag on the floor and opened it up. Inside were stacks of banded $100 bills. *Holy shit*, I breathed. *They really meant it.*

Just then I heard voices raised in the truck bay. I zipped the duffel shut and shoved it in the trash can, burying it under a pile of paper towels.

A moment later, I returned to the bay. "What was all that noise?" I asked.

"Nothing," Will said. "Andy was talking some trash about how he thinks he knows how to play poker when we all know the man can't even count." Several others in the duty section laughed.

"My man here's the one who can't count," Andy said to Will, swaggering. "Or don't want to count how much I took off him last week."

The shouts and boasts started rolling, and Will put his arm around me and gave me a squeeze.

My watch said just after 9 p.m., and I could think of nothing except the money in the trash can and the soaking tub at the Hilton. "Take me back to the hotel? My head's hurting a little."

"You think you'll be safe?"

"You're the only one who knows I'm staying there."

"I don't want anything to happen to you."

"I need to get some sleep. Don't worry. I'll be fine, if we can sneak out of here without anybody seeing me. Fred is probably halfway through a bottle of Scotch at Adolfo's by now," I said.

"Back in ten," Will said to the group. "I want in the game. Andy, give me your keys."

Andy didn't blink; he pulled a set of keys from his pocket and tossed them to Will, who caught them and went outside. I ducked into the restroom to retrieve the duffel. Will backed a mud-spattered, jacked-up Jeep through the bay doors. I climbed in the back and lay on the seat, duffel in one hand, Gucci knockoff in the other. Will eyed the duffel but said nothing.

He drove north out of the station. He carried a radio from the station so he could hear calls that might come in. If that happened, we'd have to go to the call location and my private car service would have to wait.

The engine noise enveloped us as we rolled up the road. A few blocks later, Will yelled, "I think we're being followed. There's a cab behind us I'm not sure about."

"Well, don't stop at the Hilton, then. Just keep driving," I said, in a fetal position on the back seat.

I saw the Hilton come and go. Will made a right at Anthony's Liquor Store onto Coastal Highway.

"I have an idea," he said.

"Oh good," I said. "That makes one of us."

As he made a call on his cell, I nestled my head into the duffel of cash.

A few minutes later, he turned left into a parking lot. "Be ready to jump out with all your stuff as soon as I stop," Will said. "We're pulling into the back lot of the North OC fire station. I'm parking next to a black Maxima that belongs to my buddy Ed. You're going to get out of the Jeep and get on the floor in the back of the Maxima. There's a blanket and you're going to cover yourself and sit tight. I'll go into the station, and a couple minutes later, Ed and I will both come out and drive away, me in the Jeep, him in the Maxima. He'll drive you to the Hilton while, with any luck, that cab will follow me on a drive around town."

"Wow, you're pretty good at this."

"Happens all the time," he joked, then got serious. "Please be careful, Jamie. I want to see you again. And not on a 911 call."

When the Jeep stopped, Will got out and pulled the driver's seat forward. He then opened the back passenger door of the shiny Maxima.

"Go," he said.

I jumped out of the Jeep, into the Maxima and pulled a scratchy, plaid wool blanket over me and my bags. Will slammed the two vehicle doors simultaneously. The blanket smelled like cigarette smoke.

A few seconds later, I heard the slam of the building's back door, then silence. A car passed on Coastal Highway. Then another. The storm had passed and the night was still. I felt itchy and claustrophobic. The track of the front seat was pressing uncomfortably into the side of my knee. Then I heard the station door open, and the voices of Will and another guy.

"Hey, man, I can't thank you enough," Will said.

"Don't worry about it, bubba," the other guy said with a distinctly Southern twang. "I don't care what the story is, as long as you all are buying the beers when you tell me."

"You got it."

Cold air rushed in as the driver's door opened. As he turned the key in the ignition, he said, "Y'all doin' all right back there?"

"Yeah, I'm fine."

"All right, my name's Ed. I'm going to head on down to the Hilton, see if I can get you in there without any hassles."

The voice was rough, a smoker's voice, and I could smell musty tobacco.

"Thanks a lot," I said, muffled under the blanket.

A few minutes later, Ed said, "We're coming up to the Hilton, darlin', and I think you're in the clear."

I felt the car turn into the parking lot, and I sat up on the back seat, smoothing my hair, reapplying lipstick. Ed glanced back at me. He was a middle-age, mustachioed man with a plaid driving cap. He gave me a quick nod and I smiled.

277

He pulled up the drive to the hotel entrance. I leaned over the front seat and gave him a quick peck on the cheek. "Thank you, Ed," I said, and got out of the car, duffel and purse in tow.

As I walked up the long flight of marble steps to the lobby, I began scouring my bag for my card key. Then an icy chill hit me. If Saunders and Fred had gone through my purse, they must have found the card key with the Hilton logo.

My fingers picked through hairbrush, compact, lipstick, wallet, paperback novel, lucky seashell, gloves, wadded up tissue, St. Thomas postcard from my cousin Pam, roll of stamps, pen, sunglasses, three opened packs of spearmint-flavored Trident, and two gift certificates from my big Seacrets win. No key card.

The whole time I was hunting through my purse, my eyes were scanning the lobby. I pressed myself up against the wall halfway up the wide staircase. Nobody was in the big, open lobby except the desk clerk, the beautiful Russian woman who checked me in. I looked down at my borrowed sweats, and became acutely aware of the goose-egg on my forehead. Sheesh.

I rushed up the stairs to the clerk, whose face registered surprise, then real concern. "Oh no!" she said. "My God, what happen to you?"

"It's a long story, but the guy who did this to me is probably going to show up here any minute and I need to get into my room. Problem is, he stole my pass key."

"I know who did this to you," she said, her eyes becoming dewy in sympathy. "Your husband. Ah, you poor thing."

"What? My husband?"

"Yes, your awful husband. He was here, and then he left."

"Wait, stop. My who? My husband?"

"Yes, and I will say I cannot blame you for wishing to be together with that man who came in with you yesterday. He is much more handsome, and if your husband did this to your face—dear God." Her hand flew to her cheek.

"Lady, I do not have a husband. What are you talking about?"

"Believe me, you don't have to worry about my discretion. I am a reservation specialist, after all. I have seen every person checking in with every other person, and I do not judge, and in your case, with an abusive husband, and that handsome man you were with —"

"I don't have a husband!"

"Okay!" she said, throwing her hands up in mock defeat. "You don't have a husband! So this man who is not your husband had your key. He wanted me to tell him the room number, because he said his wife, Jamie August, had given him the key and told him the number, but he had forgotten the number. I swiped the key and saw the name of your friend come up. I remember your friend," she said, smiling.

"Yes. I'm very glad you remembered my friend."

"Well, yes, so I knew this man, *this* was not the same man at all. Not at all. I asked him to present some identification, and he became very agitated, and he also smelled like drink, not so nice. He said that he urgently needed something his wife, Jamie August, had left in the room. I said I would have to check with the manager, and then, oh! Then he tried to take the key back from me!" Her eyes grew wide at the very thought.

"I would not let go of the key, and fortunately just then Francisco came out and asked if there was a problem."

"Good. Who's Francisco?"

"The manager."

"Okay. Good. So, then what happened?"

"Well, your husband —"

"He's not my husband!"

"Oh, yes. This man who is not your husband told Francisco that I was not giving good customer service and that he needed to get into his wife's room, and demanded your room number. Well, Francisco knew he was lying, because I give excellent customer service. He knows this. I won the award last month for the most consistently excellent customer service. See?" She pointed a manicured finger to a little star next to the name on her engraved nametag: Liliya.

Standing in the middle of this wide open lobby was making me increasingly nervous.

"So I explained to Francisco that I asked the man for identification, for security purposes, and Francisco agreed that we must always ask for identification for security purposes, because otherwise anyone could be walking into anyone's room and that would not be a good situation, especially in your case."

I nodded.

"The gentleman then demanded that Francisco make me give him the key card back. He did not look well, this man. He seemed not right. Drunk, for sure, of course, but also something else not right. Francisco told the man to wait a moment, and we stepped away from the desk for privacy and

then I told Francisco that I had been the one to
check in you and your friend, and that the reservation wasn't in your name at all, and it would hardly
do for me to give your husband the room number
when as far as I knew you and your friend were
upstairs and, well..."

"Right, yes, I appreciate that," I said, giving up
on divorcing myself from Fred Western. "So,
please, what happened?"

"Well, Francisco apologized, and suggested that
your husband must get in touch with you in order
to be reminded of the room number."

"So you didn't give him the room number?"

"Certainly not."

"And you kept the key?"

"Of course."

"That's wonderful, Liliya. I am so grateful to you.
I need to stay away from him, and I knew I could
feel safe here. You can understand why the room is
not in my name. Please, may I have the key?"

"Of course. May I ask you to complete one of
our customer satisfaction surveys? For your con-
venience, I have one personalized just for you." I
grabbed the key and the survey, noting that all the
top scores had been marked.

Safely tucked away in my room, door double-locked and chain-latched, I emptied the duffel and counted the cash. I stuffed the bundles into the safe. With the stuff in there, I had to rearrange it a couple of times to make it all fit. I ran the bath as I undressed. The hot water was soothing, warming my bones, uncoiling my muscles. The steam felt wonderful in my poor, cold nose, and the bath foam smelled heavenly. I floated on a cloud of calm.

After a full night's sleep, I ordered room service breakfast, then dressed and packed. The cash went back in the duffel, with a layer of clothing on top. Everything else went into a South Moon Under shopping bag, and my purse.

I wore camouflage cargo pants with a pale pink cashmere sweater and a pair of black combat boots. I did a careful job with my makeup and, though I couldn't entirely conceal the blossoming bruise over my right eye, I minimized it pretty well.

In the mirror, I saw long, dark hair pulled back and tied simply. Clothes that really fit and felt nice against my skin, unlike my usual discount mart couture. It felt kind of weird, but I liked what I saw.

"Not as much bling as before, maybe, but it's a good look," I said to my reflection. I checked out by phone, then scanned the hallway before heading to the elevators.

Behind the counter at Beach Getaway, I couldn't focus on the laptop. I kept looking out the window, expecting to see a crazed Fred Western come flying at the plate glass. So far, it was quiet. I had ducked out of the Hilton on the Boardwalk side and sprinted a block, where I caught the bus and rode north to the office. I stowed the duffel with the cash and the disk at the back of a drawer of an old enameled steel filing cabinet in the storage room. I locked the cabinet and embedded the key in the bottom of a crusty, half-used stick of margarine in the kitchenette fridge.

Now I was satisfied my story was as airtight as it could be without adding the continuing harass-ment of Larry and Dan Lombardo by Bernard Ivory.

I called Charlie's Charters.

"Charlie's Charters, Dan here."

"Dan, it's Jamie August."

"Hey Jamie, how're you doing?"

"Hangin' in there, considering."

"Yeah, Christ, that is insane about my dad's houseboat. Are you really okay?"

"Thanks, yeah, I'm doing okay but actually I'm calling because I'm finishing up the story that started the whole thing."

"Yeah, my dad said you might be calling me about this. He thinks you ought to lay off."

"It's a little late for that, don't you think?"

"I guess you could look at it that way, yeah."

"So, can we meet somewhere and talk about this?"

"I'd like to help you out, and I feel awful about what happened to you on the houseboat, but my dad wants to stay out of it and I can't say I blame him."

"Dan, listen. A bunch of stuff has happened to me this weekend and I have one hell of a story to tell about Bayview Preserve and the Ivory family. I can prove they killed off the last of the blue crabs in the bay. I can prove they bribed the professors at Eastern Maryland to falsify their environmental survey. I believe they had a woman killed, and I can tell you for sure that they tried to kill me twice."

Dan whistled. "Sounds like you've got all you need, then."

"Not quite. I know that Bernard Ivory has been coming around Charlie's Charters. I think he's trying to get his hands on the marina and the concrete plant. They're prime real estate for redevelopment. You all have some kind of a family secret or something, and Bernard Ivory has figured out what it is. Am I right?"

I could hear Dan breathing.

"I don't care about the Lombardo family's dirty laundry," I said. "I just want to stop Ivory Enterprises before they destroy another piece of waterfront, and another family."

"The concrete plant is not exactly pristine shoreline," Dan pointed out.

"Well, you've got a point there. But seriously. Talk to me about this."

He sighed, but said nothing.

"They tried to burn me out of the houseboat, then they tracked me down again the next night. The cops already know that much, and they've seen the raw data I have on the Bayview Preserve environmental stuff. The story I'm writing is going to put these guys out of business and probably get them charged with murder, attempted murder, fraud, bribery, and extortion, to name a few."

"Okay —"

"Please, help me."

Dan was chuckling. "Okay, okay, yes, I will talk to you! I told my dad we should have told you what's going on in the first place."

He told me he'd pick me up at noon. I left the cash and the disk locked in the cabinet. I carried with me a copy of the scanned photograph and a draft of my story. I'd lay all the cards on the table and see what Dan had to say.

14.

WE SAT AT A DARK BOOTH in The Angler, a seafood place at the inlet full of varnished driftwood and brass shipboard fittings. Dan was in his mid-30s with wavy hair like his dad's, in need of a trim. He wore the goatee most Maryland guys sport at some point. He was wearing jeans and a heavy wool sweater, like his dad would wear, and he looked haggard, in need of a decent night's sleep. I had some sympathy for that. He was engrossed in my story, while I scanned the restaurant for anyone taking an interest in us—or anyone working too hard to act like they weren't. The plates from our lunch, already eaten, sat in the middle of the table.

Dan looked up. "So you're saying not only did Ivory Enterprises fill in some very ecologically sensitive marshland —" he paused to take a swig from his beer— "not only that, but Bernard Ivory was at the Donnelley house, which had been the only property on the land, the day it burned down with Donnelley in it."

"Yep."

"And he subsequently bought the property for almost nothing."

"Yep."

"And a fire burned down the old Environmental Sciences building."

"It was housed in the Biology building then, but yes. Right before the falsified environmental study came out. All the supporting samples and documentation for the study went up in smoke."

"Convenient," he said.

"Mmm-hmm."

"All right, I'm going to spill it," he said. "My father is going to shit a brick when he finds out I've talked to you, but this has gone on too long. Anyway, it's my skeleton, in my closet."

I sat back and waited for Dan to collect his thoughts.

"When I was 22, I got a drug conviction," he said. "It was one of those bullshit things. I was partying a lot, too much, and I had just made a buy. I got pulled over for speeding and had enough coke for me and my three buddies. The cops found the stuff. I already had a drunk driving arrest on my record and they nailed me. I ended up doing six months in Jessup."

I stared. I never in a million years would have guessed Dan Lombardo had spent time in prison. I guess I imagined a guy with jail time would have some kind of look about them. You know, a neck tattoo or a teardrop under one eye, gangland style. Dan just looked a little rumpled. But what did I know about this? Ex-cons are never the good guys in Nancy Drew stories.

"I paroled out and came back here. My dad hired me at Lombardo Concrete. I worked hard, and kept my nose clean. So to speak. I guess my parents could see I had learned my lessons. I took on some side work at Charlie's. Before long, I was putting in more hours over there than at my dad's business. A couple of years later, old Charlie was ready to retire and he offered to sell me the business.

"I got some money from my dad, but I also had to get a business loan. Because my credit still sucked, I needed another name on the ownership papers. Dad stepped in and within three years I paid him back every dime. Charlie's Charters is still in my dad's name, but the business is all mine."

He grinned and shrugged, took a draw on his cigarette.

I shook my head, puzzled. "That's a hell of a comeback story, Dan, seriously, but what does any of that have to do with Ivory Enterprises?"

"Oh, just wait. About a year ago, lawyers from Ivory Enterprises contacted both Lombardo Concrete and Charlie's Charters. They were interested in buying the properties. This was around the time my mom was sick. Probably they knew that, and that's why they came around. But we weren't interested in selling and we told them so. Well, they kept after us. First, they sweetened their offer a bit, but then they started making references to my past. They suggested more and more blatantly that we needed to sell or something about my past was going to come back and bite me in the ass."

"I can't imagine your father putting up with that too well," I said.

"You got that right," he said. "My dad told those assholes where they could stick their offers and their threats. Then about a month ago I found a gram of coke on the dashboard of a Charlie's Charter boat."

"Wow."

"It was sitting right out in the open, plain as day."

"Holy crap. Was it just you who found it?"

"Yes, and that's what saved me. One of my guys was supposed to be going out with me to help on that day's charter, but his girlfriend went into labor the night before. I got there around 4:30 a.m. to double-check the boat, about 30 minutes before the customers arrived, and there it was. Nobody saw it but me."

"What did you do?"

"Well, I fuckin' freaked. The minute I saw it, I knew I was being set up. I got clean when I was in prison, and prison is the worst thing that can happen to you. No way was I going back."

"Yeah, I can imagine."

"I tossed the shit overboard. Later that day, another call came in to Lombardo Concrete, this one from Bernard Ivory himself, suggesting it would be an excellent time to sell, that it would be a shame if the police found out about what he called my 'sideline' business. My dad asked him what the hell he was talking about. Ivory said he heard the DEA was looking hard at charter companies these days. Drugs are coming north from Miami offshore and they're starting to look at Ocean City as a possible entry point."

293

"Is that true?"

"Who knows? But that's what Bernard Ivory said to my dad."

"How did he know about your conviction?"

"I don't know for sure, but Jonathan was partying pretty hard back in the day, too."

"You knew him?"

"No, not really, but we were probably at some of the same parties. It's a small town. Too small. Anyway, a guy like Bernard Ivory? He can probably find out anything he needs to know, or make it up if he can't find it. He's rich and he's mean."

"So that's why your dad is so afraid to blow the whistle on Ivory Enterprises. They're devious enough, they might destroy both your business and his."

"Exactly. But that's not the end of it," Dan said. "A week ago, Bernard Ivory showed up at my office with a contract of sale for the marina. He said if I didn't sign in the next 24 hours, he would be forced to report my regular drug runs to the DEA."

"Yeah, but there are no drug runs," I pointed out.

"I said the same thing. He said, don't be so sure. I told him to get the fuck out of my office, then I did an inspection of my four charter boats. In the hold of one of them, I found this."

He pulled a folded piece of paper out of his coat pocket and smoothed it on the table. On it a single handwritten word: "Cocaine."

"So he's demonstrating he can get onto your boats, put anything he wants in there."

"Exactly. I called all three of my guys in for a meeting. I didn't give them any details, but I told them we need to beef up security, and I need to hear about anybody in the marina who's not supposed to be there."

"Nobody saw anything?"

"Not a thing."

"You trust all your guys?"

"Yes."

"Are you willing to go on the record with all of this? The conviction is going to have to be part of the story."

"Yeah, I know, and that's why my dad didn't want to talk to you. But it's my deal, and I want this guy to get what's coming to him, so yes, the whole thing is fair game for your story."

Dan dropped me at Beach Getaway. I called Will to tell him about my latest discovery and my next move. Then I fetched the cash, grabbed a ring of keys, and got ready for a brisk walk through the alleyways. I knew where to hole up and write. It was just a matter of getting there undetected.

The day was warm, sunny, and bright. The earthy smell of thaw was in the air. I headed south between apartment buildings, beach bungalows, parking lots, and small hotels. A grid of alleyways threads between every oceanside block in Ocean City. I kept my eyes peeled, and the couple of times I saw a moving car, I either ducked into a building or jumped through a row of bushes to follow a different route. I saw not a single Cadillac or Camry.

When I reached 43rd, I slowly looked up and down the road. A family at the top of the street was walking toward the dune crossing to the ocean. It was the Slomkowski family from Baltimore that I had checked into Sunrise Paradise a week ago. They were wrapped in sweaters, their scarves cheerfully flapping in the light breeze. The parents were holding hands. The boy said something and they all laughed.

The exterior of Sunrise Paradise looked like a toxic woodland mushroom: wet and peeling red and orange. I walked up the stairs, which were covered in dry-rotted indoor-outdoor carpeting. On the second floor, a terrace ran the width of the building, and a door in the center opened onto steps to the third floor. I unlocked that door, carefully secured it behind me, and ascended the dimly lit stairway. I unlocked Apartment 6 and went in.

After locking the door, I closed the drapes and checked the heat. The water was running and the lights were functional. I took the cushions off of the plaid sleeper sofa and unfolded it halfway. I spread the stacks of cash evenly across the middle third of the mattress, like a fat burrito. I flattened the bag, laid it on the bills, then closed the couch.

This was the best I could do at the moment: hide out in a crappy apartment, stash the loot until I decided what to do with it, finish and file the story.

I set up my computer at the chipped dinette table and added all of the information Dan had given me. I thought some more about the series of fires that seemed to follow the Ivory clan: the Donnelley house, the Eastern Maryland Environmental Sciences building, the houseboat, the trailer—all strategically useful. But to keep using the same method suggested somebody was a firebug. Had the security guard—Alan, as Paul Saunders had called him— done the earlier ones? Who was he?

I let my mind wander. Maybe the guy was Bernard and Corinne's love child. If he was responsible for the Donnelley house fire, he would have been a teenager when he did it.

I wanted to know whether anyone had looked into the string of fires and connected them. Was there a signature method used every time?

Lost in thought, I reached into my bag for my phone to call Will. I groped, elbow deep, then remembered I had no cell because of Alan-the-Fire-Starter. The shitbag.

I peeked out the curtains and saw dusk was falling. I wanted answers, and I wanted food. Will was cooking for the duty crew at the fire station, and my stomach overpowered my common sense. I closed my computer and hid it under a pile of carry-out menus in a dusty kitchen drawer. After quietly closing the door and locking up, I tiptoed down the stairs. I don't know why, since they creaked like hell anyway. "Summer Lovin'" from the *Grease* soundtrack was wafting from under the door of the Baltimore family's apartment, along with a pleasant murmur of conversation. Something that smelled like pot roast was cooking. I was tempted to knock on the door and join in their cozy evening but instead continued down the steps and into the falling night.

I ran across Coastal Highway and waited in the shadows near the shelter until I saw a southbound bus. I stepped onto the sidewalk and the bus picked me up. Santa Claus was driving this evening. He dropped me in front of the firehouse and I went in for a noisy, friendly dinner of chili and cornbread with the duty crew. Will looked exhausted, like he had aged in the last several days.

"I seriously need some sleep," he said, slumped on the barstool next to me at the big kitchen table.

"You look pretty wrung out," I said.

"It's hard to get any real sleep around here, even when I'm not working."

"I believe it. Are you on duty now?"

"No. Would it be okay if I crashed with you for a few hours?"

"Sure, of course. Come on back to the Palace of Horrors and get some sleep."

"You wouldn't mind?"

"Of course not, Will. It's the least I can do."

I insisted Will park a block away so his truck wouldn't give away our location.

We dashed across the street and into the safety of my borrowed Sunrise Paradise apartment. Once inside, Will sank onto the couch and pulled me next to him. The sleeper was extra lumpy and hard with all those stacks of bills sandwiched inside. We rested for a moment, the silence only interrupted by the toilet, which ran continuously.

"Fred Western showed up at the firehouse after you left last night," Will said after a few minutes, casually running his fingers through my hair.

"What?" I sat up. "Ow!" My hair tangled in Will's fingers. "What happened? What did he say?" I pulled my hair together and draped it over one shoulder.

Will's face broke into a lazy grin. "He told me you stole a bunch of money from him."

"Oh, is that what he said?"

"Yep. Says he cashed out his retirement fund, and you stole it out of the trunk of his car."

Well, shit.

"Ten grand isn't much of a retirement fund," I said.

"Is that what was in that black bag? Ten grand?"

I blushed and looked away. "Yeah. I didn't tell you about it because I wasn't sure what I was going to do with it, and I didn't want to get you into trouble, you know, if I decided to maybe, I don't know, like, not turn it in..."

"So you're accepting their bribe?" Will asked, surprised.

"Hell, no! I saw a chance to hit them back, and I hit."

"Ah. So you still have the money?"

"Yeah."

"Where is it?"

"It's safe," I said, leaning back on the couch.

"Jamie, you're crazy. Those guys were already trying to kill you, so you steal their money? How is that smart? And anyway, how is that right?"

I couldn't meet his eyes. I sighed. "Fuck them. I had to hit back," I said again, halfheartedly.

Will hugged me and I breathed in his clean smell.

"You know you can't keep it," he said. "Let me take it in to the cops. I can tell him we found it in the trunk, which we checked after Western ran away."

"After trying to shoot me," I said.

"He said he didn't have a gun."

"Yeah, sure."

"Anyway, I think you should just give me the bag and I'll turn it in for you."

"You're right, Will," I conceded. "I can't keep that money. Damn it! All right, let's get a few hours of sleep, then we'll take it to the police together."

I leaned my head against Will's chest, relieved.

"Don't worry about it, Jamie. I can take care of this for you."

"Thanks, but I have already put you through too much. I can just picture it: You go in and they, like, arrest you or something for going through Fred Western's trunk."

"I know Joe Francis. He wouldn't do that."

"Plus, I need to explain the whole thing. That way, Detective Francis will hear one more piece of information to support my story."

"I'm just worried about you being out on the street any more than you have to," he persisted.

"Will. Seriously, it's fine. We'll go together."

He relented. It was only 9 p.m., but we climbed into bed. I was definitely not up for getting naked between this particular set of sheets. Will had given me a Raven's jersey earlier when he was pulling stuff out of his locker. I threw that on with some pink lace undies. I missed my old pajamas. The bed at Sunrise Paradise was weirdly soft and smelled like mothballs. Will and I curled up in the dark. I didn't feel terribly sleepy, but I closed my eyes and drifted off.

I awoke to a faint sound coming from the living room. I reached for Will, but he wasn't next to me. I heard the quiet scrape of a drawer sliding on its track, then a cabinet door opening and closing. Silently, I got out of bed. Another door opened and closed. I crept into the living room and switched on the overhead light as Will was reaching up to feel around on the top shelf of the pantry. He whirled around.

"What are you doing, Will?"

"I, uh, I was just —"

I crossed my arms over my chest as he stammered.

"Can't find what you're looking for?"

"What? No, no, what do you mean? It's not like that," he said with a forced laugh.

"No?" Angry tears welled up. "Then what the fuck are you doing?"

He opened his mouth, closed it again, came toward me with his hands outstretched, palms up, beseeching. I slid left into the kitchen, putting the table between us.

"Jamie, I have to have that money," he finally said, facing me across the table. "Otherwise, he'll kill you."

"That's bullshit. We already decided that we would go to Detective Francis with the money. Fred Western is an idiot."

Will began circling the table. "Not Fred," he said. "Alan." Fear coursed through me, icy and sharp. I circled as he did, keeping him opposite me.

"Alan? How do you know this?"

We had now done a full circle, and he stopped and faced me, fingertips on the table.

"It doesn't matter, Jamie. They know where you are."

"The only way they know where I am is if you told them," I said quietly.

"I had to talk, Jamie. I had no choice."

"What do you mean, you had no choice?"

"I tried to tell him that the cops already know everything you know, but he's not listening to me."

"What are you talking about?" I exploded.

"Jonathan Ivory and the rest of them, they want you and they want that money."

"You know them? How do you even know them?"

"I, uh, I know Jon. I owe him some money."

"Nooo," I breathed, my heart dropping. "Why? How?"

"It's a small town. There aren't that many high-stakes card games. A couple of years ago, he won big; I lost."

"A couple of *years* ago?"

"Yeah, two or three. I've been paying it back, but it's been kind of slow. Every once in a while, Jon needs something, I help him out."

I felt sick. "So you're his errand boy," I said and he winced. "After I left the firehouse, Fred never showed up, did he? You heard about the money from Jonathan, who must have spoken to Paul

Saunders. And now you're just trying to steal Fred's money."

"Fred never came back to the firehouse," Will admitted. "He's probably long gone. He's never going to get that money back—and I need it."

"So all those times you helped me over the past few days, those were all just big shows? Like, why the big production with your friend driving me to the Hilton? Why bother, when you were just going to tell them where I was anyway?"

"No, that was real. You've got to believe me! I never told them you were at the Hilton. I convinced them I didn't know where you were staying. I did everything I could to protect you."

"Fat lot of good it did, Will. Saunders and Western found the Hilton key card in my bag."

"Oh. I didn't know," he sighed. "Look, they told me to keep tabs on you, so I had to give them something. I'm into the Ivorys for a lot of money. Last month my ex-wife started getting threatening calls from them at her parents' house."

"So you made a trade? Me for your ex-wife?"

"No!"

I glared at him and he dropped his eyes. "Okay, Jamie, what choice did I have? And I gotta say, you are way more resourceful than my ex-wife. Half the time I had no idea where you were going or what you were doing."

"I was trying to protect you by keeping you out of my business."

"I'm glad, because what I didn't know, I couldn't tell them. That's the only reason you're still alive."

As he was speaking, the larger, uglier picture grew clear. "You've been in the Ivory family pocket the whole time, haven't you? You probably let Vernette Johnson die! Maybe you even killed her."

"No, Jamie, I didn't! I did everything I could, but Vernette was dead by the time we got the call. I didn't even know who she was." He seemed sincere about that, like he was flashing some kind of professional pride even as he confessed to selling me out.

"And this whole thing between us? You were just helping Jon out?" Tears were streaming.

"It started out that way, but believe me, it got way more complicated once I got to know you. He told me to keep an eye on you. He didn't tell me to—to make love to you. He doesn't know about that."

"You are weak," I said, disgusted. "Of course he knows. You played me—you had sex with me—so that I would trust you. You're —"

"I'm desperate."

"You're a whore!"

He reacted as though I had slapped him. His face grew red, his eyes shimmered with anger. "He doesn't know about us because I didn't tell him. And Jamie? You shouldn't toss that word around, considering how many people you've slept with in the last week."

"I don't fuck for money."

Will lurched across the table, which skidded with a screech across the floor. He grabbed my shoulders and backed me against the wall. "Enough. You are going to tell me where that money is, and then you are going to get out of here, before Alan shows up and things get really ugly. *Believe* me, Jamie. Believe me. I'm trying to save you."

His fingers gripped my shoulders and we glared at each other. After a second, I dropped my eyes and rounded my shoulders in defeat. When I felt his grip loosen, I brought my knee up and made sharp contact where it counts. Just like they teach you in self-defense courses at the Y. Will grunted and doubled over, gasping. I made a break for the door, but Will grabbed my leg as I ran past, and I fell with a heavy thud. A stab of pain shot through my hip.

307

He straddled me and pinned my arms against the floor. "Where is it?" he hollered.

Just then, someone started pounding on the front door. Will and I froze and looked at each other in terror. It had to be Alan, the homicidal security thug.

"Hey! What's goin' on in there?" bellowed an older, deep, and distinctly Baltimore voice.

Will attempted to clap his hand over my mouth. I bit down hard. He screamed.

"Help!" I hollered.

The door burst open with a shower of dry-rotted splinters, and Mr. Slomkowski charged in brandishing a dented fire extinguisher. He hauled Will off of me with one meaty hand and threw him on the couch.

"Don't move, you bastard," he said to Will, whose hand was bleeding.

"Okay, Christ, I'm bleeding," he said.

"I can see that," Slomkowski replied. He turned to me, smoothing down the front of his brown terry cloth bathrobe. He wore it like a smoking jacket over a pair of threadbare flannel pajama bottoms and an undershirt. "Are you okay there, miss?" I nodded. "Hey, do I know you from somewhere?"

"Yes, from Beach Getaway Rentals," I said, wiping Will's blood off my chin with my left hand, and extending my right. "I'm Jamie August. We met last week when you signed in for your apartment downstairs."

"Oh right, right," he said, shaking my hand and studiously ignoring that I had no pants on. "Merv Slomkowski. Well, what seems to be the problem here?"

"He attacked me when I caught him trying to steal —"

"She nearly bit my finger off!"

"Shut it," Slomkowski said, pointing to Will. "Is this your apartment?" he said to me.

"Yes," I said. Sort of.

"He do that to your face?" he said, eyeing the bruised lump on my forehead.

"No, that was another guy."

"Christ," he said and shook his head. "You gonna press charges?"

I thought about it for a second. "No. I just want him out of here."

Slomkowski turned to Will. "You heard the lady," he said. "Get out. And don't let me catch you around here again."

"Jamie —"

"Hey," Slomkowski said, picking up the fire extinguisher and taking a step toward Will. "She's lettin' you off easy. I suggest you quit while you're ahead."

Will backed out the ruined door. "Get out of here, Jamie," he said, then took off down the stairs. I listened to the stairs creak and the exterior door bang shut.

"Are you in law enforcement?" I asked as I stood and splashed water on my face at the kitchen tap.

"Greenlawn Mall security, 15 years."

"Ooooohh, well then. I'm sure glad you were downstairs." Baltimore's Greenlawn Mall is legendary for crime and violence. My guess is more money changes hands there in drug trades and robberies than in store sales.

"Glad to help. Why don't you get changed and come on downstairs, Jamie. Dot'll put on some coffee."

"Oh, no, I mean I don't want to keep you all up. It's almost midnight."

"Don't worry about it," he said. "We're up now. You and your pal made sure of that."

"Sorry about that."

Slomkowski waited as I went into the bedroom and threw on yesterday's camo pants, sweater, and combat boots. At the Slomkowski apartment, the stove hood light and an avocado green ceramic lamp in the living room were on. They had rearranged the furniture to make the room look warm and inviting.

"Dot, put some coffee on," he said to his wife, who was at the counter spooning grounds into the coffeemaker. "This is Jamie."

"Hi, hon," Dot Slomkowski said. "You okay?"

"I'm fine, thanks to your husband. Sorry for the disturbance."

"That's okay, hon. Things happen," she said, examining the bump on my head. "Nasty bruise. You take cream and sugar?"

The three of us sat at the kitchen table drinking coffee, and soon Merv was telling tales from his mall security days. His booming voice filled the small room, and Dot's laughter was spontaneous, like she was hearing her husband's war stories for the first time. I couldn't believe we weren't waking their two kids. Then I thought, if these were my parents, I'd probably be used to sleeping through noise and conversation at all hours.

We never heard a thing; we only smelled the smoke. I sprinted out of the apartment and up the stairs, with Merv right behind me. We skidded to a halt at the splintered door. Flames engulfed the apartment.

Merv ran down the stairs, hollering for Dot to wake the kids and call 911. I watched for a moment in the doorway as flames danced on the sofa cushions. Adios, ten thousand bucks. The kitchen, too, was bright with fire. My computer, gone. The photographs, the disk, the thumb drive: All those things I had been guarding so carefully, were destroyed. I was just relieved everything had already been turned in, backed up, copied, filed, and on and on—and that Detective Francis had seen the originals.

It was getting hard to breathe in the hallway and it felt like my hair was about to combust, so I went downstairs. The Slomkowski family was busy throwing things in shopping bags and suitcases.

"We've got to get out of here!" I called in the door.

"I know, hon, but this place is cement construction, real solid. We've got a few minutes," Dot said, calm and efficient. Merv was hauling suitcases out of the back bedroom. "Chucky, get your PlayStation," she instructed her dazed son. "Ashley, sweetheart, grab my pocketbook over on the counter. You go on, hon," she said to me. "We'll meet you in a minute."

I ran the flight down and stood on the sidewalk breathing in the cold air. I could hear the approaching sirens.

Flames danced in the windowsills of Number 6. Footsteps raced up behind me and suddenly every nerve in my body spasmed in unbelievable pain. I went stiff, then collapsed.

When I regained consciousness, I was laying on the soft leather backseat of Jonathan's Cadillac, my wrists and ankles bound by duct tape. Jonathan was driving, with Alan riding shotgun. I involuntarily cried out, and Alan calmly reached back with a chunky black and yellow taser gun and shocked me again.

I woke for the second time, still bound, on the couch in Jonathan's office. Every muscle in my body felt as though it was on fire.

I slowly opened my eyes and focused on the ceiling. I lifted my head slightly and the room swayed. Jonathan was at his desk working on papers strewn across the surface. Alan was sitting impassively in a leather chair across from the couch.

"She's awake," he said. Jonathan looked up and smiled.

"Jamie! Welcome back to the land of the living. How are you feeling?"

"Couldn't be better, dickhead."

"Charming," he muttered. Alan stood and moved to slap me. Jonathan stopped him with a casual flick of his hand. "Don't worry about it, Alan. She's from Essex. She can't help it."

"I'm from Dundalk. Asshole. Honestly, Jonathan, what the fuck are you doing?"

"I keep asking the same question about you," he said. "What makes you think you can drop in out of nowhere, and I do mean nowhere, and mess with a multi-million dollar, two-generation family corporation with ties to every political and academic organization on the eastern shore? I mean, honestly, you got a double helping of looks but came up sadly short on brains."

"If I was just making this shit up, you wouldn't really care. You'd just sue me and your life would go on. But I have already proved your company is responsible for murder, arson, bribery, gross environmental damage, and now you want to add kidnapping to the list? The game is over, Jonathan. Why add another crime to your rap sheet? The story is filed. It's done." Not strictly true, but why sweat the details?

"I don't think so," Jonathan said smoothly. "Can I get you a glass of wine? I have a terrific burgundy upstairs." I turned my head.

"I just want to talk to you for the moment," Jonathan said. "Contrary to how this might look, I really like you. Hell, you *know* I like you. I don't want to hurt you. I really don't. I'm just running out of options."

He turned to Alan, who was standing by the window. "Would you mind running up to my suite and getting the Gevrey-Chambertin from the rack?"

Alan left, and I heard the click of the reception room door closing.

Jonathan moved to the couch, and I made a show of keeping my face turned away from him. "I wish it didn't have to be like this, Jamie. You are a beautiful woman. But my God, what happened here?" He gently smoothed my hair away from the bump on my forehead.

"Your esteemed colleagues Fred Western and Paul Saunders."

"This never should have happened. I could have taken good care of you, if you had let me." He casually rested his hand on my leg. I shivered.

"But now we seem to have come to an impasse. What would you have me do, Jamie? You have already demonstrated that your word is not to be trusted. I must confess, I was shocked when I heard you had run off with $10,000 of Fred Western's money."

"I'm sure that wasn't Fred Western's personal money, and anyway, he was going to shoot me!"

"Shoot you? I seriously doubt that. Fred wouldn't hurt a fly. Anyway, his aim is probably lousy. And it was his money. He tried to talk us all into the idea of paying to keep you quiet, but frankly, none of us thought that would be effective."

"Well, it doesn't matter now."

"That is true."

"No. I mean your arsonist lackey burned the ten grand in tonight's fire," I said. Jonathan's mouth opened in an O of amused surprise. "No! Will said the money wasn't in the apartment."

"Will didn't look inside the sofa."

"Jamie, sweetheart, you are just no end of trouble."

"Yeah. You probably should have dumped me in the bay instead."

"I would never do that to you."

"Did the trick for Vernette Johnson."

"Indeed. I heard about her unfortunate accident."

I tried to keep my voice level and keep him talking.

"So tell me the story about Bayview Preserve," I said. "Presumably I'm not coming out of this in one piece —"

"No! Relax, Jamie. I like you all in one piece."

"So why not humor a curious reporter?" I plowed on. "You all burned down the Donnelley house, didn't you?"

Jonathan sighed and pasted on a face of tender regret. "No, we did not. That was a sad family tale, but it had a remarkable silver lining. We knew the property was right for Bayview Preserve, and we made Frank Donnelley an offer, but Donnelley wasn't interested in selling. So we started looking into the situation —"

"Yes, you do tend to 'look into the situation' when you want a piece of property."

"Of course! In Donnelley's case, it's a good thing we did. What we discovered was that Frank Donnelley had a son. It's one thing to ascribe to the philosophy of 'spare the rod, spoil the child,' but Donnelley was abusing this boy to the point that my father was disturbed by what he saw."

"That would have to be extreme," I said wryly. "How old was this boy?"

"He was 14, the same age as me."

I nodded.

"The boy was not going to school. He was locked in the basement, and was malnourished. My father found the boy one day —"

"Where was Frank Donnelley at the time?"

"Off at work? I don't know. He wasn't home."

"And your father broke into their house?"

"He was doing some checking, walking the property, trying to determine whether it was going to be right for Bayview Preserve."

"Even though Donnelley wasn't selling."

"My father gets what he wants. Are you not clear on that yet?" He slid his hand up my thigh. "It runs in the family."

I did not move. My expression was neutral. "So, that's when your father found the boy?"

"Yes. He heard a noise in the house. He went inside and found this poor child locked in the basement. The boy was dirty and hungry, and even though my father is a pretty hard-nosed man, he knew he had to do something."

"This is a side to your father I never would have imagined."

"None of us could, believe me. He began making regular trips there, trying to persuade Donnelley to sell. One day, he told Donnelley he knew about the boy. He told Donnelley if he didn't sell the house, he would send social services out to take the boy away."

"Touching," I said with a sneer, but Jonathan was on a roll and didn't notice.

"Donnelley ordered my father off the property."

"That's probably the picture Mrs. Mulvaney took."

"Undoubtedly. Later that day, my father returned with a shotgun, opened the basement door and told the boy to come up. The boy, poor thing, was carrying a box of matches. As Donnelley yelled at my father, the boy stood lighting one match after the other, letting them fall. I guess he had done that all the time down in the basement. It didn't matter with the dirt floor, but now, the lit matches hit the wood, one after the other. My father took an oil lamp from a shelf and smashed it on the floor. The flames caught. He told the boy to run and wait by the car. Then he made sure Donnelley was—well, he was part of the kindling when the house burned down. My father brought the boy home, and Alan has been with us ever since."

I heard the door open in the reception area, and Alan returned with the wine. He placed our glasses on the coffee table without a sound, then retreated to the corner.

"I hope that answers some of your questions, Jamie. Now, let's enjoy a glass of wine and consider how to conclude this unfortunate business in some mutually beneficial way."

He picked up his glass and took a swallow, his face breaking into a dreamy half-smile. He really thought I was an idiot, trying to sell me on the idea that I was somehow going to just walk out of there.

"Tell me about your plans for the harbor," I pressed on. "I know you want the land the marina sits on, and the cement plant."

"That's going to be the next big face-lift for Ocean City. Mixed-use development with walking bridge to connect them. Restaurants and a marina, with apartments and shops, pedestrian streets, and an open-air performance space."

"It sounds nice," I said truthfully. "All done in eco-friendly shades of brown, I presume?"

"Of course," Jonathan said with a smile.

"How did your father know about Dan Lombardo's drug conviction?"

"That was easy. Everybody knew about it because everybody partied with Dan. Including me."

"You were friends with Dan?"

"No, but you know how it is. Whatever your tastes, you're going to know everyone else who likes what you like."

"So the drug threat was your idea."

He gave a small, modest shrug.

I held up my wrists and looked at him. "I can't properly drink with my hands bound. Honestly!" I said, like being bound by duct tape was just one of those silly, everyday nuisances.

"It is a shame, isn't it? But I can't trust you, sweetheart, you know that. Here, let me help you."

He picked up the glass, leaned toward me and raised it to my lips. I took a tiny sip, and he returned the glass to the table.

Then he kissed me. I clenched my jaw and turned my face.

The strike of a wooden match sounded from behind us. Jonathan backed off and I turned to see Alan staring at me from behind the bar. He lit one match after another, dropping them into an ashtray. He didn't blink. Strike. Flame. Slow burn to his fingers as he stared at me. Drop to the ashtray. Repeat.

I realized I was about to go from the frying pan into the fire. I turned back to Jonathan.

"Jonathan?"

"Hmmmmm?" he said, savoring another mouthful of the burgundy and making an ostentatious display of relaxing.

"He's going to kill me, isn't he?"

"It's all up to you."

"But you said you couldn't trust me. What do you want from me? I'm too young to die."

"You're almost 27."

"That's pretty young," I retorted.

"Yes, but you've seen a lot. And now, you've seen too much."

"So what can I do?"

"What can you do? Well, let's see, Jamie. What are you good at?" His eyes sparkled with amusement.

"May I have some more wine?" I asked. He raised my glass to my lips and I took a big gulp. I needed a bigger shot of courage than a mouthful of burgundy, but you work with what you've got.

I lowered my voice to a husky whisper. "Have you ever talked to someone right before they're going to be killed? I mean, when they know they're going to die?"

He looked at me, fascinated.

"No, I never have."

"Can I tell you something?"

"Please." He leaned closer.

"I'm terrified. And I fucking hate you. But I hate him more," I said, with a nod toward Alan. Alan continued to stare at me impassively. "This chemistry that exists between you and me? I wish I didn't feel it, but I do. You feel it too. You understand what I'm saying."

Jonathan nodded.

"I don't want to die." Tears leaked down my cheeks, no need to fake those. "And I'll do anything you want, if it means I get to stay alive."

"Good girl." He stroked my cheek.

"But here's the weird thing, Jon. Even if I am about to die, I want to feel a human connection, I need to have that release one more time. Even with you. Especially with you. Crazy, right?" I sat up and faced him, and used my taped-together hands to take his hand and press it against my heart. Then I kissed him with everything I had.

"You *are* voracious," he said, and it sounded like the most sincere compliment he'd ever paid me.

He cupped a breast and kissed me deeply, and I leaned in, creating an awkward barrier with my wrists.

He pushed me back on the couch and climbed on top of me. Behind me I heard the matches striking. Scratch. Scratch. Scratch. Jonathan was kissing me aggressively, his teeth making hard contact with my lips. I turned my head sideways, scrunching my eyes closed.

"Get him out of here!" I said, my voice shaking. "How can you stand it with him right here?"

"He won't interfere," Jonathan said.

"Don't let him kill me," I whispered hotly into Jonathan's ear. His hard-on jumped against my leg.

He kissed me again, and one sweaty palm inserted itself under my sweater.

I started to really cry.

"If this is the last time I will ever make love, I don't want my killer to watch," I whispered, looking up at Jonathan through wet lashes. His eyes cut from me to Alan. He looked exasperated.

"Please. I can't stand this," I murmured. "Take every part of me. I want to open my whole body to you, experience things I've never tried before. I'll give you everything, because then maybe you'll give me my life." I sank a deep kiss into the base of his neck. He let out a ragged sigh.

"But I can only do that if we're alone."

"Jesus Christ!" Jonathan exploded. He stood up and faced Alan. "Get out of here for awhile. Twenty minutes."

"Twenty minutes!" I exclaimed, indignant.

"Okay, 40."

I sobbed.

"Fuck! Okay, an hour. Come back in an hour, Alan."

"I don't think that's a good idea," Alan said.

I interlaced my fingers so I could run my nails up the inside of Jonathan's thigh.

"It's fine. She's not going anywhere."

Alan looked annoyed. "I'll be back in an hour."

He left Jonathan's office and I heard the outer door click.

15.

JONATHAN PRACTICALLY FELL on me. He tried to put one knee between my legs, but my ankles were bound. He pulled my sweater over my head, but it wouldn't come off.

I looked at him, my eyes pleading. I pressed my hips hard against him, with my knees solidly together and my arms tangled in the sweater.

"Please...." I said. I raised my wrists toward him in a pleading gesture.

"No, I can't do that," he said.

"Okay," I said, kissing him deeply. "Okay, I can understand that. I would scratch your fucking eyes out. But I have an idea."

He was fumbling with the button on my pants.

"Wait, listen to me," I said, kissing all over his face. "I can't get naked with this stupid duct tape on my ankles and wrists."

He laughed and gave me a long kiss. "I'm not untaping you."

"I know, I know," I said, and gently bit his lip. "But maybe you could separate my arms and legs and bind me to something. Your desk, maybe, or your chair. I've never tried that. Have you?"

"Yes," he breathed. I didn't know if he meant yes he wanted to duct tape me to the office furniture, or yes he had been there, done that. Either way, I let out a careful sigh of relief when he got off me and made his way behind the desk. He pulled open a drawer and rooted around furiously. He picked up my cell phone and tossed it back in the drawer. Finally he took out a pair of scissors and a roll of the duct tape.

He looked up at me and I shivered with adrenaline, goose bumps rising. We locked eyes. I bit my lower lip.

Jonathan returned to the couch and knelt in front of me. I was breathing hard in anticipation. I opened my knees the few inches my taped ankles allowed and slid my hips suggestively toward his face. Then I put my hands in front of him and wiggled my fingers. He grinned, took the scissors and snipped the tape to free my hands. I pulled him to me and nibbled on his smooth, sweet-smelling neck. "My legs. Hurry."

He sat back on his heels and began to work on the tape binding my ankles. I spread my arms wide and gripped the back of the couch. As soon as my ankles were free, I planted one combat boot on the floor and smashed the other one squarely into Jonathan's face, flattening his nose. Jonathan pitched backward and landed on the coffee table. Its glass top exploded into a thousand shards.

Jonathan's face went white with shock. His eyes rolled back in his head, one arm made a jerking movement, then his body grew still.

I ran to the reception area and threw the door's deadbolt. I returned to the office and locked myself in with Jonathan. I pulled the fire alarm, starting a piercing ring. Then I called 911.

I heard the heavy wooden lobby door give way to an axe a few minutes later, above the din of the alarm bell. Then an axe blade came crashing through Jonathan's office door. Jonathan lay still in the wreckage, blood flowing from his nose. I jumped behind the big desk and tipped it forward as an added barrier, the desk accessories and Sharper Image gadgets sliding to the floor to mix with the broken glass.

The axe continued to pummel the heavy door. Shouts and footsteps came from the reception room. I heard a sharp cry of pain and a thud. A moment later, the partially splintered door swung open, and Donald rushed into the room.

"Donald!"

I vaulted over the desk and leapt into his arms.

.

16.

"I'D LIKE TO PROPOSE a toast," Donald said, standing at the head of the long, pleasantly crowded dinner table. "To the most stubborn, reckless, and unmanageable reporter ever to darken the door of the *Weekly Breeze*." Tammy grabbed my hand across the table and squeezed. "Jamie August refuses to follow her editor's explicit instructions, misses deadlines, and shows extreme disregard for the normal rules of journalistic objectivism and detachment."

He paused here and his dramatic scowl turned to a warm smile. "She also exposed corruption in our local college and brought down a multi-million dollar corporation whose leadership was responsible for murder, arson, blackmail, bribery, and grotesque environmental destruction."

I blushed and grinned from ear to ear.

"To Jamie August!" Donald raised a glass of rich, red wine.

"Hear, hear!" Glasses clinked all around the table, and Wesley kissed me on the cheek. Everyone who had played a role in breaking the Bayview Preserve story was gathered in Donald and Wesley's dining room.

"Don't forget, she won the grand prize in a bikini contest too," Tammy chimed in. She leaned into Dustin and cracked up, and everybody raised their glasses a second time.

"The girl's got talent, I always knew it," Jerry Mulvaney said, and his wife shushed and swatted him.

"I did it to escape the crazy firestarter dude!" I protested, then flipped Tammy the bird.

I looked around the room at these people who loved me—and who had saved my bacon in one way or another. The only person missing was Will, who had made a bunch of bad choices but who maybe had tried to help me as best he could. My mind flashed to the letter I had received at the *Weekly Breeze*. He wrote from a rest stop in South Carolina that he was sorry and was going to Florida for a clean start. He told me he loves me, and wants me to join him there. It was ridiculous; and I melted a little at the thought of it. He sure did make my heart beat faster.

I cleared my head of any thoughts of a new, tropical life, and beamed at Donald.

"Now I would like to propose a toast to Donald, my editor and my hero!" Cheers and laughter erupted. "How did you know where to find me?"

"I saw the security guard grab you off the sidewalk in front of that hideous apartment building."

"Hideous?" Dot Slomkowski cried. She and Merv were sitting at the far end of the table. "Oh no, hon. Sunrise Paradise is a great apartment building!"

"Indestructible," Merv Slomkowski concurred.

"Just try to burn that place down," Dot said.

"Can't be done," Merv said.

"Uh, well, yes, point taken," Donald said, ever the fair-minded news editor. "Anyway, I heard the call go out on the scanner, fire at Sunrise Paradise, and I knew with that combination you had to be there. So I hopped in the car and drove over there —"

"— and because you drive faster than the police," interjected Wesley, creating another ripple of laughter.

"— I got there ahead of the fire trucks," Donald continued seamlessly. "So I saw Jonathan and Alan grab you and take off, and I followed them. I called Detective Francis, but I waited until I saw the police pulling into the lot at the Ivory Enterprises building before I went in to find you. I mean, there's heroic and then there's suicidal."

"You rescued me!"

"Jamie, it didn't look like you needed any rescuing. By the time I got in there, the cops were right behind me, ready to grab Alan the axe-murdering arsonist, and you had everything else under control."

Between us, Donald and I managed to recount the events that followed last Friday's front-page news, much as I had been doing over the past several days on the local TV news and over the phone to a *Washington Post* reporter.

Jonathan Ivory was in the hospital with severe spinal injuries and it wasn't clear whether he would walk again. His wife was consulting divorce lawyers in Boca. Alan Donnelley and Bernard Ivory were both in jail awaiting trial. Bernard's physician came up with some story about serious heart problems, but the judge was unmoved. She deemed them both flight risks and refused to set bail.

"Jamie, you ever consider a career on the TV news?" Jerry Mulvaney broke in. "When they interviewed you on 'Good Morning Delmarva', you stole the show! You're way prettier than that anchor gal they've got over there, and I know you're smarter'n her."

I laughed and Mrs. Mulvaney gave Jerry another cheerful swat.

Donald said Paul Saunders was picked up at Dulles International as he and his family attempted to board a flight to the Cayman Islands. Fred Western was still missing, and his wife and kids had moved in with family in western Maryland.

As Donald explained Will's double-crossing to the group, I felt a tightness in my throat and kept silent. Then I pulled myself together and realized there was something much more poignant to consider than my convoluted love life. I raised my glass. "On a more serious note, I'd like to propose a toast to Vernette Johnson."

A quiet murmur ran through the group. "Dr. Johnson spent 10 years of her life—her last 10 years—trying to stop Bayview Preserve. She was outspoken, absolutely tireless, and passionate about the bay. I wish there was some way she could know that her work finally brought down Ivory Enterprises, even if it didn't stop Bayview Preserve. The world lost a treasure when she died. To Vernette Johnson." We all touched our glasses together.

"What's going to happen to Bayview Preserve?" Dustin asked.

"They're trying to figure that out now," I said.

"I was told that Eastern Maryland College has offered to put together a team of scientists to look into it," Donald said, causing the table to erupt in howls of laughter.

"Is it true Frank Donnelley locked his kid in the basement?" asked Wesley's brother Vincent.

"We have only Jonathan Ivory's word for that," Donald said. "Neither Bernard nor Alan have spoken since they've been in jail. Bernard's not talking because his lawyers told him not to, of course. Alan seems to have had some kind of breakdown. He attacked a guard the first night he was in, and now he's in solitary confinement. He sits on the floor and scratches his fingers against the concrete. He has scratched the skin off. Scratch. Scratch. Scratch." Donald told it like a ghost story.

"What a sad story," Tammy said. "That kid never had a chance."

I shivered. "Next topic," I said, grimacing.

Wesley came through and cleared everyone's dinner plates, giving my shoulder a squeeze as he passed.

"I have one additional announcement to make this evening, and—as if we needed it—one more reason to celebrate," Donald said, and we all settled back.

"This morning, I got word that Associated Press has picked up the *Weekly Breeze* story!" My jaw dropped, then I screamed with delight. Shouts erupted.

"The Chincoteague paper picks up our stuff once in a while, but AP?" I was laughing. Everyone was applauding. I spilled my wine, and didn't care.

"I don't know how much longer I'll be able to keep you at the *Weekly Breeze* writing about bake sales and surf conditions," Donald said, his voice low and sincere. "You have always wanted to be an investigative journalist, and now you have had your breakthrough. It is an honor for me to say that Jamie August got her start here."

Turn the page for a sneak preview of
Ocean City Cover-up, the second Jamie August novel.

Prologue

T HE GIRL WAS STILL PISSED OFF *but start-*
ing to feel better. The six minibottles of vodka were
kicking in, and she was finally getting to a good
part in Fast & Furious 4, *which she chose among the*
wide selection of movie options in her Lufthansa business
class seat.

Fucking business class. The girl's father cared for her
so little that he'd booked her in business instead of first.
Like he didn't know it's a sixteen-hour flight from Dubai
to Washington. She shifted impatiently, trying to get com-
fortable, but found it really disgusting to lay her seat flat
right next to some nasty businessman she didn't even
know. The plastic pod dividing her seat from his couldn't

block out the sound of his gentle snores. She clutched her Valentino purse and sniffled.

The girl's eyes grew dewy with the realization that her father no longer loved her, his one and only daughter, his princess. She opened the handbag, pulled out a tissue, and dabbed her mascara-clumped lashes.

By the time her flight touched down at Dulles International Airport, west of DC, the girl had pulled it together. Her highlighted blond hair was artfully tousled, and her lips shimmered with fresh lipstick. She'd cleaned up her mascara a little, but there was nothing like real tears to give your eye makeup that bleak, heroin-chic appearance. It looked even better than when she tried to apply it that way on purpose.

The girl wheeled a towering cart full of top-of-the-line aluminum luggage through customs, and scanned the crowd of professional drivers holding up neatly printed signs with the names of passengers they were to meet. She didn't see her name anywhere. However she heard Azeri, the language of Azerbaijan, being spoken.

A group of college-aged guys and girls were laughing and chatting with excitement. They were surrounded by a colorful riot of duffel bags and cheap vinyl suitcases. A guy who looked maybe thirty, kind of cute if you're into the patchouli-and-health-food thing, was holding a sign that read "Ocean Gateway International Student Services" and scanning the crowd.

She realized he was looking for her.

"Fucking hell," the girl said under her breath. She popped her gum and wheeled her luggage cart in their direction.

1.

MY LUNGS WERE READY TO BURST by the time I hit Tenth Street, and I slowed to a walk. I stopped to hang onto a lamppost, bent forward at the waist, and tried to catch my breath.

It was just after eight a.m. on July 1. The start of week four of my Get-Your-Ass-In-Shape campaign. Every year at the beginning of the summer season, I hit the Ocean City boardwalk shops and picked out a new bikini. This year, I'd been really irritated that I couldn't find anything that looked good on me. Everything made me look fat—or at least kind of doughy and soft.

Then I realized that the bathing suits hadn't changed. I had changed. No longer could I scarf down Slurpees and chili cheese fries and stay skinny. The late-twenties pounds were showing up. I wanted the leopard skin bikini with the fringes—it was only twelve dollars!—but I just couldn't work it the way I used to. I found myself looking at sensible one-pieces, and that's when I found Jesus, right there in the fitting room at the Bikini Depot.

"Tammy, I swear, by the fourth of July I am gonna rock this bikini," I said to my best friend, who was trying on minidresses.

"Do it!" Tammy said.

"Yeah!"

"So, how are you gonna make it happen?"

I was caught off guard thinking about the logistics of exercise. "Huh. I can't afford the gym."

"So go running. That's free."

"That sounds hideous."

Tammy arched an eyebrow, shrugged, and pulled her dressing room curtain closed.

"Shit. Okay, you're right. I'll do it."

From that day on, I went jogging every day on Ocean City's wide boardwalk. As June progressed, my runs got longer and my belly really did get flatter. Now, one month later, I was feeling pretty good about the way I looked, but that didn't mean I liked the damn running part. I stopped for a thirty-second break, hitting the stopwatch button on my plastic running watch.

"I hate my hormones," I said out loud just as three fifty-something women strolled past.

One of them turned and said, "You think you hate 'em now, honey? Just wait." They laughed and kept walking.

I was too out of breath to come up with a response. I waited for my heart rate to come down, then did a few hamstring stretches, checking out my nicely toned legs with satisfaction.

I straightened and looked down the boards, undoing and redoing the ponytail holder on my straight, dark hair, blowing my bangs out of my eyes. I spotted what I was looking for off in the distance. I hit the stopwatch button on my plastic sports watch again, squared my shoulders, and jogged on.

Finally I reached my destination: Kohr Brothers. I got in line and did another set of stretches as I waited. Despite the early hour, the line was six deep for the original, often imitated but never duplicated Kohr Brothers frozen custard. I told myself this was a healthier alternative to ice cream, that I could budget the 130 calories in that small, beautiful cone. But the truth was, if I didn't know there was a Kohr Brothers cone waiting for me at the end of every run, I wouldn't run. I just wouldn't do it. I would buy the granny one-piece, and maybe throw in some elastic-waist jeans, too.

The three teenage boys ahead of me in line finished with their order and their lame attempt to chat up the Russian summer workers behind the counter, and then I stepped up to the booth.

"Vanilla. Plain. Small. Hurry!"

"Your run was good?" one of the girls asked, smiling and tucking her cute bobbed hair behind one ear. She asked me this every morning.

"Awesome," I said. "Couldn't be better. Today I ran all the way from the other end of the boardwalk."

"That is maybe forty blocks, yes?" asked the other, more sultry girl. "That is far. How you do?"

"Brute force," I said, pulling exact change out of the little pocket in my running shorts. The cute one handed me a cone piled high with snowy vanilla soft-serve and collected the money. The sultry one twirled a long blond strand of hair.

"Knocked twenty seconds off my time today," I said, then took the first glorious bite of frozen custard. I wiped a sticky drip on my chin.

"That's great," the cute one said. "Twenty seconds off the exact same run from yesterday? You are doing very well."

"You have stopwatch on that?" the sultry one asked.

I showed her my black and safety-yellow rubber watch. "Yeah. Got it at Daffodils, eighteen bucks. Says it's a Timex, but probably a knockoff. Whatever. Really helps me track my progress."

"I have this function also," she said, extending her slender wrist and showing me a watch that looked to be completely covered in diamonds. It had small, round dials arranged within a larger analog clock face. This dial here is stopwatch," she said, delicately pointing to one of them.

"That's a fitness watch?" I said, guffawing.

"Of course. Piaget Miss Protocle XL."

The cute one whipped her head around and stared at her friend.

"Knockoff," she amended. "Of course."

"That sounds like the name of a car," I said. "Anyway, it's amazing."

"Thank you."

"One of those sure would improve my look when I'm out for my morning run."

"Yes. But I do not understand," the sultry one said. "Why you not go on diet? Would be easier than this run, run, run every day, no?"

"Are you kidding? I *am* on a diet. Otherwise I would order the waffle cone with cookie crumbles and double jimmies. I am totally cutting back."

"When I want lose weight, I just don't eat. Easy."

"I can't *just not eat*. I'd die. Well, I mean of course anyone would die if they didn't eat. What I mean is, I would kill myself."

"No, is easy," she said, one hand on a beautifully curvy hip. "Stop eat. Only smoke."

Well, she had me there. I quit smoking nearly a year before, and I knew that was a big contributor to this season's bikini crisis. Still, with only one or two minor lapses, I had kicked the habit and I wasn't about to go back. Couldn't afford it, for one thing.

"Easy for you to say." I rolled my eyes. "What are you, twenty?"

"Twenty-one."

"Just wait," I said, realizing with horror that I was mimicking those women who'd mocked me earlier. "Twenty-seven is a bitch."

2.

A N UPDATE ON SHOOTINGS outside a teen dance club and an eastern European summer worker who was knifed to death led the day's *Weekly Breeze* news roundup. Witnesses were still being sought for the incidents, which happened last week.

I put the finishing touches on a news analysis showing an upswing in gang activity and a rise in violent crime in Ocean City. Statistically much of this could be laid at the feet of young men with addresses in or near Washington, DC. I guess even gang members needed beach vacations.

I'm a staff writer at the *Breeze*. I broke a big story last winter involving a corrupt real-estate empire and a high-end housing project. A bunch of McMansions were built on some paved-over marshes that were the last remaining blue crab breeding ground in OC. The story got picked up by a major news agency and put the *Weekly Breeze* on the map as an independent local newspaper that reports actual news.

Donald Brightland, the editor and owner of the paper, often complained that my stunt ruined his relaxing routine of printing stories about American Legion scholarship winners and trends in beach-house decor. But he'd been smart enough to put me on salary and give me benefits after the story broke, to lure me into staying in his employ. Like I was going to leave. Where would I go? Back to my hometown of Baltimore, to freelance at the *Baltimore Sun*? Or take a crappy gig with some news service's rinky-dink Eastern Shore outpost? I saw plenty of news that needed reporting right here.

The phone rang, and I picked up. "*Weekly Breeze*, Jamie August."

"How are you doing, sweetheart?"

"Hi, Uncle Abe. What's goin' on?" My mother's brother owned some apartments in town and hired me to answer the phones for him in the off-season. I wouldn't do the job in the summertime because I couldn't stand the idea of fielding complaint calls for eight hours at a time. Let's just say Abe's buildings were in need of a little TLC. Okay, okay, they were all dumps, painted in migraine-inducing colors. "Those bright colors are my trademark. Everybody loves 'em," Abe always said. "They give my places a real islandy kind of atmosphere." Yeah. Atmosphere like you'd find in Haiti.

But he was family, and I didn't think he meant to be a slumlord, exactly. Plus, I lived practically for free in one of his eye-popping buildings—the Kitty Lou—down near the inlet, where the powerboats and fishing boats docked, and the Atlantic connected to the sheltered bay behind Ocean City. So I couldn't really complain.

"Jamie, I need you to do a job for me," Abe was saying on the phone.

"I don't have time."

"Come down to DaVinci's. I'll tell you about it over dinner."

DaVinci's was one of Ocean City's finest Italian restaurants. I knew this because I reviewed it—my extensive OC dining intel was gleaned exclusively from dinners paid for by the *Weekly Breeze*. It was one of my job's best perks.

353

Dinner at DaVinci's definitely sounded better than what I had planned: a PBJ standing over the sink. So I agreed to meet him.

I hung up and turned to Donald, who was tapping merrily away on his keyboard at the other desk in the *Breeze's* sunny storefront office.

"Abe's taking me to dinner at DaVinci's," I said in surprise.

Donald raised a perfectly shaped eyebrow. "Watch out, Jamie. If he's trying to get you to work him some kind of discounted advertising deal in the *Breeze*, the answer is no."

"He wouldn't even try that. He knows you're not a fan of Beach Getaway Rentals."

"Does he?"

"Um, yeah," I said, popping my gum. "Your article on the ten worst slumlords of Ocean City pretty much spelled it out. I can't believe you named Abe as the seventh worst."

"I dropped him down from the top five out of respect for you."

I thought of going home first for a quick change of clothes, but I was tight on time. I combed out my long, dark hair and considered my outfit: cut-off jeans shorts, black tank top, flip-flops. I snipped a few straggly fringes from my shorts, and changed from the flip-flops to my go-to pair of black stilettos, which I kept in my bottom desk drawer for exactly these last-minute situations. Perfect!

Donald surveyed my outfit skeptically. "Oh, hon, you can definitely pull off that look with those hot runner's legs of yours, but it's not quite... ironic enough."

"Who's being ironic?" I asked, hand on hip. "I can't get into DaVinci's with flip-flops."

He sighed. Then he stood up and removed his own belt, a white leather number studded with grommets that looked ever so jaunty with his flat-front yellow trousers and striped boater shirt. "Here, try this."

The belt was perfect with the low-rise cut of the shorts, and lent a certain '60s go-go girl style to the outfit.

"Better," he said. "Bring it back tomorrow."

3.

CAUGHT THE PACKED BUS from the *Weekly Breeze* offices uptown near the Delaware border, down to DaVinci's around Fourteenth Street. There was only standing room on the bus, it being dinner hour with everybody heading out for crabs, fries on the boardwalk, and happy-hour drinks.

A few blocks north of my stop I felt a hand inch across my thigh and cup my ass. I couldn't turn around, couldn't get away from the pervert. I looked down and spotted a grubby man's sneaker near mine. I gently picked up my foot and ground a stiletto heel into the top of the man's foot. The hand jerked away from my backside and a hoarse shriek rang out.

"This isn't Tokyo," I muttered.

"Hey kid, you're looking terrific," Abe said as I bent down to give him a brief hug. "No kidding. What the heck are you doing, Pilates? Kickboxing?"

"No, I'm doing it old-school. I'm running."

"Christ. I used to run," Abe said.

I couldn't picture it. Abe's polyester Hawaiian shirt stretched across his belly, and the bald patch under his comb-over glistened in the restaurant's subtle lighting.

I ordered a Bacardi and Diet Pepsi from the waiter, who wasn't even trying to be discreet as he ogled me in my short shorts. I couldn't tell whether he was being a lech or a snob. We perused the menu and ordered: a surf and turf special for Abe and Maryland crab ravioli for me. The waiter brought salads and blushed furiously when I looked him in the eye and recrossed my legs.

Abe seemed to miss the whole exchange, busy as he was drowning his greens in ranch dressing. I dug into my undressed lettuce.

"Since when do you like salad?" he said.

"Since never. But if I eat the salad, I might not have any room left over for dessert."

"You really got this sorted out, I gotta say."

"Thanks, Abe. So, what's this project you want to talk to me about?"

"First, I want your opinion."

"Really?" Abe was older than my dad. This was a milestone in being grown-up!

"Yeah, you're a reporter. You might know something about this."

"Right, of course. What's the situation?" I said, all cool.

"I'm buying a piece of property down near the inlet, not far from your apartment. It's back in the neighborhood. Old house with a shop front on the bottom level. Right now it's some kind of Internet cafe, or at least that's what they're calling it. Bunch of Russians in there. Lotta people in and out. I don't know what they're doing, but whatever it is, they're not doing it in English."

"Why are you buying the place?"

"It's a good price, and the place doesn't need much work. I just don't know about this tenant. They may be laundering money, running Russian prostitutes, gambling, who knows? I'm thinking of closing it down. All these Russians in town these days, I don't like it."

"But your apartment buildings are full of Russian summer workers. They're your livelihood," I said, a bit indignant.

"Yeah, but they trash the place every summer."

"All of them," I deadpanned.

"Of course not all of them. But a lot of them."

"What, and the American kids who used to come in for summer work treated your apartments better?"

"Are you kidding me? The American kids are even worse!"

"Then what's the problem?"

"Yeah, yeah, you may be right, but at least with the American kids I could go after the parents for damages. These foreigners, I got no recourse."

"So what's your question?" I took a sip of my drink.

"Can you do a little checking on this place, find out about the owner? Maybe you know something about this joint, or could ask around, see what the deal is."

"This isn't the only Internet cafe in town," I said. "I've seen one in a strip mall right on Coastal Highway."

"Exactly. How many of these places does this town need? I could get a T-shirt place in there, no problem, some kind of souvenir shop."

"That's exactly what Ocean City needs more of," I said, laughing.

Abe just grimaced.

"I gotta know what's going on in my properties, or it could be on my head. How do I know this place isn't some kind of front for the Russian Mafia or something?"

I considered this, and my thirst for conspiracy was piqued. I admit, it never took much.

"Okay, so you want to know if this place is a legit business, and worth keeping, or whether you should kick them to the curb, am I right?"

"Something like that, yeah. Can you check them out for me?"

I considered the load of stories on my desk. Not a wise move, taking on a research project on the side. But I couldn't resist.

"Okay, I'll check it out. Give me the address."

Ask for Ocean *City Cover-up* at your local bookstore, or order it on Amazon.

Author's Note

It was great fun to conjure this version of Ocean City. My own research for an Ocean City travel guide (*Ocean City: A Guide to Maryland's Seaside Resort*, a part of the Tourist Town series) forms the basis for Jamie's descriptions and opinions about various OC restaurants and hotspots. But don't let that fool you: much of Jamie August's Ocean City is pure fantasy. There is no *Weekly Breeze*, no Beach Getaway Rentals, no Bayview Preserve. There is no institution called Eastern Maryland College. I located it suspiciously close to the real Salisbury University, but I assure you I know of no corrupt environmental scientists there (or anywhere else, for that matter.)

Longtime residents of 43rd Street may recognize Sunrise Paradise, though it has since shed its crazy paint job and gone decidedly up-market.

I had plenty of assistance in bringing this novel to fruition. Any errors are mine alone. I am especially grateful to Paul Covington, who helped me coax to life the gum-cracking, acid-washed, Technicolor Jamie August. Thanks to Susanne Van Cleave and Mark Allison of Writeswell Inc. for copyediting, and to Brian Ashby for the title.

ABOUT THE AUTHOR

Kim Kash is a freelance writer and the author of the Jamie August novel series and *Ocean City: A Guide to Maryland's Seaside Resort* (2009, Channel Lake). She divides her time between Maryland and the Middle East, where she lives with her husband and a large black cat. Visit her online at www.kimkash.com

CPSIA information can be obtained
at www.ICGtesting.com
Printed in the USA
LVOW11s1619131017
552340LV00002B/447/P

Loved this book. I'm a ~~~~~~~~~~~~~~~ la Stephanie Plum fr~~
the Janet Evanovich ~~~~~~~~~~~~ Boh, Fagers Island a~
Orioles references. Too fun. – Melina Scotto

With a cast of characters as fresh as they are funny, this book will ma~
you feel like you've walked the streets of Ocean City, and it will have y~
wishing that you could hang out with Jamie August in real life. W~
written, great plot, fantastic characters, and an enjoyable story.
– Natasha Burge

Hiaasen meets Bubbles Yablonsky – Sarah D. Baker

EASTERN SHORE MARYLAND reporter Jamie August has a talent ~
unearthing more than her editor wants and a weakness for Rave~
jerseys and sparkly underwear. She is assigned to cover the gra~
opening of a big new housing development in Ocean City, Maryland. B~
instead of writing about wrap-around porches and rattan furnishin~
she uncovers kickbacks and payoffs, blackmail and murder. Jami~
tenacity, smarts, and sheer recklessness—plus some smokin' striptea~
dance moves—can get her out of some tight spots. But are they enou~
to save her from a psychopathic arsonist and two generations of corru~
real estate tycoons?

$14.99
ISBN 978-0-9895022-1-~
51499

9 780989 502214

Can't get enough Jamie August?
Find out more at kimkash.com